NOW YOU SEE ME…

"It's not him. The body in the water. It's not Danny."

I waited for the impact, for the news to sink in, to flood me with elation.

But there was nothing. Only numbness.

This was good news. So why did I feel so defeated?

Then it hit me.

A darker, deeper, buried part of me had been hoping all this was finally over.

…but can you trust me?

EMMA HAUGHTON worked as a freelance journalist, writing features for a wide variety of newspapers and glossy magazines, before becoming an author. A mother of four, she now lives and writes fiction in Dorset.

Now You See Me... is her first novel.

www.emmahaughton.com

NOW YOU SEE ME...

Emma Haughton

USBORNE

To Josh, Flan, Chip, Hetty and James.
In memory of Joan and Tom Robinson.

First published in the UK in 2014 by Usborne Publishing Ltd., Usborne House, 83-85 Saffron Hill, London EC1N 8RT, England. www.usborne.com

Copyright © Emma Haughton 2014

The right of Emma Haughton to be identified as the author of this work has been asserted by her in accordance with the Copyright, Designs and Patents Act, 1988.

Cover photography © istock/Thinkstock

The name Usborne and the devices ♀ ⊕ are Trade Marks of Usborne Publishing Ltd.

A CIP catalogue record for this book is available from the British Library.

JF AMJJASOND/14   ISBN 9781409563693   02992/1   Printed in Chatham, Kent, UK.

PROLOGUE

I never meant to be here.

I hadn't planned to be standing by the boating lake, shivering in the October breeze, watching seven men look for traces of my lost best friend.

Nor had I told anyone I was coming. Didn't mention it to Dad. Or Martha, who was boycotting the whole thing, still refusing to believe anything bad could have happened to her son.

The truth was, I didn't even want to be here. I *had* to be. When the time came, I just couldn't stay away.

And what with the sudden cold snap, I thought I'd be alone down on the seafront. But it was half-term and news had clearly got around. By the time I arrived, a small crowd had already gathered along the yellow tape sectioning off the lake. Mainly grown-ups, but a few children too, the smallest sitting on their parents' shoulders, noses nipped pink by the wind.

As I padlocked my bike to the fence by the Marine Cafe, I spotted Tom from my tutor group across from the crazy golf, next to a man I guessed was his father. Tom gave me a smile and waved, like we'd bumped into each other at the cinema or something. I pretended not to notice, pulling my hood close around my face and praying no one else would recognize me. The last thing I needed was anyone telling Martha I was here.

I walked up to the row of bathing huts, where I had a good view of the police divers as they wriggled into baggy black drysuits and heaved oxygen tanks onto their backs. With their masks on, you could barely see their faces. It made them look sinister, creepy, like something out of a horror film.

It seemed to take them for ever to get ready. All around, people shuffled and stamped, pulling scarves and coats tighter as they waited. My stomach felt raw and edgy with nerves and impatience, my cheeks red and windburned.

"Get on with it," muttered the man next to me. His head was covered by a striped bobble hat, the kind you see on little kids, pulled right down over his ears. The woman next to him wore a red anorak and an expectant look, like someone waiting for a show to begin.

As if this wasn't real, wasn't about someone's life. And the lives of everyone he'd left behind.

Finally all seven divers lined up at the end of the lake, spreading out to cover its full width. Each held a long pole in one hand, a torch in the other. I felt almost disappointed. I guess I'd expected something more dramatic – big hooks, complex equipment or something, radars perhaps.

This wasn't supposed to be exciting, I reminded myself, as bit by bit, moving together, the divers descended into the murky lake. The water barely reached their knees at first, rising to their waists as they waded deeper, step by slow, careful step, shining their torches into the depths, prodding every inch of the bottom with their poles.

Around me, the crowd thickened as dog walkers and holidaymakers paused to see what was going on. I was glad Martha wasn't here. It was boring and nerve-wracking at the same time, and something about other people's curiosity made me feel cross and spiky. This felt private somehow. None of their business.

A sudden murmur surfed the crowd. Several people pointed towards the lake as kids surged forwards for a better view. One of the divers put his hand in the air and signalled the others to stop. Adjusting his face mask, he lowered himself head first into the water.

Seconds drifted by... Nothing. I felt tense, breathless, queasy.

What if...?

Then he surfaced, one hand holding something in the air. My heart lurched as I strained to see. The police on the lakeside passed a plastic bag down the line, and the diver dropped in a solitary shoe.

"Reckon it's his?" the woman in the red anorak asked the bobble-hat man.

He shrugged. "Who knows?"

In my head, Danny pedalled across the ledge separating

the shallow from the deeper part of the lake. Like a slow-motion sequence in a film, I saw him lose his balance and fall into the water, head glancing against the side as he sank into the shadowy depths.

A shiver flowed through me, chilly as the wind. I shook the image from my mind. Turned back to watch the divers resume their slow, painstaking shuffle, my legs twitching with frustration.

Perhaps I should have asked Lianna and Maisy to come. Even Tanya or Vicky, or practically anyone else from Year Eight. At least I'd have had someone to distract me from this electric prickle in my skin, this anxious flutter in my chest.

But I knew they wouldn't have stuck it for long; all around me people were drifting away as they lost interest.

"What's going on?" asked an older woman with a dog. The bobble-hat man reeled off Danny's name and how he disappeared three weeks ago, like he was discussing an old friend. But then, thanks to the local paper, everyone round here knew what had happened.

"Do they think he drowned swimming or something?" the woman asked. She at least had the decency to look more shocked than curious.

The bobble on his hat shook. "I doubt it. It's way too shallow. They're just looking for clues."

"Unless someone dumped him there," the woman in the red anorak chipped in, her voice chirpy. "Weighed him down or something."

The older woman grimaced, and I flashed back to those times Danny and I had swum in the lake. The way the muddy water curled around your legs, cool and slippery. How you had to keep your feet tucked up high to stop them brushing against the sludge on the bottom.

I shuddered again. Martha was right. This was a mistake, I should never have come. But though my head wanted to leave, my legs refused to move. The woman and her dog moved on and through the gap she left, I spotted a man shouldering a TV camera, rotating it slowly to film the onlookers. Probably a local channel.

I pulled my hood closer and looked at my feet as the lens swung in my direction – no way did I want to appear on the regional news. When I raised my head again, the cameraman was focusing back on the divers.

"We should go," the bobble-hat man said, checking the time on his phone.

The woman in the anorak took a last lingering look at the wading men, now halfway across the lake.

"Poor kid," she sighed as she turned away.

By the time the divers reached the far wall I was almost alone, everyone else defeated by cold and boredom. Not that they'd missed much. Ranged along the walkway was a collection of rubbish. Lots of bottles and shards of glass. An old bike wheel, too small to be Danny's. A supermarket trolley.

And a rusty toy pram, dredged up from the southern side of the lake. It wasn't big, and judging by the way the diver pulled it effortlessly out of the water, it didn't weigh much.

I watched it dripping on the slipway, trying to imagine how it had ended up in there. I pictured some kid out with her parents, pushing it too close to the edge. The pram skeetering out of her grip, toppling in. Hands grasping at the water. The doll rescued perhaps, but the pram sinking without trace.

Why didn't anyone go in after it? The water barely came up to the chest of most people, even in the deeper bits. Maybe they didn't know that, I decided, or maybe they didn't think it worth the bother. You could hardly blame them. I wouldn't have gone in either, not without Danny egging me on.

Staring across the empty lake, I couldn't erase that little girl from my mind. I saw her crying, clutching the doll to her chest as her mum pulled her away. Glancing back to where dark water swallowed her pram for ever.

Something shifted and stirred inside me. A deep pain rising, like a bubble, surfacing like a gasp as I shook away the image of my mother's face. My throat closed tight and my mouth went dry. I gulped in salt air in an effort to stay standing.

I couldn't think about Mum. Not now.

I hurried back to the cafe. They hadn't found Danny, I kept telling myself. They hadn't found Danny and I should be relieved. They hadn't found Danny – and what happened to Mum didn't change a thing.

But as I fiddled with my bike lock, fingers numb and clumsy with cold, I couldn't get rid of the sudden, certain feeling that I'd lost him too.

PART
ONE

NOW

All the warning I get that my life is about to detonate is a blast of music. I recognize it from a class we did on Beethoven – "Ode to Joy", I think it's called. It fills the silent classroom, prompting thirty heads to turn and stare in my direction. It's only then I realize it's coming from nearby.

Very nearby. The bottom of my rucksack no less.

Hell. My phone. Alice has been messing with my ringtones again.

I ferret in my bag and cut the call just as Mr Harrington looks round from the quadratic equations he's writing on the whiteboard. Clocks my reddening face.

"While I applaud your taste in music, Miss Radcliffe," he barks, "I'd rather you didn't flaunt it in my lesson. Turn it off or I'll confiscate the damn thing."

Lianna and Josie both wink at me and grin. I roll my eyes and smile. As Mr Harrington turns back to his figures, I peer at the screen under the desk. The call was from Martha. A second later a text flashes up.

Janet Reynolds called. Have to leave urgently. Can you get Ally? Martha xx

That's all. But it's enough to ignite a hot lick of dread in my stomach.

I text back *Yes*, then switch off the phone. Drop it into my bag and turn to face the whiteboard, trying to act like nothing just happened at all.

Alice is sitting on the grass inside the school playground, the back of her blonde head bobbing up and down as she picks the heads off the daisies and gathers them into a pile. I nod to her teacher, who waves hello.

"Hannah!" Alice leaps up when she sees me, flinging her arms around my neck and swinging her feet off the ground.

"Hey, Ally," I gasp, collapsing onto the grass beside her. My heart is pounding and I'm out of breath. I've practically run the mile from my school to hers – no mean feat with a full rucksack. "Sorry I'm late."

"Look!" Alice holds up a crumpled piece of paper from her bag. A spiky-looking animal stares back at me, its head, body and long tail made up of lurid green and blue splodges of paint. Some stick right up from the paper and are clearly still wet.

"Kiss!" She shoves the picture so close to my face that I can smell the funny chalky scent of the paint.

"Nooo!" I squeal, pulling a pretend frightened face. "It might bite!"

Alice grins and stuffs the picture back into her bag. "Silly Hannah. It's only an Ally-gator." She falls back onto the grass giggling, then sits up again quickly. "Where's Mummy?"

"I don't know. She just sent me a message asking me to come and get you."

"Humph…" Alice grabs the daisies and throws them across the lawn.

"It must be important, Ally. She'd be here if she could."

"Don't care anyway," she says with a shrug.

"You don't mean that." I roll her back onto the grass and gently tickle her ribs, sending her into squeals of panicky delight. Then stand up and hold out my hand. "Come on, Bugsy, let's get home and wait for your mum."

She raises her hand to mine, letting her weight flop backwards as I heave her to her feet. It's not easy. Alice is seven now, and getting heavier by the day.

Soon, I think, I won't be able to lift her at all.

There's no sign of Martha's car in the driveway of Dial House, so I take the key from its hiding place under the birdbath and unlock the back door. Rudman mobs us the moment we step inside, running round our legs in little circles of joy, barking and trying to lick our knees.

I dump our school bags on a chair and look for a note. Nothing. There's a stack of plates by the dishwasher, and jam and butter still out on the kitchen table. Martha really must have left in a hurry.

"Hungry?" I ask Alice.

She shakes her head, so I make up a couple of glasses of squash, grab myself a few biscuits, and take them outside to the hammock strung between the apple trees. It's the first warm day of spring, and there's a gentle buzz of insects in the air. The garden is full of birdsong and half-forgotten smells – apple blossom and fresh green grass and something darker, more earthy.

Rudman hurtles around the lawn in ecstasy at being released, then flops panting at our feet. I'm guessing he's been shut indoors all day.

Slumped together in the hammock, Alice makes me tell her stories. It's more boring than difficult. Like a lot of kids with Down's syndrome, she wants to hear the same ones over and over. So I tell her the tale of the three goats and the troll under the bridge, and as soon as I finish she begs me to start again, her little round face a perfect blank as she listens. As if she's hearing it for the very first time.

Third go round, she falls asleep. I remove her glasses, placing them on the lawn by the base of the tree. Think about doing some English revision, but I know I'll wake her if I go back inside for my bag. So I rest my head on the side of the hammock and let my mind settle on the question it's been circling all afternoon – why Janet Reynolds has asked to see Martha.

She must have something to tell her. Something about Danny. Something she didn't want to say over the phone.

After all this time – three and a half years now – I just know that can't be anything good.

Danny.

I try to picture his face, but all that comes is the one from the photo, the one that appeared on all the posters. I've forgotten so much of him, I think, with a sinking feeling of sadness. How he looked. His voice, bright and teasing. The way he made everything seem so easy.

I feel an ache, too, at the thought of Martha. Of what she must be going through right now.

Underneath the hammock Rudman starts yipping in his sleep, his legs twitching as he chases something in his dreams. A cat maybe. Or rabbits. Alice stirs beside me, stretching an arm out so it rests on mine. I leave it there until it feels uncomfortably heavy, then shift over to give her more room, closing my eyes again and trying to settle the swirl of my thoughts.

But my mind is as restless as Rudman's dreams and keeps dragging me back to all those places I thought I'd left behind. Danny's disappearance. The search. The endless waiting, the constant hoping.

And the last time PC Janet Reynolds called Martha and Paul. When they found the body.

The memory leaves my breath catchy and raw, in contrast to Alice's slow, regular exhale. I feel suddenly trapped, airless. I want to run away, get on a bus or a boat or a train, anything to take me far from the bad news I know is waiting for me.

After all, what are the chances this will be another false alarm?

2
then

Daniel Geller disappeared on a Sunday afternoon in late September – a week after his thirteenth birthday. Not that I knew then that he'd gone. Not even that evening, when Dad stuck his head round my bedroom door.

"Any idea where Danny is?"

I put down my book on the slave trade. Dad looked distant and dishevelled, his eyes not quite meeting mine. He ran his hand over his hair, which seemed to have grown thicker and wilder in the year since Mum died.

I shrugged. "Isn't he at home?"

"Not according to his mother."

Dad removed his glasses and rubbed his eyes, staring absently at the homework scattered across my bedroom floor. He had that look about him again, like there was something on his mind he was struggling to find words for.

But then there was always something. Usually work.

"She's still on the phone. Can you speak to her, Hannah?" His mouth made the awkward movement that these days passed for a smile. "I'm rather in the middle of things at the moment…"

A few seconds later he was back with the handset, dropping it onto my bed like he couldn't get rid of it fast enough. Dad always avoided speaking to Martha. Never got beyond a perfunctory greeting, the briefest exchange of information.

I heard the closing click of his study door. I put down my pen and pressed the phone to my ear. It emitted a tiny, furious bark.

"Hi, Martha."

"Hannah, sweetheart, is Danny there?" Despite Rudman's yapping in the background, I could hear the worry in her voice.

"No. I thought he was with you."

"I haven't seen him since this morning. It's almost nine."

I glanced outside at the gathering darkness. In the house opposite, lights glowed in the upstairs windows.

Another volley of frantic barking in my ear. A groan from Martha. "Hang on a sec…" A muffled sound, then her voice scolding Rudman.

"Sorry, Hannah," she said, slightly breathless. "I've no idea what's got into that animal. Anyway, I'm a bit concerned. I've tried Danny's mobile half a dozen times, and he hasn't answered."

"He cycled back here with me hours ago. I assumed he went on home."

"Did he say so?"

I thought for a moment. "No, I don't think so."

"Any ideas where he might have gone?"

I barely had any idea where Danny got to any more, I felt like saying, but kept it to myself. "You could try Joe," I suggested, "or Ross or Ewan."

"Do you have their numbers?"

"No. Sorry."

I could almost hear Martha suppress a sigh at the other end of the line. "How about you ask some of your friends, Hannah? Maybe they'll know where he is?"

"I'll call Vicky Clough. She might."

"Thanks." Martha's voice was laced with anxiety. "Look, Hannah, if you hear anything you'll let me know, right?"

"Of course."

"Thanks. See you tomorrow after school, okay?"

"Sure. Bye then…"

An abrupt click at the end of the line. I listened to the burr of the dialling tone for a few seconds, then grabbed my phone and texted Vicky, hoping she wouldn't read anything into me asking about Danny. No matter how many times I told her he was my friend and nothing more, she clearly never believed it.

Apart from thinking that Danny would really be for it when he got home, I admit I didn't give Martha's call a second thought. It didn't even occur to me that there could actually be something wrong. Why would it? Lately Danny was always out somewhere or other, round at someone's house or off riding his bike. This was hardly the first time his mother had rung to track him down.

Even so, even now, it still seems incredible that I didn't know, that I didn't somehow sense that something wasn't right. I was his best friend, after all. Or at least had been. And not any old best friend, but the kind you get when you've practically grown up together. The kind who knows you better than you know yourself.

But there was nothing. No warning sirens going off in my head as I picked up my pen. Not even a little niggle of worry as I wrote about the slave boats and all those stolen people sent far across the world, never to see their homes or families again.

3

then

"Hey, Hannah."

I looked up to see Joe Rowling standing by my desk. He nodded at Lianna before turning his attention back to me.

"You seen Danny?"

I shook my head. "His mum was looking for him last night. Did she get hold of you?"

"Yeah. I told her we were supposed to meet up yesterday for footy, but Danny never showed up." Joe frowned and hiked his rucksack strap higher on his shoulder. "So you've no idea where he is?"

"None. I thought maybe you'd know."

"No clue," Joe sniffed. "I've tried his mobile loads. I think it's turned off."

"Maybe it's out of battery," suggested Lianna with a shrug.

"Yeah, probably." Joe glanced behind him as Mr Young marched in, register tucked under his arm.

"Well, when you see him, tell him he missed the best match ever." He punched the air. "We thrashed those idiots from Randolph's."

I grinned. Danny really would be sorry he missed that.

* * *

It was the same story all day.

"Any idea where Danny Geller might be?" Mr Young quizzed me after registration. I assumed Martha hadn't rung in or he'd have known.

Danny wasn't in assembly, and there was no sign of him at break. Or in the lunch queue. I left Maisy and Lianna to their sandwiches, and made my way to the school pool. I wasn't up to speed with where Danny hung out these days, but I did know one thing: if he was anywhere, he'd be here. Danny never missed swimming practice – not unless he was off sick or something.

I pressed my face against the glass doors separating the pool from the main sports hall. Half a dozen kids were thrashing up and down the lanes. I didn't have to wait for them to stop and lift their heads to know that none of them were Danny. You could tell by the way they cut through the water – compared with him, they made it look like hard work.

Mr Cozens strode over as I turned to go. "You seen Geller?" he snapped, not bothering to hide his annoyance. As if it was somehow my fault that Danny hadn't turned up.

"No. I'm looking for him too."

"Well, when you find him, tell him I need to speak to him," he said gruffly. "We're supposed to be sorting out teams for the trials today."

"I'll tell him." I fled before Cozens could dump anything else on me. He might be a great swimming coach, but it was beyond me how Danny put up with him three lunchtimes a week.

Danny's absence was odd, but I wasn't that worried. Most likely he was ill. Martha had probably hauled him off to the doctor and forgotten to tell the school, and now Danny was propped up in bed with a giant bottle of something fizzy, playing stupid games on his laptop. Or curled up on the sofa next to Alice watching kids' TV. Cartoons, game shows, even the baby stuff they make for toddlers – Danny loved them just as much as his sister.

So it wasn't till after school and I was halfway up the drive to Dial House that I saw the last thing I ever expected. Something which made the breath freeze in my throat and my feet jerk to a standstill.

Parked right up near the front door, under the trees, was a police car.

That was the exact moment I knew something was wrong. Very wrong indeed.

4

then

It was a proper police car, with a strip of lights on the top, and a yellow and blue chessboard pattern on the sides. I stood there, hoping perhaps I was imagining it. Or that there was some completely ordinary, everyday reason for it being there, parked under the trees, obscuring the front door of Dial House.

I didn't need this icy jolt in my stomach to tell me there was nothing good about a visit from the police.

The thought of Mum rose up again, that nagging pain that flared like toothache. I pushed it aside and focused on Danny. What the hell has he done? I wondered. A flush of anxiety made me hesitate. Maybe I should go home. Wait for someone to tell me what was going on.

But the thought of sitting around on my own, not knowing, was more than I could bear. So I went round and knocked on the back door. Normally I'd walk straight in, but somehow the police car changed everything.

No one heard me. I put my hand up to block out the reflection and peered through the window; the kitchen was empty. They must be sitting in the living room or the conservatory. I could go and ring the front doorbell, but that felt too weird; Dial House was practically my second home.

So I turned the handle and stepped inside. Sure enough, I could hear voices coming from the living room. Martha's, then another woman's. I cleared my throat quietly, heart picking up speed in my chest, and went up to the door. It was only half closed, but I tapped on it anyway.

"Yes?" Martha's voice, high and uncertain.

I walked in. Four heads turned towards me – none of them Danny's. Martha was on the sofa, her skin drawn and pale, her wavy black hair loose and untidy. Paul beside her in his work suit, looking tired and serious. In the chairs opposite, two police officers – a man and a woman.

Everyone sat straight-backed and tense, perched on the edge of their seats like they never really meant to sit down at all.

I stumbled out a hello and the officers smiled and I felt like I could breathe for the first time since I saw the police car. They weren't the same two, I could see that. They weren't the officers from before, the ones who came about Mum.

Paul rose and beckoned me over, but Martha stared at me, her face shocked and vacant, like she'd completely forgotten who I was. Then her expression collapsed and her head sunk into her hands.

I felt a flush of unease. Was she angry with me for barging in?

I cleared my throat to mumble an apology, then understood – she'd thought I was Danny. That look on Martha's face was disappointment.

Oh god. I felt giddy, my mind reeling. "Where is he?" I blurted. "Is Danny in some kind of trouble?"

Paul stepped forwards, his expression awkward, and put his hand on my shoulder, giving it a squeeze before introducing me to the police officers. "This is Hannah, the girl we were telling you about. She's always been very close to Danny."

The woman officer stood. She had brown hair and a nice face, the sort that made you feel you could say anything and she wouldn't mind. "I'm PC Janet Reynolds, the area missing persons coordinator, but that's rather a mouthful so I suggest you just call me Janet. And this is PC Simon Jenkins." The man next to her gave me a brief nod.

She said all this with a little laugh that was obviously meant to make me feel more relaxed, but it didn't work. *The missing persons coordinator?* The words rang in my head like the bell at school, loud and insistent. Suddenly I wanted to go home. To crawl into bed and read a book and pretend that everything was okay.

"Shall I go?" I said to Paul quickly. "I just came to look for Danny."

"That's why we're here, Hannah." Janet paused, waiting for me to speak. I stared at her blankly, mind racing. I felt suddenly guilty, like I'd done something wrong. Only somehow forgotten, or perhaps not realized I'd even done it.

Seeing my confusion, Janet went on: "No one has seen Danny since yesterday afternoon, Hannah. We're trying to establish where he might be."

My heart started to race, my head felt light and spacey. It *was* like Mum, I thought. It was happening all over again.

I looked at my feet, fighting the panic that threatened to engulf me, and saw one of Alice's toys beneath the sofa. The soft rag doll with the yellow hair you could tie in bunches. Where was Alice? At a friend's house maybe? Or perhaps Martha had asked someone to look after her.

"So, it's good you're here, Hannah," I heard Janet say. "We wanted to talk to you anyway. We're hoping you can help."

I forced myself to raise my eyes. She gestured towards an empty chair. I sat down.

"As far as we can tell, you were the last person to see Danny yesterday. Or at least the last person we know of." Janet paused again while I took this in. "Would you mind if we asked you some questions?"

I shook my head. "Yes. I mean, no problem."

"Do you want us to call your dad first and have him come over?"

I looked over at Martha. She was biting her lip, frowning. Wanting to get on with it, I realized.

I shook my head again. Dad would be buried in the lab somewhere at the university. It'd take ages to track him down.

"It's fine," I said.

"We're her godparents," Martha added quickly. "Hannah spends a lot of time with us."

Janet glanced at her, then nodded. I leaned forward, pressing my hands between my knees so no one could see them shaking.

I was there for over an hour. I told them everything I knew, which wasn't much. Only where Danny and I went yesterday afternoon, what we did, stuff he said, that sort of thing. Everything I could think of.

Janet asked all the questions. The policeman called Simon wrote everything down in a little notebook, which he tucked away into his pocket when we'd finished. They wanted to know details of Danny's friends, places he went, where I thought he might be. They even asked me if I knew his email and Facebook passwords so they could check his messages. I wasn't much help there either. Danny had become as distant online as he had in real life.

All the time I was talking Martha sat there, dragging her hands over her forehead, pulling the skin so tight it gave her face a startled look. You could feel the worry coming off her like a fever.

I kept trying to catch her eye. I felt nervous about saying the right things, or the wrong things; that I might somehow be letting her down. But when it was over, when Janet and Simon got in their car and drove away, Martha came over and gave me a brief hug.

"I'm sorry, Hannah. I'll speak to you later. I need to go and pick up Alice." Her words tumbled out in a rush and she almost ran out the room.

Paul gripped my arm as I stared after her. "You okay?"

I nodded. Turned to look at him. "Danny? Do you think he's all right?"

Paul's mouth twitched. His grip relaxed. "I'm sure he is, Hannah. He probably needed some time out. The police think he'll come back in a day or two."

"But why would he go off like that?" I asked, bewildered. "I mean, without telling anyone?"

And how could they be so sure he meant to go? I wanted to say. That someone hadn't made him.

Paul gazed out the window to the view across the bay. It was a cloudy day, misty, and there wasn't that much to see, but he kept his eyes fixed on the horizon like it was the most absorbing thing in the world. "I don't know, Hannah. I really can't answer that. But I'm sure we'll find him very soon."

His voice sounded convincing. Yet behind his words I thought I caught a glimpse of something. Something far less confident than he was trying to appear.

We hardly spoke all the way home. Paul seemed lost in his thoughts, driving automatically, like he could do it in his sleep. I'd told him not to bother giving me a lift. I only live half a mile away and I normally walk, but he was adamant.

Under the circumstances, he said. It was nice but crazy. I know Paul's my godfather and everything, but sometimes he behaves more like my dad than Dad ever does.

And when we arrived he insisted on waiting with me till Dad got back. This I really didn't need. I wanted to be on my own. My head was starting to ache and I didn't want to sit downstairs and think of things to say to Danny's father. But I couldn't find a way of saying this without sounding rude.

Paul lifted a pile of Dad's biology journals from the old armchair by the kitchen table, his gaze flicking around the room. Suddenly I saw it all through his eyes. The heap of pans in the sink. The cereal packets on the table. The milk left out of the fridge. All the usual chaos.

I grabbed the dirty knife and plate Dad had abandoned on top of the dishwasher this morning and shoved them inside. Paul looked embarrassed, like I'd caught him spying on us or something.

"What time is your dad home?" he asked.

I glanced at the clock above the toaster. Nearly six. Dad could be ages yet.

"I'll call him," I said, realizing Paul must want to get back to Martha and Alice. I picked up the phone and dialled Dad's number at the university.

But even before it rang, the back door swung open and Dad walked in. His face twitched in surprise when he saw Paul sitting there. And something else, just for a second. Something almost angry.

Paul got up and stepped forwards as if to shake Dad's

hand, then changed his mind, leaving his arm hanging loosely by his side. It was mad. I mean, they'd known each other for ever, since they went to university together years ago, and yet they were just standing there, Paul looking awkward and Dad bewildered. It was like everyone had forgotten what to do with themselves.

I'd had enough. I mumbled something about homework and shot up to my room. But even with the door closed, I could hear the murmur of their voices in the kitchen. Not loud enough to catch what they were saying, but I didn't care. I didn't want to know.

A bleep from my bag. I grabbed my phone and opened my messages, but the text wasn't from Danny. It was Lianna, asking me where I'd got to. Hell. I'd forgotten I was supposed to go round to hers tonight.

I thought about calling to explain, but then she'd be bound to ask me what was going on. And somehow, though Lianna's my best friend at school and the first person I'd turn to after Danny, I couldn't face all the inevitable questions. The speculation. The lame reassurances.

I sent her a text saying I'd forgotten and was sorry, then flopped on my bed and stared up at the ceiling, exhausted but not sleepy. My eyes were hot and heavy, like I needed to cry. More than anything I felt sort of frozen, as if none of this was real.

Danny would be back soon, I told myself. He'd come home tonight and he'd ring me. And I'd ask him where he'd been, and he'd snigger and say something stupid like

"Wouldn't you just love to know?" in that taunting, teasing way of his. Then he'd give in and tell me, and it would be somewhere obvious, and we'd all kick ourselves and wonder why on earth we never thought of it. And Martha would ground him for ever, but it wouldn't matter.

Because he'd be back. And that was the only thing that mattered at all.

5
NOW

I've no idea how long Alice and I sleep in the hammock, but it must be a while. I wake to the crunch of car tyres on gravel, my neck stiff and achy, the sun already sinking behind Ryall Hill. And remember why I'm here. The text from Martha, something to do with Danny. My stomach chills as I wonder again what's going on.

I guess I'm about to find out, I think, as Rudman launches himself at the garden gate in a volley of yapping. I look up, expecting to see Martha, but it's Paul striding towards us, car keys jangling in the pocket of his suit, wearing a smile that looks prepared.

"I thought you were away at a conference?" I clamber out the hammock, rousing Alice.

Paul pushes Rudman down and brushes the dirt off his trousers. "I was, but something's come up and Martha can't make it back tonight."

He bends down and scoops up his daughter, kissing her plump cheek as she blinks and yawns. Despite his cheerful manner, he looks exhausted, a glint of grey in his short hair, his skin pale and sheeny.

"You two been out here long?" Paul eyes me carefully, as if trying to read something in my face.

I shiver in the cool evening air. "A few hours at least."

"Want Mummy," Alice mumbles, pouting and rubbing her eyes. I hand over her glasses and she plonks them back on her nose.

"Tired," her dad concludes. "C'mon, let's go inside."

I follow them in, pausing in the kitchen as Paul settles Alice on the sofa in the living room. I hear the theme tune to Alice's favourite cartoon as he comes back in and slings his jacket over the chair.

"Do you want something to eat?" He scans the contents of the fridge.

I shake my head. "I'm not that hungry."

Paul grabs a can of beer and rips off the ring pull, glancing at me before taking a sip. "I'd offer you one, Hannah, but I'm not sure your dad would approve."

"Plenty of kids drink at sixteen." I grin. "Dad knows that. But you're off the hook because I hate the taste of beer."

His smile lasts about a second before his face relapses into that heavy, worried look. He runs his hand over the place where his hair is thinning, though you hardly notice because Paul always keeps it so short. It's barely more than stubble.

Sitting in the chair opposite, he takes another gulp of beer, twirling the can in his fingers and looking like he's on the verge of speaking.

"So, what's going on?" I ask, when he seems to think

better of it. "Is everything okay?" My stomach suddenly feels light and hollow. Perhaps I am hungry after all.

Paul ducks my question. "I'm afraid Martha will be gone for a couple of days."

"A couple of days?" I think of Alice. I'm not sure she's ever spent a night away from her mother.

He shrugs. "We'll manage."

"I could stay and help, if you like. Dad's deep in some research project, so he's never back till late."

His mouth twitches. I get the impression he disapproves of Dad working so much, though I can't imagine why – Paul works pretty hard himself.

"Thanks, Hannah. An hour or so would be great – I need to make a couple of calls. Then I'll run you back, okay?"

I nod, wanting to ask again what's happening. Where has Martha gone? And why did she leave so suddenly?

But I'm afraid. Not of asking, but of knowing.

I make a pile of cheese on toast and Alice and I eat it in front of the TV. I can see Paul talking on his mobile out in the garden. I can't hear what he's saying, but his face looks tense, urgent.

Alice stares at the TV, her eyes red and tired. Cartoon cats dance around a pond seething with frogs. I've always hated this one. I want to switch it off, watch something else, the news even. Anything. But I don't want to upset Ally – not right now.

I think about my upcoming exams, the revision I should be doing. But too many other thoughts crowd my head, most of them revolving around Danny and what I suspect is going on. It feels impossible to focus on anything else.

I pull my mobile out my bag and check Martha's message again, resisting the urge to text her back and ask what's happening. Whatever it is, she clearly has enough on her plate without me bugging her. I switch it off and put it back, but a second later the house phone rings.

I get to it just before the answerphone kicks in. "Hello?" I'm certain it's Martha, bracing myself for the sound of her voice.

No reply.

"Hello?" I repeat.

I stop, listening to the eerie silence at the end of the line, heavy, like expectation. With it the first prickle of fear, as always. This isn't the dead kind of silence you get when there's no one there or something's wrong with the line.

This is the silence of someone listening.

"Who is it?" I hiss into the receiver, not wanting Paul or Alice to overhear me. "Why do you keep ringing? What do you want?"

Still nothing.

Then a small noise in the background, barely audible, like someone clearing their throat. I slam the phone down so hard that for a moment I think I've broken it.

And realize I'm shaking.

6

then

Six days after Danny went missing the police were back. I opened our door to Janet Reynolds' gentle smile, another officer standing right behind her. A different man this time, bigger with a fatter face. Older.

"Hello, Hannah, is your father in?" Janet asked.

She was in luck. Even Dad didn't work on Saturday. I left the door ajar, and ran upstairs. Went straight into his study without bothering to knock. "Dad, the police are here. They want to speak to you."

Dad looked up from his screen and blinked at me through his dark-rimmed glasses. "The police?" He looked wary and, well...scared. I stared at him for a moment. He was almost trembling.

What on earth...?

Then I realized. Remembered the last time the police came to our door, and my mind shrank back from the memory like something stung.

"It's about Danny," I reminded him quickly.

"Oh, right...yes." Dad's features unfroze a little. "Of course. Just give me a moment." He turned and pressed a couple of keys on his laptop.

I paused long enough to make sure the message had sunk in, then went back down.

"He's on his way." I smiled an apology at the pair in the doorway and we waited for him to join us. Neither of them seemed to feel awkward, like they were used to standing around on people's doorsteps.

A minute later Dad appeared, a smile fixed on his face like a sticking plaster. "David Radcliffe," he said, extending a hand to each of them. "How can I help you?"

"Sorry to disturb you, Mr Radcliffe." Janet's voice was smooth and calm as she introduced herself and Detective Inspector Thompson. "We're investigating the disappearance of Danny Geller, and would like to talk to Hannah again. We think you should be present."

Dad looked at me.

"It's okay," I said.

Though in truth it wasn't, and I felt the world tip in a way that made me dizzy. I mean, I knew they hadn't found Danny yet, that he hadn't come home. There'd been no sign of him at school, and no word from Martha. But somehow the police being here again made it feel much more real, much more serious.

We sat in the lounge. I glanced at the books and magazines scattered across the table, the stains on the cover of the sofa, and felt the colour rush up to my cheeks. But if either Janet

Reynolds or Detective Thompson noticed the mess, they were nice enough not to show it.

"Is there any news?" I got in before either of them spoke. "I mean, do you know where Danny is?"

Janet hesitated, trying to find the right words. I knew they wouldn't be good. Her being here at all meant they couldn't be good.

"Nothing concrete, Hannah, but we're still at the very early stages of the investigation."

I bit my lip. I felt stupidly disappointed – though what did I expect? Because why would they be here if they knew where he was? And Martha would have called me, the minute she heard anything.

I felt a sharp pang of guilt at the thought of Martha. She must be frantic right now. I should have gone round. At least I should have rung and offered to help with Alice. After all, Martha had always been there for me, doing her best to fill the gaping hole Mum left in my life.

But I hadn't been able to face it. If I didn't have to see the desperation on Martha's face, hear it in her voice, I could still pretend that everything was okay. That Danny would be back soon and all this would melt away like a bad dream.

"Thank you for seeing us today, Hannah," Janet began, throwing in another of her reassuring smiles. "As you know, Danny has been missing for nearly a week now and we're very concerned. We want to talk to everyone who saw him last weekend, and since you were the last person we know of, we need to go over again what happened last Sunday."

I found I could look her in the eyes almost easily, lulled by their kindness. What must it be like, I wondered, walking into people's houses, always bringing bad news? How did it feel knowing that everyone you spoke to wished you weren't even there?

My thoughts veered back to that day a year ago. The knock on the door. The policemen, different, but the same uniform. Dad sending me upstairs when he saw the seriousness in their expression.

Half an hour later, when Dad came to break the news that Mum was dead, I covered my ears with a pillow. I hadn't wanted to hear it.

I still didn't.

"Hannah?" Janet's voice pulled me back. "Do you mind if we go over again exactly what happened last Sunday?"

I swallowed before I spoke. "Yes, that's fine."

"Okay, then. Let's start at the beginning. Can I ask you again what time you met up with Danny?"

I tried to picture it, to put myself there. Already that day seemed a bit less distinct, a little harder to recall. I'd woken to sunlight, I remembered that, the way it had slanted in through the window, lighting up the tiny specks of dust in the air. I read in bed for a while, ate some cereal, put on a load of washing. Was about to go up to clean my teeth when there was a knock on the door.

And it was Danny.

He grinned at me, like I was expecting him. He was dressed in the T-shirt and shorts he always wore in summer

– even when it was rainy – and his blond hair was messy and windblown from the bike ride over.

I know he saw the surprise in my eyes.

"I'm not sure," I told Janet. "About eleven, I think. I've lost my watch and there was no school. I wasn't really paying much attention. Sorry."

"No need to be," she said, giving me a look she clearly intended to be encouraging. I picked at a snagged nail on my thumb. I couldn't help feeling this was some kind of test that I might pass or fail.

And if I failed, did that mean I'd never see Danny again?

Janet made a note in her little black pad. "We're just trying to establish a timeline, Hannah. Can we go over again what you did then?"

"Not much. We hung around for a while. Danny made himself a sandwich."

"Didn't he make you one?" Detective Thompson asked. I saw from the way the corner of his mouth crooked into a smile that he wasn't serious.

I grimaced. Shook my head. "I can't stand peanut butter."

Detective Thompson laughed. "Me neither. It's like eating glue."

"Where did you go while Danny had his sandwich?" Janet asked.

I had to think for a moment. "We sat out in the garden." It was pretty hot, but you could tell summer was winding down. Danny found an old football hidden in the long grass. He sat on the bench, balancing it in the curve between his shin and his foot. He was wearing a pair of trainers I hadn't seen before. Black, with red flashes across each side. They looked new. Expensive.

"You okay?" he'd asked.

"Fine," I said, looking back up at his face, his eyes, pool-blue to my pale grey. He was smiling, friendly, trying to appear relaxed, but his gaze wouldn't quite meet mine.

Because, let's face it, that was a question he shouldn't need to ask.

"Were you alone?" Janet continued.

"Yes. I mean, no. Dad was up in his study."

Janet looked at Dad for confirmation. He squirmed a little in his chair. "I'm pretty sure I was," he said, as if there might actually be some doubt.

"You work at the university?" asked the detective. I guessed Martha must have told them. "In the department of genetics, right?"

"Human genomics," Dad corrected.

The detective frowned. "Which is…"

"DNA sequencing. Isolating the code for diseases, things like that."

"Ah," Detective Thompson nodded. "That must be interesting."

Dad opened his mouth to say more, then closed it again when he realized the detective was only being polite.

Janet turned back to me. "Did Danny come round for any reason in particular?"

"Just to hang out."

She paused, looking at the open pad on her lap. I caught sight of a plate with a half-eaten pizza crust just under the sofa beneath her feet. Jesus. How long had that been there?

"So, after Danny had finished his sandwich?"

"He suggested we go down to the seafront," I said.

"This was, what…about lunchtime? Didn't you have something to eat first?"

I shook my head. "I had something there."

"What was that then?" asked Detective Thompson, looking interested.

"We both had chips. From the kiosk by the crazy golf." I felt my cheeks redden and Detective Thompson raised an eyebrow. "Martha doesn't like us eating them. She says they're bad for us."

"Don't worry, I won't tell." He winked, and Dad actually laughed. And for a second I saw the old Dad, the one who found everything funny. Was always cracking jokes.

"Okay." Janet glanced down at her notes again. "You walked down to the beach?"

"No. We took our bikes." I had a slow puncture in my back wheel. Danny carried the pump in his backpack so he could blow it up again when it went soft.

"Where exactly did you go?"

"Um, straight down to Marine Parade and on to Sandmarsh Fields."

"Nice down there," said the detective. "I often take my kids to the playground."

"We went there, to eat our chips," I added, remembering

us sitting on the little roundabout, Danny spinning it slowly, one foot on the ground. The wide sweep of the sea, the long promenade, the playing fields and boating lake, the steep woods on Dane's Hill – round and round it all went, till it was like the world was revolving and I was perfectly still.

"I'd almost forgotten," Danny had said when he'd finished his chips, lying back on the wooden boards of the roundabout and closing his eyes. His face seemed to have grown more angular in the last year, but the tops of his cheeks were still dense with freckles. Darker than mine; larger too.

"Forgotten what?"

"How nice it is down here." He opened an eye and peeked at me, then quickly looked away.

"So why don't we come any more?"

I regretted the question the second it left my mouth. The last thing I wanted was to scare Danny off. But Danny didn't seem to hear. He sat up, pushing the roundabout faster and faster, then jumped off and stood there smirking as I twirled around in front of him.

"How long were you there?" I looked up. Saw Janet watching me carefully and for a moment, a long stupid moment, I wondered if she could see right into my head. Actually know what I was thinking.

"About an hour."

"Was anyone else around?"

I thought about it. "Just a couple of little kids with their mums," I said. "Danny was messing around on the baby swing and one of the mothers asked him to get off."

"Did you recognize them?" The detective sat up straighter.

I told him I'd never seen them before.

"And no one spoke to you apart from that?"

I shook my head. "I don't think so."

"So, what did you do next?" Janet eyed me patiently. I knew she was hoping I'd tell her something important, a bit of information they could look into. I almost thought of making something up.

"Umm…Danny chased the train."

Janet looked confused.

"The little miniature train that goes round the common. Danny raced it on his bike."

The detective laughed. "Did he win?"

"Yeah. It doesn't go very fast. But he did get told off."

Janet's head jerked up. "Told off? Who by?"

"Um…by the man driving it. He shouted at him. Said he'd tell Danny's parents."

Dad frowned, but Janet glanced over at her colleague. "We can check that out, can't we?"

He gave a brief nod.

"That's good, Hannah," Janet said. "That's what we need. Other people who will remember Danny that afternoon."

"He won't get into trouble, will he?" I didn't dare look at Dad.

Janet leaned over and squeezed my hand. "Hannah, all we're interested in is finding Danny and bringing him home. You're not to worry about getting him into trouble. We don't care what either of you got up to, but we do need to know everything – even silly little things like that. They could be important."

So I told them about the boating lake. It's not really a lake, more like a shallow lagoon that traps the seawater at high tide. A narrow concrete ledge runs right through the middle, separating the paddling section from the deeper bit for boats.

"Sounds fun," said the detective, when I described how easily Danny rode across the ledge on his bike. It's a long stretch and once you set off there's no going back, nowhere to put your feet, so you've got to keep pedalling.

I managed a smile. "It is. Until you fall in."

It was always Danny's favourite dare. He'd show other kids how easy it was, then challenge them to have a go. They'd set off and after a little way they'd lose their bottle and their balance and the next thing they were splashing around in the lake, laughing as much as we were.

"Go on, titch," Danny had said that Sunday as I paused by the edge of the water. Then he'd lifted the front wheel of his bike onto the ledge and glided expertly across. "Come on," he coaxed me from the other side.

I'd rolled forwards, ready to push off, but got no further. Something in my head wouldn't let me go.

I'd lost my nerve.

Normally Danny would never have let me hear the end of it, would have ribbed and teased me until I pulled myself together and had a go. But that day he didn't say anything. Just waved me to follow him and pedalled off towards the bandstand.

Janet and the detective stayed for several hours. I told them everything I could remember, how we cycled back past the pier, round the footpath to Ladd's Point. How we sat on the long flat ledge that surrounds the little bay, listening to the suck and swish of the waves.

Mum and Martha used to take us there all the time when we were small. I always loved exploring the caverns and crevices of the rocks, gathering up the little periwinkles and collecting them in a pool. Tiny yellow jewels against the dark rock and seaweed.

That Sunday with Danny, however, I spent my time outwitting the limpets. You can't knock them or prise them off, not without smashing their shells. But sometimes, if you sneak up and nudge them quickly, you can surprise them before they have a chance to clamp down.

I'm really good at it. I'm fast and decisive and they're dislodged before they know it, shrinking back into their tough little cones.

"You can eat them, you know," Danny had teased. "Even raw."

He laughed as I pulled a face and placed them back in

the circular ridge they made in the rock.

It was the only thing he said the whole time we were there. I'd half hoped, half dreaded him mentioning how things were between us, the fact that we'd practically been strangers this last six months. But he never did.

It was like it had never happened. Or was forgotten. At least by him.

And he'd seemed in no hurry to leave. None of the usual excuses he came up with to avoid me. Instead he suggested we push our bikes back up to Shelton Castle and cycle across to Ryall Hill, where we sat on a bench looking out over the town and the Bristol Channel, and the distant Welsh hills beyond. Danny tossed a pebble he'd picked up on the beach, catching it with one hand then the other. Over and over. Rhythmic. Kind of soothing.

And for a moment, it was like it used to be. No need for words and nothing awkward in the silence.

Just the two of us, together.

When I got to the end, to the point where Danny had cycled home with me, we went through it all over again. Janet read from her notes, checking every detail. Who did we see? Would anyone else remember seeing us? It dragged on and on, and this time it seemed harder. I felt muddled and confused and worried I'd got something wrong. What exactly did Danny say when he arrived at my house? Did we take the zigzag path to the beach or head down Clifton Road?

I kept having to stop and think. Janet never got annoyed, just told me to take my time. But it didn't help.

Then, suddenly, she changed tack, sitting back in the armchair and observing me with a serious expression. "You know the Gellers well, don't you, Hannah? You've stayed there often, I believe, especially since your mum—"

"Yes."

I said it too fast. Felt the detective's eyes studying my face.

"Paul and Martha are old friends of mine from university," Dad cut in. "Hannah has always spent a lot of time with them. They've helped me…us…out a great deal."

Janet gave Dad a sympathetic look. I guessed she knew what happened after Mum died.

She turned back to me. "You'd say you know Danny pretty well then?"

I nodded.

"So have you noticed anything different about him recently? In general, I mean."

I hesitated. "Um…not really."

"Any changes in his behaviour?"

I lifted my shoulders into what I hoped was a casual shrug. "Nothing I can think of."

"When you saw him last Sunday, did he say anything you thought was odd or out of the ordinary? Tell you he was worried about something or that he was in some kind of trouble?"

"Nothing. He was just…you know…normal." I couldn't quite look at Janet as I said it.

"Did he spend much time on his computer?" asked Detective Thompson. "Perhaps mention someone he'd met online?"

I shook my head.

Janet tapped her pen against her lips and closed her notebook. "Okay, that's great, Hannah. You've been very helpful and I'm sorry this has all taken so long."

She glanced at Dad, then back at me. "But listen, if you remember anything, anything at all, even if it doesn't seem important, get your dad to ring us straight away, okay? Don't worry that you might be wasting our time. That doesn't matter."

"Okay."

She got up, placing her hand on my shoulder as we walked towards the door.

"Hannah, think about the things you know about Danny, things he might want kept secret, things he's done that perhaps he doesn't want other people to know. You can talk to me on your own if you like." She bent her head slightly, peered right into my eyes. "Please bear in mind what's at stake here. Danny may have made you promise not to tell anyone, but it's very, very important that you do. For his sake, all right?"

I nodded again. Swallowed and blinked. "You will find him, won't you?"

Janet held my gaze. "Obviously I can't make any promises, but I think there's a very good chance we will."

She gave Dad and me a card with her name and phone

number on it. I went straight up to my room, while Dad saw them out. Threw the card into my sock drawer.

My chest felt hot and tight. I was fighting the urge to run back and tell Janet everything. That Danny *had* changed. That nothing he did made sense any more. That I no longer felt like I knew him.

And that I had no idea what I had done wrong.

Because the one question she should have asked was *why*? Why had Danny come round last Sunday when he'd been avoiding me for months?

And why was I so reluctant to tell Janet Reynolds the truth?

I sat on my bed, rubbing my forehead. I was ashamed, I realized. I didn't want to admit to anyone how strained our friendship had become, or how much that hurt me. I didn't even want to admit it to myself. It was like when you cut yourself and you didn't want to see the blood, the slice in your skin. It was too raw. Too painful to look at.

Lying back and closing my eyes, I pictured Danny. Saw him cycle off from my house, one hand steering his bike, the other lifted in a wave. The orange glow of the late afternoon sun making everything around him appear warm and golden as he rounded the bend in the road and disappeared.

And it seemed to me now that the whole day had been a gift, rich and perfect. Like nothing had ever gone wrong between us. And nothing ever would.

But now he was gone. And all I had left was his memory.

7

then

Rap, rap, rap.

I turned down the sound on the TV. Someone was knocking on the window. My heart soared as I bounded over.

Danny!

I pulled back the curtains, breath tight with joy, certain I'd see his face beaming in at me.

Martha stood in the porch, looking pale and slightly scary in her dark boots and long black coat. Disappointment cut through me, along with an insane impulse to duck down and hide.

But of course she'd seen me. I went and opened the front door, a smile ready to conceal my discomfort.

Martha's eyes flicked to mine then away. "Hello, Hannah. Can I come in?"

She followed me into the living room. I switched off the TV as Martha stood, watching me, her hands opening and clenching with agitation.

"Is it Danny?" I said quickly. "Have they found him?"

Martha didn't move, her agonized expression her only

reply. I felt a wrench of shame. I should have gone round after the police left yesterday. I should have called. I should have…

"So, how did it go yesterday?"

"What do you mean?" I asked stupidly.

"With the police, Hannah." Her voice hovered between exhaustion and irritation.

"Okay, I guess."

So that was why she was here. Martha never came round, not since Mum died, not unless it was to pick up Danny or drop something off for me – and even then you could tell she was in a hurry to leave. I guess this place reminded her too much of Mum, of all the times they'd spent drinking tea in the kitchen or sitting, feet curled up on the sofa, chatting and watching TV.

Not that I blamed her. This house was full of painful memories for me too – but it wasn't like I could avoid my own home.

I sat on the edge of the sofa, crossing my arms over my chest. The radiator was on, but the room felt cold.

"What did you tell Janet Reynolds?" Martha asked. I risked a quick glance at her face. She had the look of someone trying to hold themselves in, but losing the battle.

"I don't know. Just what happened. Everything I told them before. They wanted to go over some things."

"Such as?" There was something sharp in her tone.

"Nothing really. You know – I told you. Just where we

went and stuff." My palms began to sweat despite the chill. Why was Martha giving me the third degree?

"Just where you went and stuff," she echoed, unable to contain her impatience any longer.

I swallowed. "What do you want me to say? They asked me questions and I answered them. What else could I do?"

"I don't know, Hannah. You tell me."

I stared at her, at a loss. "What do you mean?"

"Do I have to explain?" Martha gave me an exasperated look. "You were the last person to see Danny. You're his best friend – you tell each other everything…"

"Not any mo—"

"Never mind what you said to the police. You're not seriously telling *me* you have absolutely no idea where he is?"

I shook my head vigorously. "No, Martha, really I don't…"

"Come off it, Hannah. You must know *something*."

"What do you want me to say? I told them everything I could think of. We went over and over it."

"But Danny must have said or done something. Given you some kind of clue."

"Like what?" I leaped up and faced her. "He came round. We went out. You heard me tell the police all about it the first time."

"I heard—"

"This isn't my fault," I said, a rush of feeling punching out the words. "Why are you blaming me? I mean, how do we know Danny even planned it? What if he was…?"

I stopped before I said it. The one thing no one wanted even to contemplate. That Danny hadn't chosen to leave. I felt my cheeks flush, the heat of anger in my face. But underneath I was starting to panic. The last thing I wanted was to fall out with Martha; it was hard enough coping without Mum. Especially now.

But Martha appeared not to hear me. Her voice rose, her frustration taking over. Her face was full of a mad energy I'd never seen before, her eyes narrowed, her chin jutting towards me as she spoke.

"I don't believe you," she spat. "I can't believe that you had no clue what was going on. The two of you—"

"*Back off, Martha.*"

Dad's voice made us both jump. He was standing in the doorway, watching. I couldn't be sure how long he'd been there or how much he'd heard.

"Don't tell me you actually believe any of this!" Martha asked, her voice climbing still higher. She stared at him and I sensed the tension between them, like static before a storm.

"Believe what, Martha? Danny's gone missing, and it's very distressing. But that doesn't mean that my daughter knows anything about it."

Martha's eyes never left his. She looked for a moment like she was going to say something else, then changed her mind.

"Come on, David. You can't be serious. Those two have always been as thick as thieves. They tell each other everything."

"Martha, I know you're upset—"

"Upset? Of course I'm bloody upset. My son's been missing for a week now and the last person to see him is sitting here acting all innocent…"

"She *is* innocent, Martha," Dad growled, his face rigid with anger. "*You know that.* Whatever's happened to Danny…wherever he is and whether he planned it or not, Hannah had nothing to do with it."

Martha glared at him, something twitching in her cheek.

"You're not thinking straight, Martha. Why would Hannah hide anything? She's as anxious as anyone to have Danny home."

Martha looked at me, then back at Dad. "You can believe what you like, David," she muttered. "You always have."

Dad's head jerked back as if he'd been hit. No one spoke for several seconds. Then Martha sank into the armchair, dropped her face into her hands and burst into tears.

Dad and I stood there, not moving, just listening to her awful gasping sobs.

"I'm sorry," she cried, running the heel of her hand across her cheeks, leaving a dark smear of mascara. "I'm sorry. I didn't mean… I keep thinking it's all my fault. I mean, if I hadn't…"

"Hadn't what?" Dad asked.

Martha sighed. "Oh, I don't know. Danny's been so… I can't explain it. He hardly speaks to me any more. And he totally ignores his father. He just seems so distant all the time."

"He's a teenager," Dad said, his voice more gentle. "It all sounds like pretty normal stuff."

"You think so?" Martha looked up and sniffed. "I suppose. But he's been acting so weird. Refusing to join in with things or even come down for meals. I go up to his room to get him and he simply tells me he's not hungry. The only one of us he still has any time for is Alice."

She ran her hands over her face again, pressing her fingers against her eyes for a second or two as if forcing back the tears. "You know what I mean, don't you, Hannah? You've seen how he's been."

She looked up at me appealingly, throwing in a quick, apologetic smile. I didn't know what to say. I had no idea Danny had been acting that way with Paul and Martha too. She'd never said anything before; always acted cheerful whenever I saw her, like nothing was wrong.

"I just kept thinking," Martha went on with a crack in her voice, "there must be some kind of reason. I even started checking his room when he was out. I wondered whether he was getting into drugs, something like that."

I realized I was staring at her with my mouth open. "That's crazy," I said. "He hates that kind of stuff." It was true. Danny cared far too much about his swimming to do something idiotic like that.

"I know I probably shouldn't have done it." Martha swallowed. "But I needed to find out what was going on with him. Anyway, a month or so ago he came back early from the pool and caught me going through his things. We had a terrible row."

She pulled a tissue out of her pocket and wiped her nose. She looked suddenly much older than her forty-five years.

"Did you tell Paul?" Dad asked.

Martha shook her head miserably. "I didn't want to worry him. He had enough on his plate with the business and all that trouble with those office renovations."

"He never said anything about it," I whispered, almost to myself. I felt sort of sad and sick at the same time – Danny used to tell me everything.

"I can't help thinking that's why he left." Martha was crying again. "I can't get it out of my head. I mean, why else would he disappear like this?"

Dad cleared his throat. "Have you told the police?"

Martha nodded. "I mentioned it, but they said kids act that way towards their parents all the time."

"Well, they're probably right." Dad walked over, placed a hand on her shoulder. I could tell he felt awkward doing it. That he had to force himself. "Really, Martha, there's no point blaming yourself. Or Hannah. It's not going to help."

Martha nodded again. "I know." She looked at me. "I'm sorry, Hannah. I was upset. I really didn't mean—"

"It's okay," I cut in. "I understand."

I didn't need her to explain. And I didn't want to talk

any more about it. Clearly talking was never going to get us anywhere.

Let alone bring Danny back.

8

then

"So, what do you think has happened to him then? I mean, he's been gone, what, over ten days now."

I looked up at Lianna. She and Maisy were studying me, measuring my reaction.

"Like I said, I don't know," I mumbled. "I really don't have a clue."

Maisy kept her eyes fixed on mine as she played with her long hair, pulling it forwards around her neck, then deftly weaving it into a neat brown plait. "He didn't do anything then? Say anything at all?"

I flinched inwardly at how closely her words echoed Martha's. Did even my friends think I was holding something back? I turned away, caught sight of my reflection in Lianna's bedroom mirror, my guarded, almost wary expression.

"I mean, surely if he ran away there'd have been signs or something," Maisy continued, unravelling her hair and starting again.

I felt my jaw clench and forced myself to relax. They were just trying to help, I reminded myself – after all, they've always known what a big part Danny played in my life. But somehow I could never talk to them like I could to him. Could never quite let myself open up in the same way.

"Have the police been in touch again?" Lianna asked. "Since they came round?"

I shook my head.

"What about his phone? Have you tried calling it?"

"About a thousand times," I said, swallowing down my unease. "It's always off."

"But can't they trace it or something?" asked Maisy. "Check his calls?"

"I don't know." I remembered the eeriness of hearing Danny's voice on the answerphone. I never left a message. I couldn't think of anything to say except, "Hi, it's Hannah. Call me."

And what was the point of that?

"God, it's creepy, isn't it?" Maisy gave an exaggerated little shiver. "Do you reckon he's been taken or something?"

I bit my bottom lip and looked away. It was obvious she got a little thrill out of Danny's disappearance – along with almost everyone else at school. Like it was somehow not real, just a game, something they'd seen on TV.

Out of the corner of my eye I saw Lianna flash Maisy a warning look, a frown followed by a widening of her eyes. I stared out Lianna's bedroom window, at the new house being built across the road. A man was walking across a narrow strip of scaffolding, a phone pressed against his ear.

He didn't seem bothered about the height, the fact that there was nothing more than a few planks between him and a broken neck.

"I have to go." I jumped up from the bed.

"Hey, not yet," Lianna said quickly, knowing they'd gone too far. "Stay for a bit longer. Mum's making brownies for us all."

"Yes, stay." Maisy looked genuinely sorry. "We won't talk about Danny any more – not if you don't want to."

"I've got to get home," I lied. "Dad and I are going out for a pizza."

"Do you want us to walk you back?" offered Lianna, like I was something fragile that everyone needed to protect. The girl who lost her mother. Then her best friend.

"I'm fine." I made myself smile. "It's only ten minutes away. I'll see you at school tomorrow."

Back in my empty house I headed straight upstairs and took down my jewellery box from my bedroom shelf, wiping off the film of dust with my hand. My diary was hidden inside, underneath the little tray for keeping earrings and trinkets and things. Not that I had many.

As I lifted it out, something fell on the floor. I looked down and saw it glinting on the carpet. Mum's wedding ring. The police had given it to us after the autopsy. I gazed at it for a moment, then grabbed it and dropped it back in the box, shutting the lid firmly.

Settling back on my bed, I flicked through the pages. It wasn't much of a diary, really – there were no dates or anything – just a notebook where I wrote things whenever I felt in the mood.

In one entry I'd stuck a couple of tickets from an amusement arcade – the kind you win and exchange for prizes. I ran my fingers over them, feeling a mix of warmth and sadness. Remembering that trip to Weston, three summers ago. We all went – Mum and Dad, Martha and Paul, Danny, Alice and I.

While the grown-ups lounged on blankets on the sand, drinking fizzy wine and gossiping and laughing, Danny and I had gone swimming. We'd just inched our way into the cold water when Alice woke and toddled towards us. Spotting our heads bobbing above the waves, she started wailing and screaming – wouldn't stop even when we swam back to shore.

It took nearly an hour in the arcade to cheer her up. Paul got a big bag of two-pence pieces, and Danny and I took turns to hoist Alice up so she could post them into the penny falls. Then Mum challenged everyone to an air hockey tournament, and Dad won, raising his fists in the air and whooping like an idiot.

I can't remember what we did then. I never bothered to write it down.

Leafing further forwards, I came to the page where the entries stopped a year ago. When Mum died. When there no longer seemed much point recording things like what

I ate for breakfast or who'd said what at school.

I turned to a fresh sheet. Wrote in Sunday's date two weeks ago. Best to work backwards, I decided. Start from when I last saw Danny.

Danny must have said or done something. Martha's words echoed round my head. *Given you some kind of clue.*

Half an hour later all I had was a blank page and the looming threat of a headache. I couldn't think of a single thing I hadn't already come up with. But neither could I shake the feeling that there must be something, that if I only tried hard enough I'd unearth some kind of evidence that might lead to Danny.

There was only one answer: try harder.

I stuffed the diary into my backpack and grabbed a slice of bread from the kitchen, squeezing it into a rubbery ball. I chewed it as I set off down the road, taking the footpath to Marlborough Avenue and dropping down onto Marine Parade, then skirting along to the Sandmarsh playing fields.

It was the exact route Danny and I had taken that Sunday, but it was amazing how much had already changed. Wet leaves now covered most of the path, and a brisk autumn wind bit deep through my jacket and jeans, making my eyes water and my nose run. I braced myself against the chill and concentrated on scanning the tarmac either side of me, though I knew the chances of finding anything now were worse than slim. Especially since the police had already checked.

But I had to look anyway. I had to make sure they hadn't missed anything. I couldn't sit around doing nothing any more. And maybe looking would jog my memory, bring up something I'd forgotten.

The Sandmarsh playing fields were almost deserted. Only a woman out walking a fat black dog on a lead. I paced round the outside of the miniature railway track, examining the grass. The woman with the dog paused and glanced over and I realized how odd it must look – a young girl, alone, wandering around staring at the ground. So I bent down and pretended to fiddle with the laces of my trainers, but when I finally raised my eyes, she was walking towards me.

"Have you lost something?"

I almost said yes. I almost told her who.

Easier to shake my head.

"Are you okay?" She had one of those nice faces, like Janet Reynolds. Like someone's mum. It made my chest ache just to look at her.

"Thanks. Really, I'm fine." I returned her smile, aiming for happy and confident.

She seemed unconvinced. "You sure? It'll be getting dark soon. Maybe you should think about going home."

When the woman left I carried on. Checked the path up towards Dane's Rise, going right to the bench where Danny and I had sat and watched the yachts tacking in the breeze.

Cutting back to the boating lake, I walked across the concrete ledge, peering into the dark water on either side.

Nothing. Only the sharp smell of salt and dankness. When I reached the end, I retraced my steps, just to make sure.

Still nothing.

Back along the seafront, it started spitting, a slow damp drizzle that swiftly hardened into rain. By the time I reached Ladd's Point, I was wet and seriously cold, and the light was fading fast. But I made myself scour the beach, checking up around the cliffs where we climbed, gazing into the murky rock pools, searching among the stones and pebbles.

Nothing, nothing and more nothing. Nothing but seaweed and old plastic bottles, pieces of driftwood and the odd snarly stretch of nylon rope.

The sky turned darker, the rain heavier. I huddled in the little cave beneath the cliff, waiting for it to subside. I got my diary out my rucksack. My pencil paused over the paper, then I wrote three words in capitals:

WHERE ARE YOU?

I rested my head against the cold, hard rock and tried to think, still haunted by Martha's words.

He must have said or done something.

Was she right? Had I really missed things, not paid enough attention? I couldn't get rid of the feeling that perhaps I held the missing piece that might bring Danny back, that if I just tried hard enough I could get him home and make everything all right.

I sifted again through my memories of that afternoon, worn now, a bit tatty and frayed. Closing my eyes, I tried to conjure the feeling of being here in the sunshine, but it all seemed impossibly far away.

Only…something shifted and caught at the edge of my mind. Danny sitting over on the flat rocks, watching me mess with the limpets. I'd turned and seen he was on the verge of speaking. Could see the words hovering at the corners of his mouth, like something trying to escape.

"What is it?" I asked.

Danny looked at me for a moment. Pressed his lips tight together.

"Nothing," he said finally.

Why hadn't I asked again? I wondered now, shivering in my damp clothes. My head felt muzzy and my stomach ached with frustration.

Why didn't I make him tell me what was on his mind?

I inhaled deeply and opened my eyes, blinking in the near darkness. This was pointless, I realized. I was grasping at straws, imagining things where there was nothing to see. Like someone drowning, desperate for something to cling on to.

Martha's car was parked outside my house. I could see her silhouette through the windscreen as I walked up the road.

As I approached, she leaned over and opened the passenger door.

"Hey, Hannah, get in!"

Too tired to argue, I slid into the front seat beside her. Alice was asleep in the back, her head slumped at an uncomfortable angle.

"Jesus, look at you!" Martha gasped. "You're soaked. What on earth have you been—?"

Without warning I started to cry, soundlessly, tears rolling down my cheeks, falling onto my sodden clothes. I couldn't stop. I was gulping for air, my vision blurry, my mind an almost soothing blank of anguish.

Then Martha was cradling me and I realized she was sobbing too.

"Oh, Hanny, I'm so sorry. I came round to see how you were doing." She pulled my face to look at hers. Pressed my forehead into her shoulder. "And to say again how sorry I am about what I said. You know I didn't mean it, don't you?"

I nodded, sitting up and wiping my nose on my sleeve. She brushed the wet hair from my face.

"Come and have something to eat."

Dial House, usually so tidy, was a mess. Piles of clothes heaped by the washing machine, dirty dishes crowding the space next to the dishwasher, the kitchen table covered with mugs and unopened letters. Martha settled Alice on a chair with a colouring book and some crayons, then grabbed the last couple of clean plates, pulling a sponge cake from a bag.

That surprised me. Martha hated supermarket cakes. She always said they tasted of plastic.

"I had a word with your dad before you turned up." She unwrapped the sponge and cut it into unappetizing wedges. "He's worried about you, Hannah."

She handed me a slice. It looked like coffee, but I couldn't be sure. I just hoped it wasn't ginger.

"Why?"

"He says you're taking it badly. About Danny, I mean. Says you've barely left the house except to go to school."

I thought of all the excuses I'd made to Lianna and Maisy to avoid going round before today. The headaches I'd invented. The non-existent homework. Somehow, seeing my friends made Danny's absence worse; it didn't feel right, carrying on like everything was normal.

"Your dad thinks there's been too much pressure on you," Martha continued. "From the police...from me." These last words accompanied by an apologetic pinch of her lips.

I stared at the cake on my plate. The knife hadn't so much cut the sponge as pressed its way through it. It was all scrunched up and icing was oozing out the middle. Suddenly I wasn't at all hungry.

"I know this is hard on you, Hannah." Martha leaned

over and squeezed my hand. "It's hard on all of us. But we will find Danny, I promise. We'll get him back."

I nodded, looking at Rudman. He was sitting by the back door, whining at something outside.

Martha followed my gaze and sighed. "He does that all the time, waiting for Danny to come home. And if it's not him at it, it's Alice."

Alice raised her head at the sound of her name, but didn't speak. Martha boiled the kettle, emptied the teapot and swilled it under the tap, then dropped in some fresh tea bags. I studied her face. She looked exhausted, her eyes circled with gloom.

She caught my gaze and I looked away. Saw on the other side of the table several photos of Danny, and Martha's open laptop.

"What's this?" I asked, nodding at the laptop and taking a bite of the sponge. It was coffee, but bland and much too sweet.

Martha sighed. "I'm trying to design a poster. And not getting very far. You know me and computers."

"A poster?"

"About Danny. I have to do something, Hannah. I can't just sit around waiting."

I looked at her. I knew how she felt. Doing nothing was worse than wasting your time.

"Isn't that something the police should do though?" I asked. "The poster, I mean. Isn't that their job?"

"Apparently not. They've searched the area, interviewed

everyone who might be a witness, alerted other police forces around the country. They seem to think they've done all they can at this stage."

"Do they have any idea what might have happened?" I tried to keep the tension out of my voice.

Martha shook her head and slid her tongue around her teeth. "I get the impression they think he's run away. That he'll come back when he's ready."

"And you don't agree?"

Her eyes fixed on mine. "Do you, Hannah? Do you really think Danny would do that, leave us, leave Alice, without a word to anyone?"

I flushed. Was Martha accusing me again?

"I'm sorry," she said, catching the look on my face. "Let's not get into that again. I know you would tell me if you knew anything."

Martha sighed again, heavier this time and pulled at her top lip with her fingers. "Truth is, I don't know what to think. I can't believe he'd run off, put us through all this, but then I'd rather that than…"

She stopped. Not letting herself go there. But I knew where that thought was leading – better Danny left of his own free will than was forced.

Abducted. Or worse.

"They're talking of dragging the boating lake," Martha said, her voice almost a whisper. "Just to check, Janet Reynolds said."

I thought of what I'd told them, about Danny and me

crossing the ledge on our bikes. Did they think he went back there or something?

"When?" I asked.

"Next week."

I swallowed.

"He's not there," Martha added. "I told them that." She looked at me as if for confirmation, her hands hovering restlessly in her lap.

I took a deep breath. "We'll find him." I nodded towards the computer. "I can help. I've done loads of this stuff at school."

Martha frowned. "I'm not sure, Hannah. You've got your homework to do, and your dad thinks—"

"I don't care what Dad thinks. I want to help find Danny."

"Danny." Alice lifted her head from her colouring book and smiled. "Want Danny."

I studied her face, the little pinch marks below her eyes, and felt my stomach contract – I could see how much she was missing her brother.

Pushing away the rest of my cake, I leaned forwards and dragged the laptop towards me.

9
then

The poster slipped through my hands as I tried to fix it to the street lamp. I picked it up off the pavement and brushed a smudge of dirt off the plastic sleeve. Held it back in place with my elbow. With my other hand I wound the string round the concrete post, crossing it over the plastic and tightening it into a knot.

This time the poster stayed put. Danny's face grinned back at me – and at everyone else walking down the street. I'd seen this picture a thousand times in the three weeks since he disappeared, but it still freaked me out. Every time his eyes caught mine, I couldn't help wondering where he was. What was happening to him.

I had less trouble at the bus shelter, pressing the poster against the perspex window and sticking it, top and bottom, with two lengths of tape. Then stood back and gave it a gentle tug. It held firm.

"Excuse me, young lady."

The voice made me start. I spun round and saw the old man standing behind me, eyes narrow with disapproval.

"Have you got permission to do that?" He nodded

towards the poster. "You can't put just anything up there, you know."

"I know." I picked up my bag and slung it over my shoulder, started to walk away.

"Hang on a minute…"

But I was gone, crossing the road and climbing back into the passenger seat of Martha's car. As I twisted round to grab my seat belt, I saw the man peering at Danny's photograph. Saw his face change as he realized it wasn't another ad for a local band. Saw him glance up as we pulled away, his expression half pity, half apology.

"Okay?" Martha asked.

"Uh-huh."

I didn't bother to tell her about the man. She had enough on her mind. She'd barely said a word since Paul confronted her in the kitchen this evening, staring at the bulging carrier bags, catching hold of her arm as she tried to brush past.

"For god's sake, Martha," I heard him hiss as I shot off to the car. "Just remember what Janet said, all right?"

I couldn't help wondering what exactly Janet Reynolds had said. And what she'd think about this. Was it actually legal, sticking these posters everywhere? Had Martha even checked?

"Just the shops, then we'll go home," Martha said, parking in the multistorey behind the supermarket. She sat for a moment, rubbing her forehead, looking as tired as I felt. It had taken us several hours to cover just the end of town near the leisure centre, and some of the roads leading up to the high street.

"Let's go." I grabbed a pile of envelopes and posters and led the way through the alleyway to the main shopping street. It was cold and late and everywhere had that empty, closed-up look. I shivered, pulling my scarf tight around my neck, glad Martha was with me.

"I'll do this side – you do over the road." Martha crossed to the line of shops opposite; I began working my way towards the precinct at the other end of the street. We couldn't stick the posters on the windows, so we folded them into envelopes, along with a note asking the manager to display them somewhere inside.

But not all the shops had letter boxes, particularly the larger ones. More often than not I had to shove the envelope under the door, or leave it tucked in the space around the frame.

I pushed one through the door of the bookshop, another in the place that sells vitamins and health foods. When I straightened up, I saw a group in the distance. As they got closer, I recognized Maisy and Vicky and a couple of other girls from my year. They stopped and looked at the poster I'd stuck up by the library, four heads cocked at the same angle as they read the text under Danny's photo. Then stood for a minute, talking, before heading up the street towards me.

Vicky spotted me first. I saw her tug on Maisy's arm as they approached, mumbling something I didn't catch.

My cheeks flared. All at once I felt stupidly embarrassed. Like I'd been caught shoplifting, or found naked, wandering the streets.

As they drew level, Maisy tossed me an awkward smile. "How's it going?" She nodded at the bag of posters and envelopes in my hand.

"Fine," I said.

She hesitated for a moment. "Do you want a hand?"

I shook my head. "It's fine, honestly. I'm nearly done."

"Oh, okay." Something like relief flashed across her face.

Vicky smiled fleetingly. "Sorry, Hannah," she said, then to Maisy: "We've got to go. Sophie's waiting for us."

I watched them disappear along the side street that led to the Co-op. Saw Maisy turn round and give me a small wave and a glance of something – pity? encouragement? – then quicken her pace to catch up with the others. As they passed Martha by the card shop, they all turned to stare, Vicky actually walking backwards a few paces, not bothering to hide her curiosity.

Not that Martha noticed. She was oblivious, working with a speed and fervour that made me dizzy. Ever since they dragged the boating lake a few days ago, her search to find her son had been relentless.

I glanced at the picture of Danny in my hand. Please come back, I thought. Before it's too late. Before our lives fall apart completely.

But Danny just beamed back at me. I folded his face in half and stuffed it into an envelope, posting it through the door of the hardware store. Worked my way up towards the end of the high street.

Last but one was a charity shop, with a letter box right at the bottom of the door. I bent down, struggling with the stiff flap. Managed to prise it open, but it snapped shut before I could push the envelope through, nearly trapping my fingers. I tried again. Succeeded.

As I straightened up, I saw it.

I stood there, rigid, staring at the £9.50 price tag pinned to the sleeve, unable to move or turn away or even breathe.

My mother's dress. The purple crushed silk gown she wore whenever she was going somewhere special. The one that made her look like she lived a whole other kind of life.

My heart nearly stopped. What was it doing here?

Slowly I realized, remembering Dad clearing out all her things only days after she died. I assumed he'd given them to people, to friends. But he must have brought them here. Or someone else had. After all, who wants a dead woman's clothes?

I couldn't tear my eyes from the dress. It was like she was back. Could almost see her smiling, smell her perfume as she bent forwards to kiss the top of my head.

"Love you, Hanny. Be good, won't you?"

It was what she said every time she went out. And her last words to me, an hour before they pulled her car out of the river.

Twenty minutes too late.

Suddenly I felt sick. My legs were shaky and I wanted to

sink down onto the pavement and rest the side of my head against the window, to close my eyes and go to sleep.

Mum. I miss you so much.

I felt an arm gently fold itself round my shoulder and give it a squeeze.

"Come on, sweetheart." Martha's voice was soft and gentle as she pulled me away. "I think we've done enough for one night."

I could tell she'd seen it too. And I knew that tomorrow it would be gone.

Martha wouldn't let this happen again.

10

then

Martha stepped into the porch, avoiding the broken flowerpot in front of the door, and rang the bell. The sound reverberated through the house, loud as a fire alarm.

I stood behind her, hugging myself to keep warm, trying to kill the tiredness and boredom by examining the entrance. This featured black peeling paintwork and a crack in the little window to the side. Ivy scrambled up the brickwork, and the tiles on the floor were faded and chipped. The small front garden looked almost derelict in the cold November light.

Someone elderly, I guessed, or maybe young, just renting the place, not much caring what kind of a state it was in. It was amazing how often you could tell what kind of person would open the door, long before they did. But you could never know for sure; there was always room for surprise.

A noise from inside, someone making their way to the door. The odds narrowed. They moved slowly, shuffling almost. Older, most likely. Man or a woman? I tried to guess, but already the key was turning in the lock, the sound of a bolt sliding back.

The door opened about fifteen degrees. In the gap a sliver of head appeared, grey-haired, uncertain.

A man.

"Yes?"

"Hello," Martha said in her brightest, friendliest voice. "My name's Martha Geller, and this is my god-daughter Hannah."

I dug out my most encouraging smile, glad I hadn't bothered to change after school. People always seemed reassured by the sight of my uniform.

The door opened another ten degrees. The head peeked out a little further. Martha offered a hand. A pause, then a gnarlier version clasped hers.

"Are you collecting for something?" the old man asked, adjusting his hearing aid.

Martha shook her head, holding out a photograph of Danny. "We're here about my son. He's been missing for two months now. We're just asking people in the area if they can remember seeing him."

The man brought out a pair of glasses from his shirt pocket, settled them carefully on his nose, and took the photo, squinting in the dim light of the hallway. He stood peering at it for what felt like for ever, like one of those endless TV pauses before they announce the winner.

No prize for us, though. Only the inevitable shake of the head.

"No," he said finally. "Never seen 'im."

"Would you mind if we left a copy of his picture and

details?" Martha held out a smaller version of our poster. "If there's anything you remember, anything at all, my number's on the bottom."

The man took it, nodding without speaking, and we said goodbye. Pulling the gate behind us, I glanced back at the door. It was already closed.

Seventeen houses to go. I counted as we walked down the street to the neighbouring driveway, trying not to think about how long it would be before I got home and had something decent to eat. Not to mention my homework; I still had those geography questions from last week and a pile of French verbs to learn for a test.

"You okay?" Martha asked, catching my expression. Like Dad, she had an uncanny knack of reading my mood.

"Fine," I lied.

No way was I letting her send me back. Martha did too much of this on her own as it was. Paul refused to come with her, even when he wasn't working. He didn't approve, I'd gathered – and he wasn't the only one. Janet Reynolds was far from keen. And judging by Alice's recent tantrums, you could add her to the list.

I'd even tried to broach it myself. "Haven't the police already done this?" I asked when Martha first showed me the map and told me about her door-to-door campaign.

"Yes, but only in those areas you and Danny went to. I just want to make sure we cover everywhere, that's all."

Covering everywhere in a town of over 30,000 inhabitants was easier said than done, I knew. And Martha knew it too. But where most people would have given up before they even got started, Martha ploughed on.

It was like her life had shrunk to just one thing: finding Danny.

"I have to make sure, Hannah," she'd said, looking right at me. "No matter how long that takes or what it costs, I have to try absolutely everything I can think of."

So I figured the least I could do was stand here beside her, as often as I could manage. But as we walked up the path to the next house – as smart as its neighbour was neglected – I was beginning to wonder how much more I could take. Three weeks down the line and we still had nothing – no one had seen Danny or knew anything about him. The hope I'd felt when we first started was turning into something bleaker.

Martha lifted the polished brass knocker in the centre of the door and gave it three strong raps. I glanced at the leaflets in my hand as we waited, at Danny beaming back at me from every page.

I remembered the day that photo was taken. It was cropped from a larger picture, snapped outside the local swimming pool, where Danny had just won the freestyle race in the regional championship. What you couldn't see in this fragment was me standing next to him, holding the small silver trophy over his head, as pleased as if I'd won it myself.

All you could see here was Danny, that smile, the crinkles round his eyes from laughing. A face that haunted me now, a constant reminder of his absence. Everywhere I went, it loomed out at me – from every shop and lamp post, every bus stop on the way to school, every corridor and classroom when I arrived. It was like one of those paintings where the eyes seem to follow you around the room; only I couldn't walk away – a few steps later the same set of eyes picked up where the last lot left off.

It made me sad, but it was also a little creepy. Like being spied on by your best friend.

"You sure you're okay?" Martha asked again, picking up on my fatigue. I nodded, forcing myself to look brighter. She turned back to the door and I focused on the freshly painted windows to the left of me. Through the open curtains I could see a vase of flowers sitting on the mantelpiece. Above it hung a picture, an abstract swirl of colours.

This person definitely wasn't old.

Martha rapped the knocker again, glancing at the plan in her pocket. The idea was to cover thirty houses a day, starting from the west side of town beyond the pier and moving across towards the motorway. My job was simple: "Just see if you recognize anyone," Martha had said. "Anyone who might have had anything to do with Danny."

So I stood behind her, scanning the faces that appeared. Took in their puzzled look as they found two strangers on their doorstep, sometimes half shutting the door again in case we were about to mug them. Watched their expression change to sympathy and concern as Martha explained why we were here.

Occasionally the door was opened by someone I knew. The first time was the worst. While Martha spoke to her mother, I could see Ella Thompson, a girl from my year, hovering in the background. Her incredulous look made my insides squirm, and the next day at school it was obvious everyone knew about our visit.

Though no one asked about it. Not even Lianna.

At this house, however, nothing seemed to be happening. I shuffled from side to side, chasing away the numbness in my feet. Martha examined the pretty stained glass panel in the door, probably wondering whether to knock a third time.

Chances are they were out. Another minute and we could post the leaflet through the letter box and move on. I felt a flush of relief. The ones I dreaded weren't those who were absent or slammed the door in our faces. The worst were those who tried to help. Usually women, they'd start asking questions, often recalling the reports in the paper, wanting to hear the whole story. Before we knew it, we were inside, sipping yet another mug of tea, eating another biscuit, going through it all.

Over and over and over again.

All we got were bursting bladders and a slow shake of their head. The same words, like they were reading from a script:

"I can hardly imagine how you feel."

"I'm so sorry...I would love to help, but I really can't think of anything."

"I do so hope you find him."

And they'd close the door behind us with a kind of reluctance, like we were something they were loath to give up on.

But nothing doing here, it seemed. I was about to suggest to Martha that we move on when a noise came from inside. Someone hurried down the stairs and the door swung open. A woman in dark jeans and a soft, cosy-looking cream jumper beamed out at us.

"I'm so sorry I took so long," she panted. "I was upstairs on the phone and I couldn't get away. I kept saying there was someone at the door…"

"That's okay." Martha held out the leaflet and introduced us yet again.

The woman looked at Danny's picture, then back at us, her face glowing with kindness and sympathy.

"Oh goodness. You poor things. I can't even begin to imagine how hard this must be for you." She glanced at the leaflet again, then took a small step back. "Yes, I remember reading about this. Why not come in for a minute while I take a closer look?"

Already she was moving aside, holding the door open to give us room to get past. Martha stepped forward, and I followed, my heart sinking right through the soles of my shoes.

11

NOW

"I'll be back in a couple of hours." Paul grabs his jacket and a few of Martha's reusable shopping bags from the peg on the back door.

"No problem," I say. "Take your time. Alice and I will be fine."

I don't blame him for not wanting to take her. Alice isn't good in supermarkets; she wants everything she sees and can be pretty vocal if she can't have it.

"Thanks." He looks at me like he wants to add something else. I assume it's about Martha and why she's still away, and steel myself for news.

"I was wondering…" Paul sounds artificially breezy, the way you do when you're pretending something has just occurred to you. "Maybe when I get back, we might go down to the seafront for a bit of lunch? The three of us, I mean."

I can't tell if he's asking or assuming. To be honest I'd rather go home and get on with some revision, but something in Paul's expression tells me he really wants me to stay. So I nod. "Sure."

"Fish and chips it is then," he says, with what I can tell is an effort to sound relaxed and cheerful. Whatever's going on with Martha is clearly playing on his mind as much as mine.

Alice, however, is oblivious to the tension. "Hurrah!" she yells, raising both hands in the air and shaking them around, her face a manic grin of delight.

She reminds me so much of her brother I have to look away.

When Alice gets bored of cartoons, I suggest taking Rudman out for a walk. Alice groans, then warms to the idea, grabbing Rudman's lead and running to put on her shoes. But right as we're leaving, the phone rings.

I remember yesterday's call, the silence at the end of the line, and my stomach chills. I pick the receiver up cautiously, bracing myself.

"Hannah… Hannah?"

Martha's voice sounds crackly, uncertain. The reception keeps cutting in and out. She must be on her mobile.

"I can't really hear you."

"Hang on." There's a few muffled sounds as she adjusts the phone. "Is that better?" Her voice is echoey, but at least I can make out what she's saying.

"Better."

"The signal here isn't very good. Sorry."

"Where are you?" I ask before I can stop myself.

"Paris," says Martha quickly. "Listen, I can't explain now, sweetheart. But I will. I just wanted to check everything's okay. Paul said you were minding Alice. How is she?"

"Fine. Missing you. Keeps asking where you are. We're about to take Rudman for a walk."

"Good. I'll be back the day after tomorrow hopefully."

In the background I can hear voices. Men's voices. Foreign accents. One of them calls Martha's name, and I get a flash of dread. What's going on?

"I also wanted to say thank you, Hannah, for all your help. I know you've got enough on your plate with your exams." Martha's voice is suddenly wobbly with emotion. "I really appreciate it."

"It's fine," I say. "Really. I can study here."

I mean it. I love coming over to help with Ally. When Danny vanished it left a hole in Ally's life that I've tried my best to fill. Just as Martha did when my mother died.

"Look, sweetheart, I have to go." Martha sounds rushed. "Give Ally a big kiss for me, will you?"

"I will."

The line goes dead before I can say goodbye.

We take Rudman out along the path that zigzags up through Church Woods. I'm walking and talking all the time to Alice, but another part of my mind is trying to figure out what on earth Martha's doing in France.

I'm stumped. I can't think of a single reason that makes any sense, but my feeling of unease is growing.

Whatever's going on, it must be something big.

Rudman heads off into the undergrowth that borders the path. There's no sign of him for ages, only the occasional yip of excitement as he flushes out a rabbit.

"Stupid dog," says Alice solemnly, making me smile. Stupid dog indeed. Rudman never appears to learn that rabbits are much faster than him, especially now he's getting on a bit. Not that he cares – all the fun is in the chase.

As if on cue he emerges, panting, from a thicket of brambles, wearing a broad doggy grin and a fair bit of foliage in his fur. Alice giggles, and I put him on the lead so we don't lose him again.

We head through the beech woods behind the old castle, the sun breaking out through the clouds, making everything bright and fresh. Danny and I used to come up here all the time. We'd drag our bikes right up to the top of the hill and Danny would yell "Race ya!" and off we'd go, hurtling down, wheels bouncing over stones and tree roots, bikes flying over humps and landing with a breath-jolting thump.

By the time you got to the bottom you felt like your teeth had been rattled loose in your head. I'd be trailing him by miles and he'd wait for me at the bottom, grinning, victorious. I didn't mind. I wasn't bothered about winning. I just liked being with him.

As Alice and I zigzag down the path, I get a cramp in my heart, an actual physical ache. I miss all that, even though it was nearly four years ago and I'm now too old for bikes. I miss spending half my life outside – here or down on the beach or over on the salt marshes. I miss those long days, those endless hours where you completely lose track of time.

Most of all I miss Danny. And I still wonder why all that stopped, so suddenly, a few months after Mum died. The fun, easy times we had together, the connection I thought could never be broken. Why did it end?

Or rather, why did Danny end it? Quite suddenly, like he'd developed an allergy to everything we used to do. Like he'd developed an allergy to *me*. He wasn't rude or anything, just sort of made himself scarce. Left the room as soon as I walked in. Invented excuses if I suggested we go do something together. He'd disappear off to his bedroom, or leave the house on his own, staying away for ages and never telling me where he'd been.

I had no idea what was going on. I tried asking him once, about what I'd done wrong, what had made him change. He just looked at me. He didn't try to deny it or pretend that everything was okay. He simply gazed at me in a helpless sort of way.

"It's not you," was all he said.

But I could never quite shake off the feeling that it was.

12

then

"Budge up a bit."

I shifted over to give her some room and Lianna plonked herself down on the sofa next to me and Maisy. It was a bit of a squash and I had to curl up my legs to keep them out the way. My whole body felt fidgety and awkward. Nervous.

"Only a few minutes to go." Maisy grinned, hardly able to keep the anticipation from her voice. I saw Dad glance at her, and regretted again agreeing to have them over. Part of me was grateful they'd asked – in the six months since Danny disappeared, they were the only friends I had, and I appreciated them sticking by me. But another part felt exposed, like everything inside me was on show.

The documentary about Danny's disappearance was a big deal. All over town other kids and their parents were sitting, like us, waiting for it to begin. At school everyone had been talking about it for weeks, the excitement building as the scheduled date approached.

"Are you going to be in it?" Rebekah Collins had asked me in history.

When I shook my head, she gave me a sort of pitying

look, like I was missing out on something exciting. It didn't make me feel any better.

The truth was I could have been involved. I'd wanted to do it, but Dad had said no. "She's done enough," he told Martha when she tried to convince him.

I'd opened my mouth to object, but Martha got in first. "It's just a TV programme, David. They only want to talk to her. What harm could it do?" Her voice was taut with frustration. "Couldn't Hannah—?"

"Drop it, Martha," Dad cut in, his expression morphing into anger. "It's up to me, not you, to decide what's best for my daughter."

Martha gave him a furious look, but she didn't argue. Nor did I. So as the adverts ended and the announcer introduced the programme, I was as much in the dark as anyone. I had no idea what we were about to see. Martha had never mentioned it since, and somehow I'd felt it better not to ask.

As the opening credits rolled down the screen, Lianna and Maisy turned and gave me encouraging smiles. I managed a thin one in return, but my attention was caught up with the music. It was haunting, sort of serious and eerie at the same time.

I glanced at Dad. He was staring at the screen, his lips pressed firmly together. He looked nearly as tense as me.

It turned out the programme wasn't only about Danny, but missing teenagers in general. It featured various kids who'd disappeared over the last year or so. A boy who took the bus home from school, but never got off the other end. Another boy who vanished seven months ago – just a few weeks before Danny. And a girl called Jenny who went missing after a house party last summer. They kept showing this photo of her, dark hair, dressed up in a short skirt with lots of black eye make-up, pouting at whoever took the picture.

But it was Jenny's best friend who stuck in my mind, the one who was with her the night she vanished. Jenny's friend didn't look in the least bit excited about being on TV. Halfway through describing the last moment she saw Jenny, she started crying.

"I keep thinking it's all my fault," she said, covering her eyes with her hands, hiding her tears. "I go round and round, wondering what I've missed, wondering what I might have done to stop it." I watched her, my own eyes welling, feeling like someone had climbed into my head and borrowed my thoughts.

Teens ran away for all sorts of reasons, said an expert psychologist, a man with wiry hair and huge bushy eyebrows. He listed the main ones: bullying at school, stress, depression, addiction, and physical or sexual abuse. I caught Maisy and Lianna exchanging a wide-eyed look, and my cheeks flamed – Martha and Paul were certainly watching this over at Dial House.

Could any of those things be true? I wondered, as they switched to an interview with one of the parents. Did any apply to Danny? And if they did – if he had been depressed or bullied or somehow abused – how come I didn't realize? How come he didn't tell me?

On the TV, the psychologist reappeared. While most teens ran away, he said, you could never rule out abduction.

Another furtive look between my friends. I felt my chest tighten and I almost didn't notice when the scene changed again. All at once I recognized the boating lake. Two kids on bikes riding around the edge of it. A girl and a boy, about my age.

A prickly, electric sort of sensation ran through my body. Danny and me.

Not really us of course. People pretending to be us. Which was even weirder somehow. I stared at the girl. She was exactly like me. Same light brown straggly hair and pale grey eyes, kind of skinny.

It was like looking in the mirror. Or at the twin sister I never knew I had.

I glanced at Dad. He was watching intently, a stiffness in his jaw, his forehead knotted into a frown. I knew just what he was thinking.

Martha must have given them a photo.

I looked back at the screen. Still the boating lake, but Danny and I had gone. It was last October, the policemen wading across the water, the crowd in the background. The cameraman, I thought with a frisson of panic – he hadn't been filming for the news after all.

I held my breath as the camera panned over the crowd, praying it wouldn't fix on me, but the image dissolved before I could even appear in shot. Now we were looking at Dial House, filmed from the bottom of the drive. The camera zoomed in slowly to the front door, then the scene switched to Martha and Paul, sitting together on the sofa in the lounge.

"Martha, could you tell us how you felt when you first discovered your son had gone missing?"

The room looked strange somehow. It took me a moment to figure out why. They'd swapped the furniture around so Martha and Paul were sitting with their backs to the window, a flat blue line of sea visible in the background.

But it wasn't just that. Everything looked smaller, and sort of fake, like it was a film set, a place made up for a story.

"It's hard to describe." Martha's voice sounded different too – uncertain, nervous. She was wearing some kind of make-up, and her skin looked too smooth, too perfect.

"At first you don't really believe it. You think he's going to come back at any moment. But at the same time there's this sense of increasing panic, this constant need to look, to try and find him."

She kept tugging at her hair as she spoke, pulling it back in that way that made her appear stern and angry. Paul was clearly on edge too, his thumb twitching as his wife talked. He looked like someone who would rather be anywhere but there.

No sign of Alice.

"So at what point did you realize he wasn't coming home?" the interviewer asked Paul.

But it was Martha who replied, a pained expression around her eyes. "If we'd reached that point," she snapped, "we wouldn't be sitting here now."

The camera panned in on her face. "We still believe Danny will come back," she explained. "That's why we're here, doing this programme. To raise awareness." Martha paused. "Someone, somewhere, must know where he is."

"So, if your son is watching this, Martha, what would you like to say to him?" the interviewer asked.

Lianna and Maisy swapped "as if" looks. They'd clearly come to some conclusion of their own.

On the screen, Paul coughed, but Martha's expression didn't change. She stared directly into the camera. It was like peering right into her eyes.

"Danny…" she said, then stopped.

"Go on," said the interviewer encouragingly, but Martha shook her head.

"It doesn't matter. If Danny's watching this, he'll know exactly what he needs to do."

13

then

Six weeks later Paul turned up on our doorstep, Alice bundled in a blanket, asleep in his arms, a carrier bag hanging from his elbow. It was gone nine on a Friday night but he was still in his work suit, the jacket crumpled from clutching his daughter.

"Hi, Hannah." His smile was warm, but the strain in his face was obvious. "Listen, could you get your dad? I need to ask you both a favour."

I turned to go upstairs, but found Dad standing right behind me, fixing Paul with a stony glare.

"What is it?" Dad asked, his tone abrupt.

I felt like kicking him for being so rude, but Paul acted as if he hadn't noticed, though I could hardly imagine how. Dad's expression was as cold as his question.

"I wondered if you'd mind having Alice for the night?" Paul asked.

"Why?" said Dad. "What's going on?"

Paul sighed, shifting Alice's weight in his arms. "I'm really sorry, David. You know I wouldn't ask if we weren't desperate. Can I come in for a moment?"

Dad hesitated for a second or two, then stepped back from the door to let Paul through.

"Bring Ally upstairs," I said, not even glancing at Dad for permission. "She can sleep in my bed."

Paul smiled at me gratefully and Dad had the sense not to object. How could he, given how often I'd stayed over at Dial House? I followed Paul up to my room, pulling back the duvet. Alice didn't even stir as he rolled her onto the bed, her face sinking into my pillow. Paul handed me the bag stuffed with various toys and books.

It was only as I trailed him back down to the kitchen that I started to feel really anxious. What had happened? I wanted to ask.

But I didn't have to.

"Are you going to tell us what's going on?" Dad's tone was borderline aggressive. I stared at his face, dark with stubble. Compared to Paul, he looked untidy, wild even.

Paul sighed and ran his hand across his scalp. "It's Martha," he said. "She's a bit upset."

By a bit, I knew he meant a lot. Martha never did anything by halves.

"Why?" I burst out. "What's happened?"

Paul frowned, hesitated. Studied me for a moment before coming to a decision. "I suppose you're going to find out sooner or later. It may as well be now."

I sat on the chair next to Dad, a light sweat breaking out all over my skin. I felt hot and clammy, my mouth suddenly dry.

Paul raised both hands up to the back of his head, like someone surrendering. "God, I don't know how to tell you this." He exhaled slowly, lowering his arms to his sides. They hung there, defeated.

"They've found a body."

A gasp like air escaping from a tyre valve. I realized it came from me. No one spoke for ages. I tried to keep breathing but my chest felt stiff and tight. I looked at Dad, saw the agitation on his face, as if he were deciding how to react. Then he turned and reached inside the cupboard, pulling out the bottle of whisky; the one he kept for special occasions – or emergencies.

He nodded at the empty chair in front of Paul, who sat without protest. Dad got a couple of glasses and poured a finger's depth into each. Paul downed his in one swallow, wincing slightly, and cleared his throat.

"A fisherman discovered the body in the channel, about ten miles downstream, between Weston and Brean. It... he was male, young. Janet Reynolds came round to tell us this evening."

I stared at him, slack-mouthed, trying to find some words. My lungs felt empty, useless, like deflated balloons.

"Is it...?" Even Dad couldn't bring himself to ask.

"We don't know for sure, not yet. But reading between the lines of what Janet said, it's likely to be Danny."

"Can they tell?" Dad asked. "Danny has been missing, what...eight months now."

Paul glanced at me, hesitating. I held his gaze.

"They…er…they've got to check the dental records," he said. "We won't know for sure for a day or two."

"So you can't be certain?" Dad said slowly.

Paul shifted in his chair. "No, not till the results are back. But no one else has been reported missing locally. Janet thinks we should prepare for the worst."

A tidal wave of panic rose from my stomach, stopping just short of my throat. For a moment I thought I might pass out. I didn't dare look at Dad. It was all I could do to keep upright.

"I'm sorry." Paul gave me a lingering, concerned look. "I didn't want to dump this on you. Not till we knew for sure. But Martha…she's taken this pretty badly… I thought it best to get Alice away."

"Of course." This time there was no hostility in Dad's voice.

"Is she okay?" I managed to stammer. "Martha, I mean…"

Paul sighed, long and slow, and lifted his hand to massage the back of his neck. His fingers were trembling.

"A bit better now, Hannah, thank you. The doctor came and gave her something to calm her down. I left her asleep in bed."

"Shall I come round?" The second I offered I knew it was the last thing I wanted to do. I didn't want to see Martha right now. I wasn't sure I could bear it.

Paul shook his head. "If you could just look after Alice tonight. Give Martha a chance to rest."

I lay awake, listening to the muffled sounds of Alice breathing, the unaccustomed warmth radiating off her little curled body. A faint light came in from the street outside, leaking round the edge of the curtains and casting a network of shadows on the opposite wall. Now and then a car passed, bathing the room in a momentary sweep of brilliance before plunging us back into night.

I'd been awake for hours. My stomach hurt every time I thought of Danny. Was he really…? I wouldn't let myself finish that thought. Wouldn't let myself go there until the time came when I had no choice.

I kept remembering Martha, too. All those times when she thought we'd found him. That glow of excitement, her voice vibrating with certainty as she described the latest sighting. The press release she sent out to the papers and the website she set up had attracted lots of attention. Danny had been everywhere, it seemed. And not only in England – he'd been spotted across half a dozen countries in Europe, as well as America, Australia, even Brazil. Each week Martha received emails via the website or the missing persons forums, and in every single one someone claimed to have seen him.

They were convinced – and convincing.

But it had never led anywhere. Most times the police couldn't find out who they'd actually seen – and when they did, it was never Danny. Martha would be pinched and silent for a day or two, until another message set her off all over again.

I learned not to get my hopes up, but Martha never did.

Though this time, I thought as I watched the room slowly brightening around me, felt different. This time didn't feel like another wild goose chase.

This time it looked like we really had found Danny.

Paul came back for Alice late the next morning, his face haggard and pasty from lack of sleep. Alice screamed and clung to my legs, refusing to go. Paul stared at her, bewildered, looking helpless with exhaustion.

"I'll come too," I said.

"You sure?" Paul glanced at Dad for confirmation, but I didn't give him a chance to object.

"I'm sure," I said firmly.

Alice sucked her thumb the whole way, staring out the car window at the dog walkers braving the rain. It was one of those wet, drizzly Saturday mornings that made you wonder why you even bothered with weekends – you might as well be at school.

I sat in the back with Alice, crossing my fingers and tucking them under my knees so Paul couldn't see. Please let everything be okay, I repeated silently to myself, over and over, until the words felt flat and drained of meaning. Please. Please. Please.

As soon as we got into the house I saw my prayers had gone unanswered. Everything was most definitely not okay.

Martha was standing in the hallway, the phone in her hand, tears rolling down her face, her dark hair loose and messy and her expression so anguished it made my stomach curl.

"Jesus, Martha..." Paul strode over and grabbed the receiver, listened for a moment before setting it back in its cradle.

"Who was it? The police?"

Martha shook her head miserably.

"Who then?"

I flinched. Paul seemed annoyed, almost angry.

"I don't know." She sank onto the bench near the front door. Alice scowled and marched into the lounge. Seconds later a children's channel boomed in the background. By the sound of it, she'd turned the volume up as high as it would go.

"What do you mean, you don't know?" Paul persisted. "Didn't they tell you?"

"He...they...didn't say anything."

"And you didn't ask?"

"Of course I did," Martha sobbed. "I always do. But he never answers."

She spoke so quietly that I nearly didn't catch what she said against the noise of the TV. But I heard enough to send shivers right through me.

The phone calls.

"Martha, what are you talking about?" Paul looked at the very edge of his patience. Clearly he'd been up half the night, churning over the news from the police.

Martha swiped her hand across her eyes. "It rings. I answer, but there's just silence."

"A wrong number then? One of those automated marketing calls?"

Martha shook her head again. "No, there's definitely someone there. Listening, I mean."

"You're telling me this has happened before?"

"Yes. I...normally it doesn't bother me, it's just right now...today..." She started crying again, her brow creasing into lines that seemed to have deepened overnight.

"How many times, Martha?"

"I don't know. Perhaps a dozen."

Paul was almost glaring at her, his expression incredulous.

"And me."

I blurted it out before I could change my mind. Martha and Paul both turned and stared, Paul frowning in confusion.

"When?" Martha gasped.

"I'm not sure. A few times, maybe three. Once at home."

"Hannah, sweetheart, why didn't you tell us?" Martha grabbed my hand and pulled me to face her.

I shrugged. "I don't know. I just assumed they were from someone at school, messing around." It was easier to ignore them; we all had enough on our plate as it was.

"So how long has this been going on?" Paul turned back to his wife.

"A few months. Maybe a bit longer."

"Christ, Martha, this is crazy. Why the hell didn't you say anything?"

"Because I knew you'd be like this," she said quietly. "I knew you'd never believe me."

Time to go. I picked up my bag, but Martha hung onto my hand and shot me a pleading look.

"Believe you about what? Why wouldn't I believe we've been getting prank calls, Martha?" Paul's voice had softened, but only a little.

"You don't understand," she said after a pause. "I thought it was Danny. I know it's crazy but I thought maybe he couldn't speak to me, that he just wanted to hear my voice. Our voices," she added with a quick glance at me.

"So why didn't you tell the police? Ask them to trace the calls."

"I did," Martha wailed, "and they can't. I checked 1471 every time, but the number is always unavailable. And all the police could find out was that the calls are coming from abroad, probably using one of those phonecards. They're untraceable."

Paul looked at the floor and clenched his fingers into his palms. Closed his eyes briefly before fixing them back on his wife. "And did they think it was Danny?"

She pressed her lips together, blinking back tears. "Janet reckons it's someone who heard about him and gets a kick out of calling us."

"But you don't agree?"

Martha didn't answer.

Paul said nothing for almost a minute, but a vein on his

forehead started to pulse. "Face it, Martha, it isn't him. It can't be him, can it?"

Another long silence while we listened to a chirpy song coming from the living room. It sounded like that programme about the chimpanzees.

"Alice seems okay," I said, handing Martha the plastic bag with Alice's teddy and books. "I really ought to get home." She nodded mutely, releasing my hand with a little squeeze. Her face was crumpled with misery as I turned to let myself out the front door.

Right at that moment the phone rang.

All three of us froze, watching the flashing light on the receiver, listening to the shrill scream of the ringtone.

No one moved to answer it.

Several moments later, Alice appeared, her face dark with fury. "Shut up!" she yelled, picking up the receiver and throwing it at her father. Paul lifted it to his ear, his hand pressed against the other side of his head to block out the noise of the TV. I could see a tremor in his jaw, a twitch of raw emotion.

"Hello?"

Martha and I watched him. Most of me wanted to run out the door and never look back. But I simply couldn't move.

Paul stood there, saying nothing. Just listening. It seemed to go on for ever, and I remembered that silence at the end of the line, the way it made the back of my neck prickle with dread.

Suddenly Paul spoke. "You're sure? There can't be any mistake?"

He dragged his thumb and forefinger across his brow, pulling the skin into a pleat above his nose. A ball of ice formed in my stomach.

This wasn't another of those calls.

"Right, okay." Paul's voice was shaky, uncertain. "Yes… fine…thank you. Thank you for letting us know."

I looked at Martha. Saw my own panic reflected on her features.

Paul placed the phone down gently, staring at the floor for a moment, then turned towards both of us. The colour had seeped right out of his face, leaving it ashy and sheeny with sweat.

Martha spoke first. Firmly, almost calmly.

"Paul, just tell us."

He gazed at her, finding the words.

"It's not him. The body in the water. It's not Danny."

I watched the alteration in Martha's face like it was in slow motion. Relief washed across it in a deluge, tears of gratitude springing to her eyes as she gazed at her husband, open-mouthed, like someone who'd just witnessed a miracle.

I stared at her, unable to move or look away. It wasn't him. It wasn't Danny. I waited for the impact, for the news to sink in, to flood me with the elation I saw on Martha's features.

But there was nothing. Only numbness. Empty space. Like the silence on the end of the phone line.

This was good news, I told myself fiercely. *Good news.*

So why did I feel so defeated? Then it hit me, and a hot prickle of shame flared up inside.

A darker, deeper, buried part of me had been hoping all this was finally over.

15

then

There was something approaching silence in the assembly hall. It was unnerving. None of the usual hum of whispered conversations and barely suppressed giggles; just the occasional cough or scrape of chairs as people shuffled in their seats.

Mr Givens, the head, stood at the front, hands in pockets, rocking backwards and forwards on the soles of his feet as he waited for the stragglers to find a place. Behind him, the teachers sat in semicircles, staring out at us with faces drained of expression.

Givens cleared his throat to get our attention then treated us to his oiliest smile. Even before he opened his mouth, I had the urge to leave. Pretend I felt faint and take myself off to the sickroom or something. No one would blame me, after all. Not today.

But I was stuck right in the middle of a row, between Lianna and Georgia from my tutor group. The whole school was here and it was a crush. There was no way out without creating a disturbance.

"All of you knew Daniel Geller," Givens began, "and are

aware of his unfortunate disappearance last September." He paused and scanned the nine hundred faces staring up at him, like an actor surveying his audience. "I'm sure you are also aware, despite a nationwide search and the tireless efforts of his parents, that Daniel is still missing nearly one year on."

A few heads craned around the hall, presumably looking for Paul or Martha. They settled on me instead. I sank lower into my seat, training my gaze on the head's receding hairline as he got into his stride.

"So I felt it appropriate that we mark this today by taking a moment to reflect upon him and what his absence has meant for all of us…"

In front of me Robby Burchill yawned and fidgeted with the knot of his tie. I bit the inside of my cheek, fighting the urge to thump him. After all, if Danny had been here, he'd have been just as bad. Danny had the lowest boredom threshold of anyone I'd ever known – including Alice.

"He had the kind of outlook on life we all aspire to, always willing to participate, never afraid to make mistakes…"

Several of the more sensitive teachers had the decency to look embarrassed at the head's careless use of the past tense. He'd obviously made up his mind that Danny was dead.

"He was always a most friendly and good-humoured member of the school. Indeed I never saw him without a smile upon his face…"

Lianna turned to me and grinned, and I almost laughed. Danny said Givens looked like a chipmunk. He never could walk past him without smirking.

"…the sort of boy who set an example to everyone, who put his all into everything – his studies, his swimming, his friendships…"

His studies? Jeez. Had the head got Danny mixed up with someone else? I tuned out, watching the clock at the front of the hall, the second hand idling its way through a minute, and let his voice melt into a background drone. I was no longer interested in anything he had to say about Danny – after all, Givens had probably never uttered more than ten words to him the whole time he was here.

It was like the vicar who spoke at Mum's funeral – the more he went on, the more he told you how wonderful she was, how thoughtful and kind, the more you realized he didn't know a single genuine thing about her. It wasn't that those things weren't true; just that he made her sound too perfect to be real. More like someone in an advert than an actual person.

"Before we bow our heads and say a prayer for Daniel and his family, Mr Cozens would just like to add a few words."

A dull murmuring filled the hall, as everyone took a welcome opportunity to stretch and whisper to their neighbours. I kept my eyes fixed on Mr Cozens. He was clutching a small pile of notes, which he balanced on the lectern in front of him. He'd lost his usual fierce expression.

His face was beet red and the overhead lights bounced off the sweat on his forehead, making him look like he'd just completed several laps of the top pitch.

Cozens looked up and coughed into his fist. We all stared back at him and waited for him to speak.

The silence lengthened. Mr Givens gave him an anxious glance. Someone sneezed loudly at the back of the hall, and finally Mr Cozens seemed to come to. He picked up his notes and shoved them in his pocket, stepping aside from the lectern to give himself a clear view across the hall.

"So…I've thought a lot about what I want to say about Danny…" He stopped and cleared his throat again. "But now I find I don't want to say very much. I'm not going to try and convince you that Danny was some kind of saint. Most of you knew him, some of you better than others. You knew he was a good lad – and a superb swimmer. But in many ways…most ways…he was just an ordinary boy."

A couple of girls in the rows in front of me turned and checked out my expression. I dug my teeth into my bottom lip, pretending not to notice.

"Not that there's anything wrong with being ordinary," continued Mr Cozens. "Not at all. And it doesn't mean we feel his absence any the less. Every swimming practice, every day, I look at the pool and I feel there's something missing. That there's *someone* missing. It's worse in a way *because* Danny was an ordinary kid, someone just like all of us."

A burning sensation started behind my eyes. I blinked

hard and leaned forward, allowing my hair to fall across my face. I could feel Lianna watching me intently.

"But Danny wasn't the kind of person to look back. If he were here now, I'm sure he'd be laughing at us all. At our straight faces, all this serious talk."

A tear broke free and rolled down my cheek. I swiped it away with my fingers. I felt Lianna's hand take mine and give it a squeeze. I blinked hard and held my breath, willing myself not to cry.

"That's all I want to say, really," said Mr Cozens, looking sheepish as the head stared at him in astonishment. "I don't think Danny would want us moping around missing him. I'm sure that Danny – wherever he's got to – is getting on with life. And I know that's exactly what he'd want the rest of us to do too."

16

then

We were trapped round the dining-room table at Dial House, all watching Martha trying to light the candles on Danny's cake. Fourteen of them. And twelve of Danny's friends, each thinking exactly the same thing.

Who the hell was going to blow them out?

I glanced at Joe, who was observing Martha's struggle with the matches with increasing alarm. She struck one and it flared and dropped to the floor. Joe stamped on it quickly, then reached for the box.

Martha shook her head, taking another and lighting it with a determined look that reminded me of Alice. I wished again that Paul hadn't refused to have anything to do with this. Somehow his not being here made the whole thing feel more precarious. Hazardous, even, like anything might happen.

I eyed the others, gauging their reaction. Ewan was staring out across the garden, faking an interest in the apple trees, and Ross was studying his feet. Lizzie Jenkins and Vicky Clough sat between Martha and Jamie, examining their nails and fiddling with their hair. Beside them were the twins from Danny's tutor group. The other three were from the swimming club.

Everyone Martha invited had come; I don't think anyone dared not to.

"Here's to Danny," Martha said, as the flame on the last candle finally took hold.

I swallowed, feeling giddy with awkwardness. Was Martha going to make us all sing "Happy Birthday"? One glance at the panicked look on Lizzie and Vicky's faces told me something similar had crossed their minds too.

But Martha just sat with Alice on her lap, gazing at the candles for a minute or two in a lost sort of way.

"Me do it." Alice pointed at the cake and Martha let her lean forward to blow them out. It took almost as long as lighting them, Alice pursing her lips and puffing noisily, with little effect on the flames. In the end, Martha had to do it herself.

"Who would like a slice?" she asked in an overly upbeat voice, knife poised over the cake. Chocolate with raspberry jam and buttercream filling. Danny's favourite, though I always found it way too rich.

Everyone said yes in unison. Everyone except Lizzie, who put up her hand like she was still in school, slowly lowering it once she realized what she'd done. She looked nearly as embarrassed as Jamie, who'd actually brought Danny a card. One of those jokey ones with a hamster with boggle eyes and a silly message. It was standing on the shelf above the sink, like some kind of crazy memorial.

There was nothing sane about any of this, I thought, as I bit into my cake. Paul had told her as much, but Martha wouldn't listen.

"He's my son. We're going to celebrate his birthday." It was all she'd say.

Everyone ate in silence, and I remembered Danny's birthday the year before last. Him insisting we play traditional party games, even though we were getting way too old. It was a riot. Joe and Ross got so competitive over musical cushions, pushing and shoving, that Martha had to stop the game and declare them both winners.

Best of all was pass-the-parcel. Danny had let Alice rip open every layer, relishing the look on her face as she discovered the sweets hidden between the sheets of paper. The way she fingered each one in wonder, like a treasure hunter unearthing precious gems.

Oh, Danny. I couldn't help thinking he'd be the only person who'd actually enjoy any of this. If he could see us all now, sitting around eating birthday cake for a boy who wasn't even here, he'd crack up. Danny would think it was the funniest thing in the world.

Almost as soon as I swallowed the last bite of cake, I started to feel queasy. And hot, like someone had turned up the heating too high. I mumbled an "Excuse me" and made my way to the downstairs loo to splash some cold water on my face.

On the way I passed the little room that Martha used as an office. It had everything in there. Recipe and gardening books, piles of fabric, baskets of wool, jars of buttons and a box crammed with dozens of reels of bright-coloured cotton. In a large cabinet at the far end, Martha kept rolls of wrapping paper and ribbon, and a locked section for the presents she hid away for birthdays and Christmas.

We weren't supposed to go in there. Especially Alice, who would rip through the place like a small tornado, meddling with everything and putting nothing away. But today the door was ajar and, as I walked past, I caught sight of something. I paused. Pushed the door open and peered inside.

There, on the old pine table Martha used as a desk, was a box wrapped in blue and red stripy paper, topped with a gift tag and a big red bow. And from its size and shape I could guess exactly what it was. That games console, the one Danny had begged for and Martha dismissed as a complete waste of money.

Back in the kitchen, I could hear the tense murmurs of eleven kids desperately trying to act like all this was normal. I slipped into the room and turned over the label.

Danny, Happy 14th Birthday, it said, in Martha's handwriting. *All our love, Mum and Dad xxx*

That was all. I don't know what I expected really, but the very ordinariness of it was worse somehow. My stomach felt heavy, rebellious. My skin sticky with discomfort.

"Hannah, are you okay?"

Martha's voice made me start. It sounded closer than the kitchen and, as I swung round, I saw her hovering just across the hallway. She stopped when she saw where I was.

"Yes, sorry," I mumbled, backing out the room and closing the door behind me. "I was…um…"

I couldn't think of anything to say. It was obvious what I'd been doing.

Martha just looked at me, her expression unreadable.

"I'm sorry," I muttered again. "I'm not sure I feel very well."

"You're very pale, Hannah. You look like you've seen a ghost."

I almost laughed at the irony, but I felt too sick. "I think I ate a bit too much cake."

"Do you want to lie down?"

"No…no, I'm fine…" But suddenly I wasn't, as a rush of nausea sent me running towards the loo.

I barely reached it before my stomach began to contract. I kneeled over and threw up, the terrible force of it making my ribs ache and my eyes water in pain.

I hate being sick, but this time I didn't fight it. I let the tears run down my face as I hunched over the toilet bowl and heaved, over and over, until every last bit of Danny's birthday cake had gone.

17
NOW

"You're sure about this?"

Paul is lingering by the back door of Dial House, fiddling with his car keys. "It's not too late for me to get someone else to mind Alice. I could always ask Sophie's mum."

"It's fine," I repeat. "You go and meet Martha."

I want him gone. With every moment he remains, the temptation to make him tell me what's going on grows stronger. What's happening with Martha, why Paul has to go up to London to meet her, what any of this has to do with Danny – the need to know is becoming unbearable. Like an itch that grows stronger the longer you resist the urge to scratch.

But Paul is still wavering, eyeing my pile of books on the kitchen table. "How long before your exams start?"

"A couple of months."

"You think you'll do all right?" He looks genuinely concerned, and I wonder why. Maybe I'm a reminder that Danny should be here, going through the same thing.

"I'll be fine." I nod at the kitchen clock. "You'll miss your train."

Paul glances up and sighs. "Okay, but ring if there are any problems. Anything at all. Promise?"

"I already have. About ten times."

He manages a smile. "I'll try not to be late. No later than nine, I hope."

"Don't worry about it. Dad's working tonight anyway."

Paul raises an eyebrow.

"Some project that's gone over deadline," I explain. "He's been stuck in the lab for days."

Paul bites his lip, his hand gripping the door handle. "You're a great girl, Hannah. Your dad…you know…he's very lucky to have you."

His eyes fix on my face and I feel suddenly self-conscious. Scrutinized.

"Go!" I say quickly. And this time he does.

"Ninety-seven…ninety-eight…ninety-nine…a hundred. Ready or not, here I come," I yell.

There's an excited squeal from somewhere upstairs, but I've no intention of going up straight away. Alice's hiding spots are never the most imaginative, so half the point of playing hide-and-seek with her is making sure you don't find her too quickly. I'm pretty good at looking in all the wrong places – under the blanket in Rudman's basket, in the cupboard beneath the kitchen sink, behind the thin silk curtains in the lounge.

I work my way through the downstairs rooms, making

sure to bang plenty of doors and drawers as I go. I'm wondering how long I can spin this out and keep Alice off the topic of why both her parents have now gone away.

Because the answer is, I don't know. Or rather I have an awful feeling that I do, and it's not something that is going to make Alice – or me – feel any better.

Finally I climb the stairs, thumping my feet so that she hears me coming. It works. There's a barely suppressed giggle of apprehension.

"Fee…fi…fo…fum… I smell the blood of a juicy little girl!"

Another squeal, but I'm not sure where from. I'm pretty sure it's not the bathroom, so I go in there first. I open the top of the laundry basket, now way too small to contain Alice, then let it drop with a clatter. Peek under the lid of the toilet. Glance in the airing cupboard in the hallway, even though the boiler and shelving above take up most of the space.

"Where is she…?" I give a theatrical bellow before going into Martha and Paul's room and peering inside all the closets. I open the drawers on Martha's dresser, making sure to give them a good rattle. Finally I check under the bed – nine times out of ten it's where Alice will be hidden – but today there's nothing but dust on the bare floorboards.

I repeat the whole process in the spare room, though there aren't so many places to look. Then go into Alice's bedroom, knowing she's there. I start with her toy cupboard. Several games and puzzles fall out as I open the door – there's barely space for another doll or teddy bear, let alone Alice. I check the drawers of her chest, each bulging with clothes. I look in her wardrobe, sweeping aside all the coat hangers with a dramatic swish.

It's under the bed then. I lower myself chest first onto her duvet and slowly drop my head over the edge.

"Raaaaaaaaaaaarrrrrggggggghhhhhhh!" I roar, peering right underneath.

Nothing.

I blink with surprise. I so expected to see her beaming up at me, thrilled and terrified in equal measure.

Where on earth is she?

Clambering back onto my feet, I look around. I'm fairly sure I've checked everywhere that might hide a seven-year-old girl.

Then I hear another giggle. And finally work out where it's coming from.

Danny's room.

With a sinking heart, I push on the door. The hinge makes the funny squeaking noise that somehow reminds me of Danny. He always refused to let Paul or Martha do anything about it; said it was his early warning system in case anyone crept up on him.

I open the door just enough to stick my head in, but it's too dark to see much. I fumble for the light switch. Suddenly it's me who feels scared. I hate coming in here.

"Alice. Come on out."

Silence. No movement. Crap.

I take a step inside, trying not to look at all Danny's stuff. This place is wrong. Barely changed from the day he left, though Martha did at least clean up. Washed the bed linen and rearranged the pillows. Picked up the usual clutter that trailed Danny everywhere, certain he'd be back soon to mess it up again.

But it's all still here, three and a half years on. All those football magazines and DVDs, those silly horror novels with lurid covers. His swimming trophies and the Bristol Rovers posters on the wall. His laptop, finally returned by the police.

It's like Danny just left the room, not our lives. I half expect him to sneak up behind me and jab me in the ribs. "Poking around my stuff, eh, titch?"

I know it's normal in a way, that lots of people can't bear to get rid of someone's things after they die, but it still gives me the creeps.

More to the point, neither of us is supposed to be in here. Martha would kill us if she knew.

"Alice?" I whisper, though I've no idea why. There's no one else to hear us.

Still nothing. Oh god, I am going to have to look.

I check under the bed, which is oddly pristine, then in the wardrobe. Seeing the clumps of Danny's clothes stuffed on the shelves, his few smart shirts lined up on hangers, makes me shiver.

I can't help thinking about when we got back from Mum's funeral and Dad grabbed loads of carrier bags and cardboard boxes and marched from room to room, throwing in everything she'd ever owned. Clothes, books, CDs, ornaments, pictures, even the plants she grew on the kitchen window sill. Anything that reminded him of her.

He didn't stop, even when he saw me crying. He didn't stop even after I'd called Martha and begged her to come round. He didn't stop because he couldn't – not until he'd removed every last trace of her.

Right now I'm wishing Martha had done the same.

"Alice?"

I open another cupboard, but there's nothing except more crumpled magazines and boxes of games. I shut the doors fast before too many memories surface. Why can't Martha get rid of some of this stuff? What's the point of hanging on to it all?

It's not like we'd forget him without all these things to remind us. Or that we'd stop missing him if they were gone.

"Alice!" I hiss. "Where are you? Come on, you know Mummy doesn't want people in here."

I can't keep the impatience from my voice. I want to get the hell out of here before I end up as crazy as Martha.

"Alice! For god's sake…"

"Yarrrrrrrrrrr!"

I actually scream. Spin round and see Danny's dressing gown billowing from the back of the door and shriek in panic before Alice emerges from behind it.

"I won!" She punches the air in the same way her brother always did, but her victorious look melts to concern when I sink to the floor and burst into tears. She crouches down beside me and strokes my hair as I sob and try to pull myself together.

"You sad about Danny?"

"What?" I wipe my tears on my sleeve and gaze up at her, holding my breath. Have Martha and Paul told her what's happening? I search her face for clues. But I can't bear to ask.

"I know," she says, sitting on the floor beside me. "I know you sad about Danny."

I stare at her in horror. She knows... Oh god, they've told her. So it's really true. This time there's no mistake.

Alice nods her head, then leans forward and peers right into my eyes. "I sad too cos Danny is still hiding. I look everywhere, but I can't find him, Hannah. I can't never, ever find him."

18
NOW

At ten past nine I hear a car pull up in the drive of Dial House. A minute later the sound of the key in the door. But it's not Paul's face that appears.

It's Martha's.

"Hi." I jump up from the sofa, flustered. "I didn't think you were coming back yet."

Martha smiles. "Sorry, Hannah. I tried to ring to tell you, but the battery went flat on my mobile. Paul's staying up in London overnight. There are a few things to sort out."

She stands there, jangling the car keys. "Alice in bed?"

"Yep. She fell asleep about an hour ago."

"Thanks, hun." She steps over and touches my cheek. "God knows what we'd do without you."

I manage a quick smile. "It's no problem. I don't mind – I love Alice."

I pick up my books and stuff them into my rucksack, catching the corner of my maths textbook in my hurry, making a large crease across the cover.

"Actually, Hannah, I was wondering if you could stay a moment longer. I need to talk to you."

Oh god. I look at Martha blankly, searching for an excuse to leave. At the same time knowing it's hopeless.

You can't run away from the truth. Not for ever.

"There's something important I need to tell you. And Alice. But I want to tell you now because I know it will come as a bit of a shock and I want to give you enough time to take it in before…"

"Before what?" I stammer.

But I can guess what she's going to say. Before the funeral. Danny's funeral. Because it's obvious what all this is about. Finally admitting this to myself is terrible. Because now I'm not sure I feel anything at all. Just numb, dizzy. Vacant.

Martha watches me, reading the anguish on my face.

"Hannah, sit down, sweetheart. Just for a minute."

I sink back onto the sofa and force myself to meet her gaze. I don't understand why Martha doesn't seem more upset. Her eyes are puffy and tired, but there's no sign of redness there, and her mouth is restless, as if she's trying not to smile.

"Hannah, I'm sorry, we should have told you before, but I…we didn't want to say anything until we were absolutely certain."

Martha pauses for a second, obviously trying to think of the best way to break the news. I clench my hands, digging my nails hard into my palms.

"That's why I've been in France, you see. I had to go and see, and then Paul came up to London and he too…

well, we're sure." She bites her bottom lip, but the corners of her mouth still curl back upwards.

"Sure of what?"

"That it's him. Danny."

I stare at her. She *is* smiling.

This is *mad*.

"Oh, Hannah, don't look so upset," Martha laughs, leaning forward to tuck away the strand of hair that always flops in front of my face. "It's true, sweetheart. It's him. We've found Danny."

"You've f-found him?" I stutter. "You mean you've found his body…?"

Martha reels back, eyes wide with astonishment. "No. Christ, no. Why would you think that? Oh god…" She cups both hands around my face, forcing me to look at her.

"No, Hannah. He's alive, sweetheart. He's coming home."

With those words, the air whooshes right out of me. I sort of fold up like a deckchair, unable to keep myself upright.

"Hannah?"

I can't respond. There's a pain in my chest where my lungs should be. Breathe, I tell myself. Breathe.

And the blood sings in my head as Martha pulls me round and hugs me tight against her.

"It's true, sweetheart, it's really true. Danny's coming home."

PART
TWO

FROM
NOW
ON...

Dad gets up around seven. I wait until I hear the sound of the kettle boiling before pulling on my dressing gown and catching him in the kitchen.

"Dad?"

"Mmmm…" He looks at me, bleary-eyed. Not enough sleep – it was gone midnight when he got back from the lab.

"I've got something to tell you. Something important."

That gets his attention. I see him clock my excited expression. "What's going on, Hannah? Is everything okay?"

"Fine," I nod. "Better than okay, actually."

I take a deep breath. Even after a night of tossing and turning, trying to take in Martha's news, I can hardly believe what I'm about to say.

"They've found Danny."

"What?" Dad looks perplexed. Like I've uttered some kind of riddle.

"Danny's coming home. They've found him."

I watch as a wave of comprehension finally breaks across

Dad's face. His eyes widen and his eyebrows contract to a frown.

"*Danny?*"

"Yes."

Dad stares at me. "They've found him? You mean alive?"

"Yes." I grin. "Alive and well. Okay, a bit the worse for wear, Martha said. But he's all right. And he's coming home."

"Good grief." Dad sits down. He looks truly stunned. "When did this happen?"

"Yesterday," I say, sitting in the chair opposite. "Or rather a few days ago. Martha told me last night when she got back."

Dad doesn't speak for a moment. Just gazes at me.

"Jesus."

"I would have told you last night but you were back so late." I feel my cheeks redden a little. That's not quite the truth. I was so dizzy and happy and shocked and elated, there was such a confusion of things going on in my head, that I needed time alone for it all to settle. To let myself finally believe it was real.

Like a secret, a gift of happiness I wanted to savour.

"I see." Dad chews the inside of his lip. I give him another minute or two to let the news sink in. "Okay," he says. "So start from the beginning. What exactly did Martha say?"

I summarize everything she told me. How Danny had emailed the missing persons website to say where he was, and how the French police had picked him up a couple of days later. That he'd been attacked and was now recovering in hospital in London.

"And he's all right?" Dad asks.

"Apparently. Martha says it's only a few cuts and bruises, but he did get a bang to the head. They want to check that out before they let him come home."

Dad stares down at the kitchen table before raising his eyes back up to mine. "Is she really sure this time?"

I nod. "She flew over to France to see him."

He still doesn't look convinced.

"Martha's *seen* him, Dad," I say, my voice bubbling over. "Talked to him. And Paul has. He went up to London yesterday to meet them from the airport."

I pause to feel the weight of my own words. It's almost like I'm trying to convince myself. Martha and Paul have met Danny. *They've actually spoken to him.*

It still doesn't seem possible.

"So why now?" Dad asks.

"Why now what?"

"Danny. What made him get in touch now, after so long?"

"I don't know." I shrug. "But I guess we'll find out."

"So, what's he said then?" Dad persists. "Where's he been all this time? What was he doing in France?"

"I don't know."

"Didn't Martha tell you?"

"Yes. I mean, no, not really. I did ask, but she said all that can wait till he's home."

"Right." Dad remembers his tea and takes a sip. He lets his gaze drift out the window as he considers everything I've said. I study the stain on his jumper, the hair that badly needs a cut, the sides sticking out and the fringe nearly covering his eyes, and wonder again what happened to the old Dad who used to look so smart and keep his hair tight and short.

Will he, too, just reappear one day?

Then Dad looks up and asks me a question that throws me into a tailspin. "So, how do you feel?"

"Feel?" I echo.

"I mean, this must be something of a shock, right? After all this time. So suddenly."

I swallow, my smile fading a little. "I suppose."

"So?"

"Um…well, I'm happy, Dad, of course. I'm delighted. Thrilled. Why wouldn't I be?"

He makes a small shrugging movement with his mouth. "I just thought it must be a lot to take in." He holds my gaze until I look back down at the table, picking a crumb off the wood and flicking it onto the floor. "You seem a bit jittery, that's all."

"I didn't sleep that well."

Understatement. I barely slept at all. The moment I got back home, the numbness I'd felt with Martha gave way to a riot of feelings that kept me wide awake.

"So when's he coming home?" Dad asks.

"In a few days, I think. A social worker is bringing him down."

"And when do you reckon you'll get to see him? You must be rather nervous."

I have to look away. How does Dad do that? I mean, we spend weeks barely setting eyes on each other, yet he has this uncanny knack of knowing exactly what's going on in my head. As if he can prise it open and peer inside, decoding my thoughts like DNA.

"I don't know." My heart races at the thought of seeing Danny again. It's a weird anxious feeling, uncomfortable almost.

I get up and grab a glass of water, gulp it down and bolt upstairs before Dad can interrogate me any further. I feel sticky and sweaty from lack of sleep. I need a bath, filled deep and hot. With lots and lots of bubble foam.

As I climb in, I catch sight of myself in the mirror. My hair lank and tangled, my face pale with a guarded expression, like I've caught myself doing something wrong. I squeeze my eyes shut and lower my body into the water, letting the heat seep into me and loosen the knot of my feelings.

Danny.

I try to summon his face, but nothing comes. The last few years have almost erased the features of my best friend, and all that floats before me now is like an image from an old film, scratched and faded by time. The back of a boy with chlorine-bleached hair, his feet resting on the pedals of his bike as it carries him off around the hill and out of my view.

I sink deeper into the water, let the bubbles tickle my chin. I think about Dad's question. I am happy, yes. Happy in that delirious way when nothing quite seems real. Like you imagine people feel when they discover they've won the lottery, or they've been cured of some terrible illness.

But underneath, there's something else. Why does the prospect of seeing Danny make me feel so anxious? So apprehensive?

After all, isn't this what I'd hoped, wished, prayed would happen?

It's not until the bubbles have disappeared, leaving the water scummy with soap, that the knot finally unravels. The thing is, I'd thought Danny had gone for good. Not at first, of course. At first I'd expected him back at any moment. Imagined it over and over, could actually *see* him walking through the door, acting like he'd never been away.

But slowly, gradually, despite myself, I came to believe the one thing I was determined would never even cross my mind. That Danny was never, ever coming home.

Only I was wrong.

As the bath water cools around me, I remember that Bible story, the one where Lazarus dies and is brought back to life. In the version we read at primary school, everyone was so happy to see him. There were pictures of them giving thanks and laughing and crying with joy.

I always thought that was stupid. Because, let's face it, if that really happened, if someone really came back from the dead, all you'd be is scared.

2

Six days. Who knew it could feel like for ever?

Six days while the hospital makes sure Danny is okay and all the paperwork is sorted and social services are happy for him to come home. Given that I've waited three and a half years to see my best friend, what's six days more?

A lifetime.

I don't even have school to distract me. Just the long drag of the Easter holidays, and revision, and Dad either stuck in the lab at the university or holed up in his study. Lianna and Maisy text a few times asking me round, but I make an excuse. I know all they'll want to talk about is Danny, and that will only make it worse.

And the more I think about him, the harder it feels to have to wait till Sunday, and Martha's big welcome home meal.

When Sunday morning finally arrives, I'm so nervous I can't do anything. If I sit, I have to stand up again. If I stand, I have to walk. I try going over my French revision, but the words shape-shift on the page, refusing to make sense.

When I can't handle it any longer, I go and knock on Dad's study door. Hear something like a grunt.

"We should leave," I say through the door. The sound of his chair scraping across the floor, then Dad appears, his face blank with thought.

"Lunch," I remind him. "We're going to meet Danny. Remember?"

Dad glances at his laptop, the screen crammed with the usual muddle of figures and footnotes. Looks back at me, stricken. I can tell he's weighing it up.

Genetics wins. "Could you just give me half an hour?"

I look at my watch. It's already gone twelve.

"You go ahead," he says. "Tell Martha I'll be there soon. An hour tops, I promise."

"Okay," I sigh. "See you there."

I don't take the short cut, but the road that runs round the back of the park. Now, when it comes to it, I want to put this off a little bit longer. That's the trouble, I think, as I turn down Palace Avenue. You want something so badly, so deeply, so much for so long, that when it actually arrives, you just don't feel ready.

I walk fast. The blood pumping, the rhythm of my breathing helping to settle the jittery sensation in my stomach. I don't even mind when it begins to rain. There's no one around, just the odd car passing with a sizzle of tyres on wet tarmac. As I pass I glance in all the windows of the houses, hoping for a glimpse of other lives. I want to see people doing normal things – eating, watching TV, chatting over cups of tea.

Right now, suddenly, I would happily settle for an ordinary life – not this extraordinary one I seem to be living.

In the white house near the end of the road I catch sight of a woman and a child. They're standing in the kitchen, the woman grasping the girl round the waist, holding her up so she can stir something in a bowl. I stop for a moment. See the girl stick her finger into the mixture and offer it to her mother, who jerks her head back, laughing.

A twist in my heart, sharp as glass. We used to do stuff like that, Mum and I. Make brownies and biscuits. Big fluffy scones. Once a giant birthday cake for Dad, decorated top to bottom with tiny silver balls and pastel-coloured sugar flowers.

Five years on and this is how my mother comes back to me. In the small things. Moments that meant so little at the time, and so much now.

And in the big things too, I realize. Like today. Needing her more than ever.

Martha is stooped over, arranging pans, dressed in a blue and yellow patterned skirt I've never seen before. And make-up.

Her voice, when she sees me, is glittery and cheerful. Bright as sunshine. "Hannah! Don't just stand there. Come in, you silly thing. You'll get soaked."

I shrug off my coat and hang it in the little lobby by the back door. Inhale the rich, tempting smell coming from the oven. Through the glass doors leading into the dining room I can see the large oak table, busy with plates and cutlery and several posies of flowers. And wine glasses, I notice – the best crystal ones Danny and I were never allowed anywhere near. Everything is gleaming, as if it were new, recently unwrapped.

Like old times, I think, remembering the lunches we used to have here. All of us, Mum and Dad, Martha and Paul, Danny and Alice and I, sat around this same table.

It all feels so long ago.

"Your dad not with you?" Martha asks.

"He'll be along in a bit. He had something important to finish first." I have no idea if this is true.

"You look frozen." Martha checks out my skirt and thin summer top – the only halfway smart things I could find in my wardrobe. "Go and warm up. Paul's lit the fire."

I glance through the doorway into the living room. I can see several people. Paul in a crisp blue shirt, though he's dispensed with the usual tie. Beside him a short man dressed in a leather jacket and beige trousers, and one of those strange manicured beards that looks like it's been painted on. To his left, sideways on, a tall man wearing a baseball cap, its peak pulled low over his face.

No sign of Danny. Or Alice. I'm guessing she's playing up in her room.

"You sure you don't want any help?" I ask.

Martha stirs something in a saucepan, then wipes her hands on a tea towel. "Thanks, sweetheart, but it's all sorted. I was running late though. Had to persuade Danny to shower and have a shave. And find him something decent to wear."

"A shave?" I frown, remembering Danny's smooth, tanned face.

"I know," Martha laughs. "I nearly choked when I saw all that stubble... And how much he's grown. It's amazing how quickly boys change at this age." She flashes a smile and grabs my hand. "Ready?"

My stomach flips. I feel almost queasy with nerves.

"Oh, Hannah." Martha pauses to brush the hair away from my face. "Always so shy."

No one seems to notice us at first. The bearded man is saying something about the government and funding cuts, gesturing wildly as he speaks, while the other one stands with his legs wide apart and his hands thrust deep into his pockets, nodding in agreement. I hover to the side, not wanting to interrupt.

Paul catches my eye and comes over. Placing a hand on each shoulder, he turns me towards the man with the beard. "This is Hannah, Danny's oldest friend. More like one of the family really."

"Tony Dickson." The man takes my hand and shakes it vigorously. "Very pleased to meet you."

"Mr Dickson brought Danny down from London," Paul explains.

I nod, trying to think of something to say in return. I attempt a smile, but it comes out all wobbly. I'm conscious of the taller man studying me. I turn to face him, taking in the NYC logo on his baseball cap and the clean line of his jaw. He's wearing a pair of dark jeans that look like they might be Paul's, and a polo shirt that's clearly several sizes too big.

Everyone looks at me expectantly, waiting for me to say something. My mind stalls. My knees feel weak and shaky, like they're about to let the rest of me flop to the floor.

"Go on," Martha nudges. I raise my eyes, cheeks hot, fighting the urge to look away. The tall man is smiling at me. A big wide smile, with lots of teeth.

He takes a step forwards. "Hannah," he says, his voice low and confident.

I lift my hand, assuming he'll want to shake it too, but he raises his arms towards me.

I stare at him vacantly. What on earth am I supposed to do?

Then I realize, with a jolt that almost stops my heart.

Danny?

I freeze, eyes locked on his face. I can't get over how different he looks. I mean, I know he's older now. I knew he must have changed, of course I understood that. But the difference between the boy in my head and this…this *man* towering over me leaves me paralysed and winded with shock.

"Hannah!" Martha hisses behind me. I glance back, bewildered. She narrows her eyes and nods towards the man. I face him again, taking in the faint line of stubble around his cheeks.

And suddenly I see it. A glimpse of the Danny I still have in my head. Those blue-sky eyes. The familiar mess of blond hair, barely visible under his cap.

And that smile. How could I ever forget that smile?

Danny.

My breath quickens into a gasp, crushing my voice to a whisper.

"Danny… Oh god… Danny… Is that really you?"

"Hey, titch!"

Danny's grin widens as he moves towards me, arms still outstretched. Stupidly, inexplicably, I flinch, stepping backwards. Danny's hands drop to his sides.

"Hannah!" Martha's tone is sharper.

I take a deep breath and pull myself together. "Oh god, I'm sorry," I mumble. "It's just that you look... I mean, you look so..."

"Different?" Danny laughs, his mouth slackening into something between a smile and a grimace. "I guess I do."

He falls silent for a moment, examining me with a strange, almost wolfish expression. "For that matter, so do you, Hannah. We might have passed on the street and I'd never have known it was you. You're taller and you look much more..." He lets the sentence tail off.

I stare back at him, my heart still pounding, my head spinning. It isn't just that Danny has grown so tall. He was always tall for his age, even before – people assumed he was older than me, though there's only six months' difference. No, it's more that everything about him has changed – his manner, the way he holds himself, the slight stoop in his shoulders.

And his voice… A man's voice now, deep and unfamiliar. That's what throws me more than anything; he doesn't even *sound* like Danny any more.

"You look like you need to sit down." Paul grasps my elbow and guides me towards the sofa. I sink onto the far end, near the warmth and crackle of the fire. Realize I'm shivering.

"So…" Danny lowers himself into the armchair opposite. "Nothing to say, titch? I mean, it's been a while."

"I…I…god…sorry…it's all a bit of a shock." I clear my throat and start again. "Sorry, Danny. I mean, how are you? Really, are you okay?"

"Fine." He sniffs, flashing a smile at his mother. "Never better."

Everyone laughs, though I'm not sure any of us could say why. Least of all me. I'm dazed. Not happy. Not pleased, excited, or any of those things I always imagined I'd feel if…when I saw Danny again. I just feel flat, like after Christmas lunch, when you've eaten too much and opened all your presents and there's nothing left to do but watch TV. Or the last day of a holiday, when going home hangs over you like a cloud and there no longer seems any point trying to enjoy yourself.

For a moment, it feels like disappointment. Because only now, seeing Danny in the flesh, do I grasp how much has changed.

"Didn't I tell you, Hannah?" Martha's eyes are gleaming with triumph. "Didn't I always say Danny would come home?"

Over and over, I think. Though I stopped listening years ago.

Danny watches the pair of us, a strange expression twitching across his lips. He looks nearly as on edge as I am. "I guess she's a bit overwhelmed, Mum. It's a lot to take in." He glances at me for confirmation. "I know how she feels."

"Yes, it's all been rather dramatic," says Paul. "As I'm sure Hannah can imagine."

And I can. I see Danny walking in, that big silly grin spread wide across his face. See him drop his bag on the floor and stride over to his mother, hugging her tight and hard. Hear Martha's squeals, first of disbelief, then delight, and Alice running downstairs and charging at him like a cannonball. I can see Rudman spinning round in ecstasy, barking and whimpering and thumping his tail against the furniture.

Of course I know it didn't really happen that way – I just like to think it did.

At that moment there's a knock on the door, then Dad appears, looking rushed and apologetic. And untidy, his trousers creased and his jacket looking like it should have been thrown away years ago. Though he's changed his shirt, at least, and brushed his hair. He takes in the room, saying hello to Martha and nodding at Paul, before turning to me and Danny.

A slight grimace of surprise, then Dad strides over, offering his hand. "Good to see you again, Daniel."

Danny stands for the handshake. "You too." He looks a little nervous, his fingers twitching as they fall back to his side.

"Hannah's been on tenterhooks all week," Dad says. "Waiting for the big day."

I raise an eyebrow. Surprised he's noticed.

All at once Danny's face relaxes. "It's great to see you again, Mr Radcliffe."

"You've never called me that before." Dad frowns. "Let's stick to David."

Danny reddens a little. "Sorry. It's just…you know… hard to tell whether everything's still the same…"

"We understand, darling," Martha cuts in, offering Dad a drink.

I turn back to Danny. "So…honestly, how are you?" I ask again. This time really wanting to know.

Danny wrinkles up his nose. "I dunno. Tired, I guess. Glad to be back."

My eyes never leave his face. I can't get over how much he's changed. His features are sharper somehow…leaner, with hollows that were never there before. The same broad tanned cheeks, however, and turquoise eyes, though underneath you can see the exhaustion.

It's Danny, I can see that now. The same, but different. Older.

I nod towards him. "When did you get that?"

A puzzled look eclipses his smile.

"The baseball cap," I say. "I thought you hated them. You always said they made people look dopey."

Danny lifts it enough to reveal a large bruise around his left eye, just beginning to fade to yellow. Then pulls it back over his brow. "Doesn't it suit me?"

"Sure." I grin. "You look great. Dopey, but great."

He laughs. "You look good too. Seriously. I mean the last time I saw you, titch, you were just a skinny girl on a bike. Now look at you, all grown up."

I feel my face flush with pleasure, my breathing settle.

"You remember that trip?" Danny asks. "Down to the lake? When you chickened out of riding the ledge."

"How could I forget?" Warmth spreads through me as my anxiety drains away. Danny's back, I tell myself. Danny's back. And finally I can let myself believe it.

Upstairs there's a sudden high-pitched wail. All heads turn towards the door, then Martha hurries out. Moments later the muffled sound of Alice's protests.

Several silent minutes pass before Martha reappears, cheeks flushed, and bends to whisper something to Paul.

"Leave it," he replies, shaking his head. "Just give her time."

Mr Dickson talks a lot, but somehow doesn't say very much. I gather it's his job as a social worker to make sure

Danny settles back in okay, but he seems more interested in Martha's food than in Danny or the rest of us.

Not that I blame him. Martha's really gone to town. There's a huge quiche with salad, and tons of fresh herb bread and roasted vegetables. And a large, golden-skinned rice pudding, still baking in the oven.

I know exactly why that's there. Rice pudding was always Danny's favourite. One birthday he insisted on it instead of cake; when Martha tried sticking in the candles, they tilted and sank before she could light them.

Danny wasn't bothered – he simply pulled them out and tucked in.

I pick at the pile of food on my plate, listening to everyone talking about the weather, the price of houses, Paul's business. Chatting away like nothing ever happened, like Danny didn't disappear for years, then reappear as abruptly as he left.

Like there isn't one great enormous thing we all need to know more than anything: where the hell has Danny been?

I watch him, stealthily, searching for clues. Notice Paul doing the same, chatting to Mr Dickson but eyeing Danny every few seconds, as if he still can't believe he's actually there. Dad, on the other hand, keeps his head down, eating silently and ignoring everyone – I can tell he's counting the minutes till he can make a polite exit.

Danny doesn't say much either, just eats and nods and smiles when anyone speaks to him. Though I can see by the strain in his face that he's finding this hard. I keep trying to catch his eye, hoping to start a conversation, but it's like he's forgotten I'm here.

I'm just going to ask him about France when Mr Dickson gets in first. "Daniel, I guess you'll soon be old enough to learn to drive. Your dad here says he's planning to teach you."

Paul smiles encouragingly at his son. "I thought you could have Martha's old car. It wouldn't cost too much to insure."

"Sounds great, Dad," says Danny, his tone unenthusiastic, like his father had suggested he mow the lawn or help him clean out the garage.

Paul blinks, clearly surprised by his reaction. Danny had always wanted to learn to drive. When he was little, he'd ride his bike round the back garden making revving noises, pulling on the handlebars like he was steering a car.

"Actually I'm planning to teach Hannah next year," Dad chips in out of nowhere, lifting his eyes to Paul's.

I stare at him. He is? Dad's never mentioned it before.

Paul glances at Dad then looks away, a stiffness in his features he can't quite suppress. Dad carries on eating, oblivious to Martha's tight-lipped expression. I turn to see Danny studying the three of them, coming to some kind of conclusion of his own. Clearly the tension between them all isn't lost on him either.

"Hannah behind a wheel?" he declares suddenly. "Now that I *have* to see."

Everyone smiles and I feel something lift inside me.

Danny could always do that, defuse a situation with his refusal to take anything seriously. At school he ran rings round the teachers, making them laugh at stuff that would get most kids a detention.

I give him a grateful look, then cut a piece of pastry from the edge of my quiche and slide it under the table, waiting for the cold touch of Rudman's nose. But the food remains uneaten in my hand. I lean down and peer underneath. Nothing but human legs and feet.

"I've put him outside," Martha says as I sit up.

I frown before I can stop myself. Martha adores Rudman. He's always allowed to hover under the table at meals. Why would she shut him out in the rain?

She pretends not to notice, getting up to clear the plates. Danny picks up the salad bowl and starts to follow her out to the kitchen, but she waves him back. "You stay put," she beams. "After all, you're the guest of honour."

Danny sits back down and a minute later his mother returns, the rice pudding suspended between two oven gloves.

"Now that looks fabulous." Mr Dickson leans back in his chair, patting the swell of his belly. "It's not often in my job that I get fed like this."

Martha spoons him a large portion into a bowl. It gives off a warm, heavy scent of vanilla. She fills another and hands it to me, nodding at Danny. I pass it across and just catch his expression. A small involuntary curl of his lip.

I tuck into mine. It's perfect, creamy and delicious. But

as Martha offers seconds, I see Danny has barely touched what he already has. I lean over.

"I thought you loved rice pudding," I whisper, glancing at Martha.

Danny gives his mother an apologetic shrug. "I guess I'm just full," he says. "But it was lovely."

"No problem, sweetheart," she replies. "I'll save you some for later."

As soon as the meal ends Dad excuses himself and bolts home to his study. Mr Dickson starts talking to Martha and Danny about getting him back to school, so I slip upstairs with some rice pudding in a bowl and tap lightly on Alice's door.

No answer. I push it open and peer inside. Alice is lying, fully clothed, asleep on the bed, the pink and yellow satin of her best dress crumpled under her bare legs.

A lump rises in my throat. She looks so small somehow, and I can see from the red around her eyes that she's been crying. I want to crawl onto the bed, pull her alphabet quilt over the pair of us and go to sleep beside her. I feel shattered suddenly, like I've climbed a mountain or run a marathon, or swum right across the Bristol Channel.

"Don't worry, Hannah. She's okay."

Paul's voice makes me jump. I spin round. He's standing on the landing, watching me watch his daughter.

I nod. "I just wanted to say hello. Why didn't she come down for lunch?"

"She refused. Point-blank," he laughs. "In that way only Alice can."

I know what he means. Alice looks a bit different and finds it harder to learn stuff, but otherwise she's much the same as anyone else. Only, sometimes, if she can't get her head around something, she can get rather stroppy.

Paul sighs and comes into the room. "I'll be honest, Hannah, she's having a hard time with it all," he says, keeping his voice low. "She got really upset when Danny arrived. She's barely spoken to him."

"Upset?"

"We told her Danny was coming back. We tried to explain, to prepare her so it wouldn't be such a surprise, but the moment she saw him she started screaming."

"Really?" I study her, concerned.

Paul sits on the end of her bed, his shoulders slumping. He rubs his hand over his chin, as if squeezing away the pressure of the last few days. "It was awful. The worst I've ever seen her. In the end I had to carry her up here and sit with her until she calmed down."

I stare at him. I don't know what to say.

He shuts his eyes, dropping his voice to a whisper. "I don't think she recognizes him any more."

"God, poor Alice. I guess it's the shock. I mean, he has changed a lot."

Paul sighs. "I know. We were all taken aback when we

first saw him, how grown-up he looks now, how much older. But of course he is... I mean, he's getting on for seventeen, and god only knows what he's been through..."

"Any idea?" I venture.

Paul shakes his head. "John Dickson says to leave it for a bit. Let him get back into the flow of things. It's important that Danny tells us in his own time."

He puts his hands on both knees, kneading them for a moment before getting back up to his feet. "Anyway, it was all too much for Alice. I suppose she thought he'd look exactly how he did before. How she remembers him."

I trail Paul back downstairs. I guess we all thought that.

Everyone is still sitting around the table, finishing the wine. Danny must be on his second or third glass, I reckon. I look at Martha – she's doing a very good impression of not having noticed.

She catches my glance. "You look tired."

"I am," I say, with an apologetic shrug of my mouth. "I think I'll go, if that's okay. I've got loads of homework and stuff to do."

Martha nods. "Thank you for coming, Hannah."

"And thanks for lunch, it was great," I say, wondering why everything feels so strange and formal all of a sudden.

I turn to say goodbye to Danny, but he drains the rest of his glass and follows me into the kitchen.

"So what's up, titch? Why *are* you leaving so early?"

I look at him. It sounds more like an accusation than a question. He stares back at me, something almost defiant in his eyes.

"Sorry," I mumble. "It's just all a bit…"

He gazes at me for a few more seconds before his expression softens. "A bit much. Yeah, I know."

I make an effort to smile. "You really okay?" I examine his face, drawn again to those eyes, the same disconcerting shade of blue.

"I will be. Now I'm home."

"It must be a relief."

Danny smiles but doesn't reply.

"Looks painful." I point towards the bruise just visible between his cap and his eyebrow.

He raises his hand to touch it, running his fingers carefully over the skin. "Yeah. It's getting better though."

"Who attacked you?"

He shrugs. "I dunno. A bunch of men laid into me. I can't remember much about it. Or anything really."

I chew the inside of my lip. "Weren't you scared? Out there. On your own."

He doesn't reply.

"I mean, how did you survive? What did you do all that time you were away?"

Danny's eyes flick away from mine. "Like I said, titch, I can't really remember."

I watch him, feeling an unexpected wave of frustration.

I hadn't realized how many questions I had buzzing around my head. How badly I needed some answers.

"I missed you," I blurt, not meaning to say it, but knowing if I don't now, I never will. "We all did," I add, to cover my embarrassment when he doesn't respond.

And from nowhere my frustration curdles into anger. How can Danny just stand there, so casually, as if nothing has happened? Has he no idea what we've been through?

Doesn't he care?

His cheeks flush. He looks past me, trying to hide the emotion in his face. All at once I see the old Danny again and my anger fades. I want to hug him, to shrug off this awkwardness and start again.

"Danny, I—"

At that moment a yelp sounds from outside, followed by the scratch of Rudman's claws on the back door. Without thinking, I move to let him in. He shoots into the house, shaking off the rain, tail wagging furiously, then his big brown eyes fix on Danny and he freezes. He takes a step forwards, a low deep growl emerging from his throat.

"Rudman!" I grab hold of his collar and yank him back.

Rudman stops growling, but his eyes never leave Danny.

"Come on, Rudders, old boy. It's me, Danny." He squats down and holds out his hand towards the dog, palm turned up, as if offering him something. But Rudman's hackles rise still further, and his lips curl into an ugly snarl.

"Rudman! Bad dog! What's got into you?" I shove him back out the door with my foot, then turn around. Danny's standing there, hands in his pockets, wearing a bemused expression.

"He'll get used to you again – he's just a bit freaked out," I say. "I guess we all are."

Danny shrugs. "And they say dogs never forget."

"I think you'll find that's elephants," I joke, trying to shake off the gloom that seems to have settled between us.

There's an odd expression on Danny's face. A kind of pleading. Like he wants something from me.

"Okay." I grab my coat from the door hook. Suddenly I can't take any more. All I want to do is leave. "Bye then."

Danny observes my retreat. "See ya, wouldn't wanna be ya," he says abruptly, and heads back towards the dining room.

I stop. I can't move. My throat feels tight and my eyes hot and stingy.

Just six words, and I'm back there, that Sunday afternoon, watching Danny push off on his bike and head down the road, the front wheel wobbling as he lifts his hand to wave goodbye.

"See ya, wouldn't wanna be ya."

The very last thing he said to me.

4

"Come on, Hannah, 'fess up." Sophie Fox leans over my desk, her face all smiles and dimples. "Tell us about Danny. You must have seen him."

"Yeah, go on, Radcliffe, spill. Give us all the gory details." Vicky Clough pulls out a chair and sits beside me, her skirt riding up her thighs. Lianna raises her eyebrows at me, suppressing a smile. Across the classroom, curious stares minnow around us.

News of Danny's return has travelled fast – even during the Easter holidays. Everyone in the school knows, it seems, and everyone in the school wants to know more.

"How is he?" Vicky is practically breathless with excitement. "Is he okay?"

Vicky always had a crush on Danny. She once spent a whole term wanting to hang out, only to drop me overnight when Rick Thomas asked her out instead.

I give in. "Yes, I've seen him. And he's fine."

"So, how does he look?"

"Good, I guess. Great."

"How do you mean, 'great'?" demands Vicky, her

expression guarded. Clearly she still hasn't accepted Danny and I are just friends.

"Taller." I shrug. "Older."

Vicky's gaze drifts to mid-air. I can tell she's trying out this new version of Danny in her head; from the way she purses her lips and smiles to herself, she clearly likes what she sees.

"But the real question," Sophie glances round the classroom before leaning in confidentially, "is where—"

"I don't know," I cut in, saving her the bother of asking. "I have no idea where he's been."

Sophie snorts. "Oh, come on…"

At that moment Mr Young walks in, his harassed expression and brusque glare at the three of us sparing me further interrogation. Sophie gives me a reproachful look before sidling back to her desk, but Vicky nudges me gently.

"Tell him 'hi' from me, will you?" She flashes me a quick smile before Mr Young orders her to sit down.

5

After school I find Danny slumped on the sofa in front of some programme about Canadian truckers, eyes fixed on a lingering shot of an articulated lorry sinking into a vast frozen lake. I stand to the side, waiting for him to notice me.

"Hey," I say, when he doesn't. "How are you?"

He yawns, glancing up then back at the half-submerged truck. "What's up, titch?"

"Nothing. Just wondered how you're doing. Everyone's been asking about you at school."

"Yeah?"

I lower myself into the armchair, since Danny isn't showing any sign of giving me room on the sofa. Besides, it means I can study him while pretending to watch TV.

I still can't take my eyes off him. Danny's been back a couple of weeks now, and already he looks different. The bruise above his eye has faded and his face has filled out, losing that lean, tired look. I let my gaze loiter over the faint line of stubble covering his chin and top lip, the smooth planes of his cheeks.

He's wearing that cap again, but the hair curling around

its edges seems thinner, straighter somehow, and longer, covering his ears. Danny always kept it short before, so it dried quickly after swimming.

"Vicky sends her love."

I wait for him to laugh, but he doesn't even look up. Vicky's crush on Danny was something I always teased him about, winding him up by copying that slurry way she talks.

"She's practically bursting at the prospect of seeing you again."

"That's nice."

"You'll see her next Saturday," I say, "and all the others." Martha's invited everyone to the party to celebrate Danny's return – half our year seems to be going. "You looking forward to it?"

"Of course." Danny flicks to a news programme. I can tell he's barely listening to me. "So will you be coming back? To school, I mean?"

"I guess so."

"But you've missed loads. And the exams start soon. It hardly seems worth it."

Danny shrugs. "Mum still thinks I should go back. I've got to sit some tests and stuff to see what level I'm at."

Something snags his attention and he leans forward, turning up the volume. A reporter is describing a riot in Marseilles – there's concern it might spread to other areas of France. I sit there, scrutinizing Danny as he watches the screen.

"*…as the unrest has extended to the districts surrounding the city, the police have mobilized…*"

I think about all the times I've pictured this moment. How it would be when he got back, all the things I would ask him, and all the things I'd have to tell him. I never imagined it would be like this.

Give him a chance, the voice in my head reminds me. But I can't help myself. I'm determined to get him to talk.

"Danny?"

He looks at me like he'd forgotten I was even here. "Mmmm?"

"Are you sure you can't remember anything? I mean, surely some of it must be coming back?"

Danny's focus returns to the room. He sucks in a breath and slowly releases it, finally turning his shoulders to give me his full attention. "Yes. I mean, not really. Nothing concrete."

"Concrete?"

"Just odd impressions. Strange dreams."

"What kind of dreams?"

Danny stares at me in open annoyance. There's something else in his eyes. Something guarded. "I don't know, Hannah. Bad dreams. Running, being scared. Alone."

He turns back. The news has moved on to a story about the Middle East. Soldiers in sand-coloured uniforms run across a desert landscape. He switches to another channel.

"But you can remember before? I mean, before you left?"

"Of course."

"So it's just the stuff after you disappeared."

"Yeah."

"Up till when you got beaten up in France. Just before the police found you."

Danny doesn't answer. Just points the remote at the TV and plays with the volume. I notice his hand twitching as he does it.

"I mean, that's a bit odd, isn't it? Why only then? Why not all your life?"

"How should I know?" Danny spins round again, his voice hard. "What's with the cross-examination, Hannah? So many people asking me questions. How about you leave all this stuff to the shrink?"

"You're seeing a psychiatrist?" I know I sound surprised.

"Yeah. Mum's orders. Leave no stone unturned and all that. So I don't need the third degree from you as well, okay?"

I look at him, stunned. I've never seen Danny like this. Never heard him so...so *angry*. My face flushes with heat. "Sorry," I mumble, "I didn't mean to upset you."

I feel crushed. My chest actually hurts. Danny regards me coolly, running his tongue over his teeth. I wait for him to say something, to break the gulf of silence between us.

Instead he leans forward and turns off the telly, heading out the door without a word, the sound of his footsteps resounding all the way up to his room.

* * *

"What's up?"

Dad stands over the sofa, eyeing me with concern. I've been lying here for over an hour, picking my nails and staring out the window. Across the road, the neighbours are repainting their house, one of them up a ladder doing the bit above the front door. There doesn't seem much point – it looks exactly the same shade of cream it was before.

"Hey, Hannah, I asked you a question."

Dad leans over and dumps a pile of journals on the coffee table. I glance at the one on top. *Human Genomics and Proteomics*. Good grief. That should keep him happy for hours.

"Nothing's up."

Dad raises an eyebrow.

"Okay," I sigh. "I went to see Danny. It didn't go well."

"How so?"

"I tried talking to him."

"What about?"

"Everything. What happened, what he can remember. He got pissed off."

"Ah." Dad sits down in the armchair opposite and balances his elbows on his knees. He spreads his fingers and presses them together, resting his chin on top. His thinking pose.

"I don't know. I just feel…" I struggle to find the words, then give up. "I don't know what to feel."

Dad doesn't speak for a moment.

"Sounds natural, Hannah. After all, this isn't exactly a

typical situation, is it? Everyone is bound to be upset and confused. It'll settle down."

"I suppose. I only want to help. Get things back to normal."

As soon as I say this I recognize how absurd it sounds. And how very much I want it to be true. I guess part of me had been hoping that Danny and I could pick up where we left off.

Or rather start afresh, erasing those months of weirdness before he left.

But now I understand, with a chill in my stomach, that there's no way back to how things were before. And it hurts.

It's like losing him all over again.

6

Martha is standing in Danny's room, rooting through a jumble of stuff on the bed. My heart gives a little start of surprise. Danny's clothes. The ones that sat in the wardrobe, untouched, all this time.

"Hello, Hannah." She beckons me over. "Want to give me a hand?"

"I was looking for Danny." I haven't seen him since our confrontation several days ago and I want to make up. Try and get things back on track between us.

"You just missed him, sweetheart. He's gone out with Paul. Something about getting a new phone."

I scan the room. Already so much has changed. The football posters have disappeared from the wall, along with the magazines and DVDs scattered across his desk. There's no sign of Danny's swimming trophies, and it smells different – fresher, faintly lemony.

"I don't suppose this still fits?" I pick up a T-shirt from the heap on the bed, running my hand across the front. It's the one Paul brought back from Sydney with the picture of the kangaroo – always Danny's favourite. "Tie me kangaroo down, sport," he sang whenever he wore it. Even the time we had a non-uniform day at school and that exchange teacher from Australia accused him of taking the piss.

"Strewth, no," Danny drawled in the worst Aussie accent you ever heard, and the whole class collapsed into hysterics and even the teacher had to laugh.

"Miles too small." Martha takes the T-shirt and puts it into a bag, then dangles a pair of black trousers in front of me. "Good enough for charity?"

I nod, catching sight of a couple of paint swatches standing on the window sill – one a slatey shade of grey-blue, the other more green in tone.

Martha follows my gaze. "I'm redecorating. Something a bit more grown-up."

I smile to hide my unease. A few weeks ago, Danny's mother wouldn't have dreamed of touching anything in this room – now she's repainting and tossing out his things like they're rags.

"Has he grown out of everything?" I finger a pair of shorts; they look almost new.

"Pretty much. I don't think there's anything here we can salvage." She folds another pair of trousers and puts them in a bag. "Anyway, it's time for a fresh start."

A squeal in the doorway. Alice runs in, leaping onto the bed and trampolining towards me, a small whirlwind of excitement. "Hannah, Hannah, Hannah!"

I grab her before she sends me flying.

"Love you, Hannah." Alice wraps her arms round my neck and squeezes tight.

I laugh. "Love you too, Bugsy."

She flops back onto the bed, stretching out her legs and staring at her feet. Her mouth makes a cross shape.

"You okay?" I pull at one of her toes through her tights.

She kicks my hand away. "Don't like that bad man."

"Bad man?"

"Alice!" Martha snaps, with a sharpness that makes me wince. "I've told you not to say that."

Alice's eyes shine with defiance, her bottom lip trembling. She jumps up, sticks her tongue out at her mother, then runs back out the room.

Martha rests her hands on the bed and sighs. "I've no idea what's up with her."

"Does she mean Danny?"

Martha nods and her face clouds. "It's really thrown her, his coming back out of the blue. She still doesn't seem to recognize him."

I flashback to the months after he disappeared, the way Alice carried round that photo of him, cuddling it like a teddy bear. "Danny back?" she asked, over and over, never satisfied with any answer you gave her.

"I suppose it's not surprising," Martha says. "She was so small when he left."

I look at her, unsure what to say. Could Alice really have forgotten Danny, even after all this time? From the moment she could crawl, she trailed her brother with a devotion not even Rudman could equal. Danny would get back from school to find her waiting at the back gate, knuckles white from gripping the ironwork, eyes fixed on the drive. There for hours, Martha said.

"Still, there's good news," she cuts in. "The doctor's given Danny a clean bill of health. There's nothing physically wrong with him, as far as they can tell. Though all he seems to do is eat and sleep."

"I guess that's a good thing. It means he's recovering."

"Yes. Dr Wilson said that's all he could prescribe – food and rest."

I watch her sort through a pile of shoes, some going into the bag for charity, the others into a pile for recycling. "Such a shame," Martha mutters, looking over a pair of black leather boots. "These were brand new." She gives them one last regretful glance and stuffs them into the charity bag.

I watch for a minute, then clear my throat and take the plunge. "Has he said yet what happened? I mean, where he's been?"

Martha stiffens slightly. "No, Hannah. He hasn't." She pauses, looking out the window across the bay. "He still says he can't remember, though I don't think he likes me asking."

Me neither, I think.

"It's all a blank apparently. Just odd scenes and things, impressions. Nothing coherent."

I look at her, dumbfounded. "But is that possible? I mean, to forget so much?"

"Dr Wilson says it is. He thinks Danny was knocked out when he was attacked, though there's no sign of lasting damage. He believes Danny will remember after a while."

How long is a while? I wonder. I mean, it's already been nearly four weeks since the attack.

"It could be months, according to Dr Wilson," Martha says, reading my mind. "Even longer. It's impossible to tell." She pulls her eyes from the view and meets mine. "I don't suppose Danny's mentioned anything to you?"

"Nothing," I reply, thinking of his resentment when I asked. The look he gave me. Cold and hostile.

Martha's eyes linger on me for a moment, then she picks up a pile of socks and throws them into the bin. "Anyway, Dr Wilson has booked him in for an MRI scan. Just to make sure."

"Okay."

"Well, I don't think we should push it. Danny clearly doesn't like it and Dr Wilson thinks we should just give him time." Her tone contains a hint of warning. Danny must have told her I was bugging him.

"Okay," I say again, looking away. After all, she's right. We waited long enough for Danny to come home.

It won't kill us to wait a little longer to find out why he left.

7

"Penny for them."

I find Dad sitting in the corner right at the end of the hallway. He's got a glass of champagne in his hand, but doesn't exactly look like he's celebrating. I get a pang of guilt for making him come.

"They're not even worth that."

"C'mon, Dad. Make an effort."

He examines me in my new dress and something comes into his eyes. "You look lovely," he says after a pause. "Just like…" He stops. Swallows.

I sit down beside him. He turns and gives me a weak smile. I know he's thinking about Mum.

"Sorry," he says. "You know parties aren't really my thing."

They used to be, I think, remembering when Dad was always up for a bit of fun. He and Mum loved fancy dress. They went to one party as a flamenco dancer and a matador – while Mum looked gorgeous in her ruffly black dress, Danny and I almost died laughing at the sight of Dad in his red braided jacket and knee-length gold trousers.

Looking at him now, though, you'd think that was someone else entirely.

I want to hug him. Tell him I'm happy he's here, even just for half an hour. But Dad's sitting there so stiff and tense I lose heart. We don't seem to do the touching thing any more. Another thing that disappeared with Mum.

"I see Danny's on good form."

Dad nods towards the front door, where Danny stands with his mother, greeting people as they arrive. I watch for a while. Some hold him at arm's-length, examining him like a painting in an exhibition, or slapping him on the back and exclaiming how much he's grown. Others are sneakier, doing the standard hugs and handshakes and pecks on the cheek, but all the while eyeing Danny furtively, soaking in every detail of what has changed.

One or two actually finger his hair, like they can't quite believe he's real. It's as if they're compelled to reach out and touch him, like pinching yourself to check you're not dreaming.

Danny's shaking hands, smiling and letting people hug him, but I can tell he's uncomfortable by the way he's shifting from one leg to the other. Like he's itching to get away.

"He certainly looks well," Dad says.

"Amazing."

I mean it. Dressed in a pair of beige chinos and a long-sleeved shirt he once wouldn't have been seen dead in, Danny looks really grown-up. If it wasn't for the baseball cap, you'd think he was way older than sixteen.

"Daniel!"

A smartly-dressed woman around Martha's age walks

up, taking both his hands, then steps back and looks him up and down. "God, I'm sorry I'm so late. You wouldn't believe the traffic on the motorway."

She raises one eyebrow, waiting for his reaction. I study Danny's face. Something flits across it, a moment's discomfort chased away by his widening smile. He's more nervous than he's letting on.

"Hey!" he replies, only the slightest hesitation in his voice.

The woman cocks her head to one side. "Well?"

Danny's smile barely wavers, but I see him glance round for his mother. He's out of luck. Martha's busy greeting another group of late arrivals.

"Come now, Danny, you remember me, don't you?" the woman purrs, seemingly more amused than offended.

Danny laughs. "Of course I do."

"Well, I must say, I expected more of a welcome than that!" Her voice is playful as she drops his hands and offers up her cheek for a kiss.

Danny's still smiling, but I can read the tension in his posture. He isn't enjoying this at all. He turns and grabs a glass of champagne from the tray Paul is passing round, and takes a deep gulp, oblivious to the woman's frown of surprise.

That's what's so odd, I think. Not so much that Danny is drinking – or that he's getting away with it – but the *way* he's doing it. Confidently, like it hasn't even occurred to him that he shouldn't.

"Millie!" Martha's voice rings out as she spots the woman Danny just embraced. "Millie! Finally!"

Millie laughs. "Well, I'm glad someone knows me. I think Daniel here is at a loss."

"Don't be absurd." Martha turns to her son. "He's only playing. How could he possibly forget *you*?"

Millie? Then I remember. Martha's old schoolfriend, the one from London. I've never met her, but Danny always came back from visits full of tales of river trips and the Science Museum and tea at the Ritz.

"Of course I remember you, Millie." Danny grins, the fingers of his free hand drumming against his thigh. "I couldn't resist teasing you a little, that's all."

Millie beams back at him. "Same old Danny. Some things never change."

Martha laughs, slipping an arm round her friend's waist and giving it a squeeze. Her face is radiant. I don't think I've ever seen her looking so happy.

When it happens, I'm sure I am the only person who sees it. Though later, I can't be completely certain I did.

Danny, quite deliberately, spills his drink right over himself.

"Damn!" He looks down at the spreading stain on his trouser leg with feigned surprise, then back up at Martha and Millie. "Sorry. I have to go and change." He touches Millie's arm. "It's really good to see you again."

With that he turns and heads straight upstairs, barely glancing at us as he passes.

8

Out in the garden, in the marquee taking up half the lawn, the party is in full swing. The hired band is blasting out cheesy hits from the eighties. People are jiggling and swaying on the dance floor, bumping into each other and laughing and apologizing. Small kids dart between them, hiding under tables, helping themselves to what's left of the food.

Uncles and aunts and other relatives of Danny's I barely remember stand chatting in clumps, along with family friends I've never met before. Martha is one of those people who never loses touch with anyone – and it looks like no one in her bulging address book turned down the invitation to Danny's homecoming bash.

I spot Danny standing by an older couple, wearing clean trousers and an expression like nothing ever happened. Behind him all the kids from school are huddled together in the corner, leaning across to speak to one another and throwing stealthy looks in his direction. I see Lianna talking to Maisy and Olivia Richmond. I'm about to go over when Joe Rowling gets up and weaves his way to my side.

"You look nice." His eyes give me a quick once-over. "That dress really suits you."

I put on a pleased face. "Thanks. Danny's mum got it for me."

It is lovely, the material light and swishy, a beautiful swirl of yellows and greens, colours I wouldn't usually wear.

Joe glances over at Danny. "Everyone's frantic to meet him, but I can't seem to pin him down. Every time I get near him he's dragged off somewhere."

"Wait here," I say, and go over and slip my hand through Danny's arm, smiling an apology for breaking into the conversation. I stand on tiptoe so I can whisper in his ear. "Come and say hi to everyone from school. They're all dying to see you."

Danny's mouth turns up at the corners, but his eyes narrow as they flick towards the group in the corner.

"Come on. They won't bite." I give him a tug and he lets me lead him across the floor. Everyone stares as we approach, while trying to look like that's exactly what they're not doing.

"Hey, Danny!" Joe says in a hearty voice that doesn't quite cover his nerves. He steps forward with his hand outstretched, hesitates, then throws his arms around his old friend.

Danny's face morphs into a grin as Joe releases him. "Boy, have you changed. Some power in that grip now."

"I don't know what you mean," Joe beams and flexes his arm to make his bicep look bigger. "Just the same old Joe."

"Yeah, still an idiot." Danny laughs before turning and pointing towards Sophie. "Vicky, right?"

"As if!" Sophie shrieks, and Vicky punches her on the arm. "She's Vicky – I'm Sophie. You know, the gorgeous, genius one." She strikes a pose, pouting her lips, and Vicky rolls her eyes.

"Jesus, sorry." Danny slaps his hand against his forehead. "Of course. I mean, you both look so different with make-up on. Fantastic, actually."

Vicky and Sophie both beam with pleasure.

"That's okay," Vicky says, ogling him. "To be honest, I'd hardly have recognized you either. You look amazing. So tall!"

Lianna turns and smirks at me. She knows all about Vicky's crush on Danny. I have to bite my lip to stop myself grinning.

Ross Jacobs steps forward and grabs Danny's hand. "You haven't forgotten me, right? Not after that drubbing I gave you in that last footy match. Face it, Geller, you never could tackle for shit."

"Yeah, Ross. And you never could quite get the ball between the goalposts, if I remember right."

Everyone's face relaxes into laughter. "So, how are you?"

Vicky asks, her eyes glued to Danny's. At the edge of my vision, I see Dad walk right past Martha and Paul, ignoring them both. Paul stiffens slightly in his wake.

What is it between them? I wonder, for the thousandth time. This tension, this...stand-off. More like people avoiding each other than people who were friends for years.

"Hey, Hannah, you remember that, don't you?" The sound of Joe's voice drags me back into the conversation. I turn to face him.

"You know, that time in Year Seven when Danny pretended he was drowning."

I smile. "Yeah."

"It was John Whittaker who dared you to do it, wasn't it?"

Danny laughs. "The bastard."

"Go on," says Vicky, "I love that story."

"Nah, Joe's version is much funnier," says Danny.

So Joe recounts the whole incident, from the moment where Danny pretended he had cramp, sinking to the bottom of the pool and playing dead, to the bit where Mr Cozens jumped in and dragged him out.

"I loved how you suddenly sprang back to life right before he gave you mouth-to-mouth," says Joe, wiping the tears from his eyes.

"Can you blame me?" says Danny. "I mean, would you fancy the kiss of life from old Cozens?"

Everyone laughs again, and Joe shoots me a grateful look. I realize just how apprehensive he was about meeting Danny again.

Over his shoulder I see Dad give me a brief wave then head towards the gate. I have a sudden urge to go after him. To ask him what's going on between him and Martha and Paul. Why things seem to have gone so bad that he can hardly bear more than half an hour in the same place as them.

But then I spot Alice sitting at a nearby table, a plate of untouched food beside her, picking at a scab on her knee. She looks so forlorn I can't bring myself to ignore her. I excuse myself and walk over.

"Hey, Ally, how are you doing?"

Alice just stares ahead, her expression blank.

"Good party?"

Still no response. I've never seen her so subdued. The stubborn jut of her chin, the hint of sulkiness around her mouth. Everything about her looks cross and miserable.

I sit down beside her. "What's up, little one?"

Alice pouts, still refusing to even look at me. "Want him back."

"Who?"

"Rudman."

"Hey, where is he?" I realize I haven't seen him all day.

"In the shed." Alice's finger returns to the scab. "Mummy put him in the shed again because he's naughty."

"Naughty? What's he done?"

"Woofing," Alice says solemnly. "And *he* don't like it so Mummy put Rudman in the shed. She put his basket in the shed too, but it's all dark and Rudman don't like it."

Tears well in the corners of her eyes. I don't know who I feel sorrier for, Alice or Rudman.

"Don't worry," I bend over and whisper in her ear. "He'll be fine. I expect Mummy put him in there so he wouldn't get fed up with all this noise."

Alice chews her bottom lip and says nothing. Even through the thick lens of her glasses I can see her eyes look hollow and tired.

"Fancy some ice cream?"

She shakes her head.

"You sure? I think there's chocolate *and* strawberry."

Her eyes finally lift to mine. But her flicker of interest is eclipsed by a scowl. I glance round and see Danny walking straight past, not even glancing in our direction.

I watch him disappear into the house, then look at Alice. What's going on with her and Danny? I wonder. Does she still not remember him?

Then it hits me. Alice hasn't forgotten Danny at all – she's *angry* with him. Angry for abandoning her, as she sees it.

This is her way of punishing him.

I study the slump of her shoulders, my mind buzzing with confusion. But that doesn't explain why Danny is acting so cool towards his sister, persists an unwelcome voice in my head. Surely he understands how she feels? Surely he'd forgive *her* of all people?

From the moment Martha brought Alice back from the hospital, a tiny bundle swamped by her babygrow, Danny worshipped her. He showed her off to everyone. He didn't care that she had Down's; just the opposite, he seemed to love her all the more because of it.

The only time I ever saw him lose his temper was when John Harding called Alice a spastic at primary school; Danny walked straight up and punched him in the face.

"Want old Danny back," she says, echoing my own thoughts. "Not this one. Hate this one."

"You won't always, Ally. We just need more time to get used to each other again. That's all."

"No," she mutters, her face darkening. "No, not ever. And not Rudman too."

I sigh and tussle her hair. "A bowl of ice cream, I reckon, then maybe a story?"

I stand up, offering my hand. Alice looks at it for a moment, then climbs off her chair and slips hers into mine.

9

By the time Alice is asleep, most of the guests have vanished into the darkness. Just a hard core of friends and relatives remain gathered in the living room.

"Hey, Hannah, come and join us." Paul waves me in, nodding towards an empty chair. Hands me a glass of Coke I don't really want.

On the sofa Martha's sitting on one side of Danny, Millie on the other, both examining a large photo album balanced on his lap.

"See, here's one of you, Hanny!" Martha tips the album and points to the picture of a little girl standing just behind Danny, trying to hide her face.

"Goodness, how alike you two were," says Millie.

It's true. People often mistook us for brother and sister. Danny and I exchange glances, both clearly thinking the same thing – we don't look anything like each other now.

Martha turns the page and Danny points to a different picture of me with a short, wonky fringe. "Hey, titch, I remember that haircut! Didn't your mum do it?"

I nod dumbly, then lift my head and catch Paul's eye.

Get that feeling again, that he's quietly observing me, gauging my reactions.

Martha points out a blurry snapshot of a dark-haired boy in shorts. "Oh, there's…um…Danny, you remember, that kid you were friends with at primary school. What was his name?"

"Er…" Danny leans forward for a better look, peering under the rim of his cap to examine the photograph.

"Oh, you know," Martha says. "He used to have that funny way of walking, picking his feet right off the ground like a prowling cat…"

"Sure," says Danny, still staring at the picture.

"Billy," I say, "Billy Crossland."

Danny shoots me a grateful smile. "Thanks, titch. Right on the tip of my tongue."

A flush of pleasure flows through me. Danny always had that way of making you feel like the sun had come out whenever he paid you attention. Clearly he hadn't lost any of his charm.

"Remember when he threw that cricket ball and it hit the greenhouse?" Martha giggles. "And you pretended you'd done it."

Danny laughs. "How could I forget? He was so scared he offered me his PlayStation to cover up for him."

"I wasn't fooled, darling." Martha leans into him and squeezes his arm. "I knew it was him all along."

Danny touches the side of his head to hers and I see his mother glow with happiness. Millie turns over the next page, revealing a picture of the two of us, short and skinny, wading in the sea. We both look grey and shrunken with cold.

"I remember when that was taken." Martha glances up at me. "It was just after you hurt your arm."

I smile. "No thanks to Danny." I hold up my left arm, showing off the small scar near the wrist.

Martha laughs, but Millie looks puzzled. "What was that all about?"

"Ask Danny," Martha says. "He'll tell you."

Millie turns to him.

"Oh god, not that old one," Danny groans.

"Come on, Danny. I'm dying to hear it," Millie says.

Danny leans down and picks up his glass from the floor, draining the last third of his wine in one gulp. Then sits back and takes a deep breath, like someone preparing for a performance. There's a long silence as everyone waits for him to speak. I watch his face, the concentration in his eyes. And something more. A glimmer of agitation.

Across the room, I notice Paul studying his son with a frown.

I'm about to open my mouth to come to his rescue again when Danny stands and walks into the centre of the room. Sticking out his arms like he's balancing on a skateboard, he relates the tale of how he dared me to go down the steep path on the west side of the park. When he gets to the bit where I lost control and shot into Mr Campbell's garden, he mimes me teetering, then falling head first into the pond.

Everyone laughs. I'm laughing too, though to be honest I never thought it was that funny. Especially when you were the one crumpled in all that water with a gash in your arm.

"Tell us another," Millie coos as Danny goes back to his seat.

Danny shakes his head.

"Oh, go on," Martha squeezes his arm. "There was that time you and Andy Summers climbed onto the roof of the cricket pavilion. Do you remember?"

I glance back up at Paul. His eyes are still fixed on Danny as his son leans forward and drops the photo album on the coffee table and gets up abruptly.

"Show's over," Danny says, and turns and walks out the door, followed by Martha's look of astonishment.

An awkward silence fills the room. Millie leans across and places a well-manicured hand on Martha's arm. "Forget it, darling. It's nothing. Danny's tired, that's all. It's been a long day."

Martha's gaze lingers on the open doorway. As she rises to collect the empty glasses, I try and catch her eye, wanting to offer a smile of sympathy.

But the moment she sees me, she looks away, as if even the sight of me reminds her of something she'd rather forget.

10

A sharp trill from my mobile as I'm walking home from school. A voice sounding hurried, anxious. Martha.

"Have you seen Rudman?"

"No…why?"

"He's gone. I left him here in the house while I went out shopping. I got back a few minutes ago and there's no sign of him." A heavy sigh on the end of the line. "I thought maybe you'd come round and taken him out or something."

"Nope. Maybe Danny did."

The moment I say it, I know it sounds stupid, though I'm not sure why. I guess because Danny's been back nearly a month now and I don't think he's taken Rudman for a walk in all that time.

"I already asked him," Martha says over a noise in the background. Someone wailing. Alice. "Maybe I left Rudman in the garden. I don't think so, but I can't be sure."

"Even if you did, he wouldn't run off, would he?"

"Well, I suppose there's always a first time."

The wails grow louder. Alice shouting something about a man.

"For god's sake," mutters Martha. "That's all I need."

"Do you want me to go out and look? I could check the park."

"Oh, Hannah, would you, sweetheart? As you can hear, I've got enough on my plate with Alice. And Danny's gone out – I've no idea where.

"Come round for supper afterwards, Hannah," she adds, almost as an afterthought. "There's still loads of food left from the party."

I hesitate. I'd planned on talking to Dad tonight. Tackle this rift between him and Martha and Paul. Now that Danny's home, I'm hoping we can sort it out and all start afresh.

Then again, I'd also like the chance to spend some time with Danny. I never seem to catch him in these days – though I've no idea where he goes off to.

"Okay," I say to Martha. "See you later."

That conversation with Dad will have to wait.

I go out round the back of the house. We've not got much of a garden – just a small patio leading to a patch of lawn with two straight flower beds either side. When Mum was alive it was all kept neat and trim, but now the grass has romped into the borders and all you can see are a few flower heads poking through. The lawn is so overgrown I have to trample it down to reach the gate at the end.

I head off towards the playground, skirting the cricket

pitch, and pick up the path winding up to Ryall Hill. The sun is low in the sky, but it's warm enough to make me wish I'd left my jacket at home.

As I walk, I scan each side of me, alert for Rudman's little brown body. "Ruddddeeerrrrrssss," I yell, adding a long, slow whistle with a quick trill at the end. The way Danny and I always called him.

Skirting round the hill, I head for the warrens that litter the higher ground. Rudman loves chasing rabbits, more for fun than anything, always slowing up at the last moment or taking a wrong turn, letting them dart off in another direction. He doesn't really want to catch one; he wouldn't know what to do with it if he did.

I check the burrows anyway. Sometimes dogs follow rabbits so deep into a hole they have to be dug out, their owners guided by their muffled barks for help. Bending at the mouth of every tunnel, I peer inside and whistle, listening for a responding bark.

Silence.

I make my way to the top of the hill. I'm really starting to worry. Rudman's not the kind of dog to run off. He's older now, and lazier. Sometimes you take him out and he sits down, right in the middle of the pavement, refusing to walk any further. Presenting you with a choice – to carry or literally drag him home.

A pause to catch my breath. The air smells fresh up here, only faintly salty, and the view is amazing. You can see right across the town and the channel to the distant glint of factories and the hazier Welsh hills beyond. I stand for a moment, taking it all in – the tiny stick figures walking along the promenade, the tankers heading to and from the docks, the mauve-grey islands of Steep Holm and Flat Holm.

I haven't been up here for a year or more, I think with a pang. We used to come most days, Danny and I. We knew every inch of the place, the bramble thickets and copses of birch and blackthorn, the concrete monolith of the trig point that marks the top of the hill. We brought Alice up here as soon as she could walk. And Rudman too, for his first run as a puppy.

"Nice view, eh?"

His voice makes me swing round, heart leaping. Danny is sitting on the grass just behind me, leaning against the trig point. How come I didn't see him on the way up?

"You should see your face, titch," he laughs. "Like a startled animal."

I squint down at him. A half-burned cigarette hangs from his left hand. I stare at it in shock. "I didn't know you smoked."

Danny shrugs. "I guess we've still got a lot of catching up to do." He takes another puff and turns his face back towards the sun. "So, what brings you up here?"

"I'm looking for Rudman. He's disappeared."

Danny says nothing.

"Have you seen him?"

He breathes in deeply, exhales slowly, an extended sigh. "Nope."

I stare at him. Irritation rises and catches in my throat. My next words come out croaky. "Aren't you bothered? I mean, Rudman was *your* dog, Danny. You used to adore him."

Even as I say it I flashback to the pair of them, asleep on the same bed. Officially Martha banned Rudman from the upstairs rooms, but somehow he always ended up on Danny's duvet, head resting on the pillow next to his. It's a wonder Danny never got fleas.

"Not to mention that Alice is really upset," I add. "Don't you even care?"

He takes another drag on his cigarette. "I guess we just grew apart."

"Who? You and Rudman? Or you and Alice?" Or you and me? I wonder, staring at him. Was that what he meant?

Danny doesn't answer.

"Jesus, what's happened to you, Danny? Why come back if you don't give a shit about anything any more?" My voice is louder now, Danny's indifference getting to me. I'm on the brink, I realize, on the edge of venting stuff I never even knew I felt.

Danny turns, blue eyes glinting. He tosses the remains of the cigarette onto the grass in front of him and extinguishes it with the heel of his boot. He looks at me with an intense, almost piercing expression.

"Give me a break, Hannah. I've only been home a few weeks. It takes time to, you know...adjust."

The truth in this stings and my anger instantly deflates.

I take a deep breath. "I'm sorry," I say. "It's just that... that... God, I don't know..."

"That things are different now?" Danny finishes my sentence for me. "Well, of course they are. People grow up, they change. You've just got to go with it, titch – no use clinging on to the past."

I think of that photo of us in Martha's album. How alike we were. And realize there's more than one way to grow apart.

"Is that what happened?" I ask suddenly, before I can think better of it. "Is that why you avoided me all the time, you know, before you left? You just grew out of me?" My heart starts to race again, reacting to this new swell of emotion. "I mean, what the hell, Danny? Did you even consider how that made me feel...what with Mum...?"

I stop. Aware I'm about to cry.

Danny eyes me carefully. I see the corner of his mouth twitch. If he smiles, I think, I'm going to kick him.

But he doesn't. He doesn't move. Or speak. I wait for him to explain, but he stays silent.

It's not you.

That was what he'd said when I asked him this before, back before he left. *It's not you.*

So why am I still convinced it was?

Danny sucks at his teeth, presses his lips together. "You need to chill, Hannah. Seriously."

Chill?

I'm trying to read his features, but his eyes give nothing away. I can't tell if Danny is serious or only teasing. There's a mocking, almost malicious edge to his sarcasm now that was never there before. How could someone change so much? I wonder again.

What on earth happened to make him like this?

Something big, says a voice in my head. Something dark. Something bad. Something he can't stand even to remember.

Like drugs, maybe. Gangs. Danny must have survived out there somehow, and what could a boy his age have lived on, except crime? It's not like he could have got a real job or anything.

And how did he get over to France without a passport? However he managed that, it couldn't have been legal.

The more I think about it, the more it makes sense. And it explains why Danny decided to come back when he did.

Danny was running away again – only this time in the other direction.

"I've got to go," I say, feeling a sudden need to get away. "I've got to look for Rudman."

Danny doesn't even bother to reply and all the way down the hill, as I half walk, half run along the path leading back to the road, I feel his eyes watching me.

11

In the end, it happens outside the supermarket. Hardly the place to have a heart-to-heart with anyone, let alone your dad. And I'm already feeling low and edgy from seeing Alice, red-eyed and withdrawn after three days without Rudman.

But this is my first chance to speak to Dad when he's not got a head full of DNA. And with Danny back, I'm determined to get this sorted out. I've had enough drama for one lifetime.

I wait till we've loaded all the carrier bags into the boot – the usual mix of bread and pizza and frozen stuff you can stick in the oven or the microwave. Dad climbs into the driver's seat and slides his key into the ignition. Pauses and sighs, like we've just accomplished something monumental, not just the weekly shop.

"Can I ask you something?" I say quickly, before he starts the engine.

Dad looks at me. Or rather half looks at me, his eyes veering away from mine, then back again, his expression wary.

"You and Martha and Paul. What's going on?"

Dad stiffens, his shoulders going rigid. He turns back to stare out the windscreen. "What do you mean?"

A woman edges past our bumper with a trolley piled high with food in big canvas eco bags. She's manoeuvring carefully, avoiding scraping our car, though it would hardly matter if she did. It's old and grubby, the green paintwork beginning to flake off in places, worn patches appearing on the fabric of the seats.

"You know what I mean. You used to be such good friends before Mum…" I break off, feeling I don't really need to explain.

Dad doesn't speak. He's going to make me spell it out.

"And now you…I don't know," I go on, my jaw tightening. "It's like you can hardly bear to be around each other."

I watch Dad inhale slowly, his chest rising with the effort. Wait for him to say something.

He doesn't.

"Dad?"

He exhales loudly. "Hannah, I'm sorry."

"What for?"

"I don't know. Everything. I haven't been much of a father, have I?"

"I wasn't saying that," I blunder, flustered. "I wasn't saying it's your fault. I just want to know what it's all about."

"I know I haven't been there for you. Not properly. Not since…" He stops. He doesn't need to say it.

"Okay. But that's not what I'm on about, Dad."

We both stare at the woman with the trolley, now heaving the food into the boot of the adjacent car. One of those smart people carriers where the kids peer down at you as they overtake. I can see vegetables sticking out the bags, leeks and carrots, a couple of globe artichokes like huge green flower heads, and an enormous cauliflower, fat as a football. Stuff you actually have to wash and chop and cook.

"Martha and Paul have been good to me," I continue, since Dad has clearly gone mute. "Good to *us*. They were your friends, Mum's friends. It's awkward, being stuck in the middle of whatever's gone bad between you. I think we should try and sort it."

More silence. Part of my mind starts to worry about the tub of vanilla ice cream defrosting in the back. Isn't there something about not being able to refreeze it?

"Why now?" Dad asks. "Why bring this up now?"

I consider his question. "Danny," I say. "I don't know… now he's home it feels like a second chance. I mean, to get things right." I nearly say to get things back to how they used to be, though with Mum gone I know that can't happen.

Dad relapses into silence. A minute ticks by, then he lets out a long sigh. "Okay…" he begins. Pauses. "We just had something of a disagreement. That's all."

"What about?"

"Nothing really. I can hardly remember."

I feel the frustration start to build inside, hot and heavy. "You must be able to remember something." Christ, this is like talking to Danny.

Dad clears his throat. "It was a long time ago, before your mum..." His hands grip the steering wheel. "Just before it all happened. I suppose we never really got over it."

"So why don't you just talk to them? Sort it out? I mean that was nearly five years ago now. I'm sure they're—"

"Hannah," Dad turns to me. There's a look on his face I'm not sure I've ever seen before. A kind of desperation. Like someone on the edge. "Please," he says, his voice wavering. "Hannah, please can we just leave it?"

A heat behind my eyes that's almost painful.

"Sometimes friendships just run their course, that's all," adds Dad. "It's not worth trying to go back and pick up all the pieces."

I blink, thinking of Danny again. Maybe Dad's right. Maybe there is no way back and it's all best left alone.

"It's not just them, it's us." The words fall out of my mouth before I'm aware I'll say them. Before I'm even aware I mean them. "Since Mum died. It's like..." The tears start to roll down my cheeks, unstoppable now. "I don't know...sometimes it feels like we're strangers. Like people just sharing a house."

An image of Dad chasing me on Weston beach. Me running and giggling so hard I can hardly breathe, Dad catching me and swooping me up into the air, then spinning round and round, both of us laughing until we collapse onto the sand, panting and gasping.

"I don't understand what I've done wrong," I say quietly, my voice sounding ridiculously small. I suddenly feel alone, abandoned. Like I lost both parents in that river five years ago.

"Oh god, Hannah." Dad lowers his forehead against the steering wheel. He sits like that for a full minute while I try to pull myself together. Then he turns round in his seat, and puts his hand under my chin and makes me look at him. "I'm so sorry. Really I am."

He leans forward and holds me in an awkward hug. "You're the most precious thing in the world to me, Hannah. I may not always be very good at showing that, I know. And I'm sorry."

His arms linger for a few seconds, but I can tell he feels uncomfortable. I pull away. Make myself smile.

"Thanks," I say, though I'm not exactly sure what I'm thanking him for. It's not like I'm any the wiser.

Dad sits back in his seat and turns the key in the ignition. Looks at me for another second or two with the engine idling.

"It won't always be this hard, Hannah," he says, his voice soft yet serious. "I promise. Things will get easier."

I hope so, I think, as he drives us home. I really bloody hope so.

12

"Geller!"

Mr Richards bangs the end of his marker pen down hard on the desk. Most of the class jump in alarm, eyes swivelling in unison to see how Danny has strayed into the line of fire.

Danny is leaning back in his chair, legs stretched out in front of him, hands forming a headrest behind his head. He looks round from the football match he's watching out the window, and gives Mr Richards an indifferent stare. A long, lazy smile breaks across his face.

"Yes?"

"Sir!" Mr Richards snarls. "Yes, *sir.*" He pauses for emphasis. "Would it be asking too much, Geller, for you to pay a little bit of attention in my class? After all, it's you who's got to sit the exam. I'm only obliged to help you revise."

Mr Richards' lips are always a barometer of his temper; right now they're stretched as thin as a pencil line, on the very threshold of quivering.

"Not at all..." Danny looks back at him with cool unconcern. "Sir."

My stomach tightens. Mr Richards is not the kind of teacher you wind up – not unless you want to spend the rest of your life in detention. Or worse.

Danny's manner isn't lost on Mr Richards. He places the marker back on the desk and walks slowly towards him, glaring with an intensity that makes me fidget. While most of the teachers are clearly unnerved by the casual, almost cocky way Danny now treats them, they're also wary of confronting him – afraid he's still fragile, I guess, or that he might vanish again at any moment.

But Mr Richards is different. Mr Richards clearly isn't going to make any kind of allowances for Danny, even if he's only been back at school a few days.

Danny has plainly pushed him too far.

"In that case, Geller" – he leans forwards, both hands on the desk, and growls in Danny's face – "would you care to read out the sentences I've just written on the board and tell me exactly what they mean?"

"Certainly, sir."

Danny glances at the board, reeling off each sentence in what sounds like a perfect French accent, then translating them fluently into English. Not a single error, as far as I can tell. Everyone gazes at him in amazement. No one in the class can speak like that – not even Robert Chasson, whose dad actually *is* French.

I'm open-mouthed with astonishment. The thing is, I never really spent much time in class with Danny before – I was in higher sets for everything except PE. But since he sat those tests to see how much he needed to catch up, Danny has appeared in most of my revision sessions. And he's sitting most of the exams, even though he's been absent since Year Eight.

Whatever Danny missed while he was gone, it clearly wasn't schoolwork.

"Will that do, sir?"

Mr Richards stands in front of Danny, considering his next move. Then snorts, turns round and walks back to the whiteboard.

"Sir?"

Mr Richards stops.

"Second sentence down, sir. There should be an extra 'e' after the adjective, sir, because '*lapin*' is feminine, sir. And you've forgotten the grave accent in '*l'élève*'. *Sir.*"

Danny's final "sir" is so slow and deliberate that no one could miss its challenge. The whole class holds its breath.

Mr Richards walks up to the whiteboard and stands in front of it, colour rising slowly up the back of his neck, a creeping tide of red. Thirty pairs of eyes are fixed on him, waiting to see what he'll do next.

When he reaches round to pick up the marker pen, I almost flinch. Is he going to throw it at Danny? Or literally drag him out the classroom by the collar, like that time he caught Josh Crawford spitting at Liam Penfold?

An abrupt slump in his shoulders indicates Mr Richards has come to a decision. Without a word, he steps up to the board and makes the corrections.

I look back at Danny. Arms crossed in front of his chest, legs outstretched, he's gazing back out the window as if nothing has happened.

From then on, Mr Richards pretends not to notice.

13

Ten days after vanishing, Rudman reappears as suddenly as he left. When I get Martha's text and go round to Dial House, he's lying in his basket, looking like he's been in some kind of canine war zone. Alice is slumped on the floor beside him, cradling his head.

She looks up at me miserably. "Rudman hurt, Hannah. Hurt bad."

I bend down to stroke him. His coat is all matted, and there are patches where it's missing altogether. He has a deep scratch on his nose, and one on his side, near his back leg.

I tickle him gently behind the ears, riffling my fingers through the silky fur in that way he loves. He doesn't even raise his head, just lifts his tail feebly a few times and lets it flop back to the floor.

"Rudman hurt," Alice says again.

"She wants to come to the vet," Martha whispers when Alice is finally persuaded to sit and have something to eat. "But I don't think it's a good idea. I'm not sure what's wrong with him and I don't want her there if it's bad news. If the vet says it's best to…"

She doesn't have to finish. I know what she means.

"You don't mind, do you? Looking after her till I get back?"

"Of course not," I say. "How did you find him?"

"We didn't. He just came home. Paul heard a scratching in the night and there he was, sitting outside the back door."

"God, poor Rudman."

"Paul thinks he got himself trapped somewhere, that it's taken all this time to get himself free."

"But he must have had some food," I say, puzzled. "And water. He couldn't survive that long without water."

At that moment, Danny strolls into the kitchen, wearing only an open dressing gown, exposing his chest and the jeans slouched low around his hips. Alice freezes, a piece of toast halfway into her mouth.

Danny glances at us both then walks over to Rudman, crouching down and patting his head. "Poor old thing."

Rudman lowers his eyes and doesn't move. Danny looks at Alice, crooking his mouth into a smile, then turns to his mother. "Do you want some help? I can take Rudman to the vet if you like."

"Don't worry, darling," Martha says. "I can manage."

"Or I could look after Alice," he offers, getting to his feet.

Martha hesitates, her eyes darting towards Alice then back at her brother. "Thanks, but Hannah's already said she'll stay." She presses her lips together. "In case you want to go out, I mean."

"Whatever," shrugs Danny, leaving us to it.

What's that all about? I wonder as I hear him retreat back upstairs. Why did Martha asked me to mind Alice, instead of Danny? I mean, would it kill him to stick around for an hour or so?

I glance over at Alice, her eyes fixed on the space Danny just vacated. Then she turns to Rudman, an expression I can't quite read on her face. It takes a moment to register what it is.

She looks terrified.

"It's all right, sweetheart." Martha bends over to give her a hug. "He'll be okay."

Alice bites her lips together. I think she's going to say something, but she just nods. More tears roll down her cheeks.

"I'd better go," Martha says, picking up Rudman's basket. Normally he'd try to jump out, but today he lies still and lets her carry him towards the door.

"Thanks for taking care of Alice, Hanny. If I'm not back by six, could you run her a bath? Paul's working late."

"No problem," I say, as she closes the back door behind her.

Alice stares after her mother. I'm certain she's about to try and run after her, but she just sits there, looking shell-shocked.

"Come on." I stroke her hair. "Let's go and play cards."

* * *

"Can I join in?"

Alice and I both look up from our game of Snap to see Danny towering over us. He's got his cap on backwards and the bright overhead light of the living room casts shadows across the stubble edging his chin. I can't help thinking it makes him look a bit sinister.

"Sure." I shift my chair to give Danny space, hoping he hasn't noticed my surprise.

What's this all about? He's never shown the slightest interest in playing with us since his return, though Danny and I often used to play cards together – Rummy and Go Fish and Strip-Jack-Naked. Danny won nearly every game, even when it was all down to luck. I sometimes wondered if he cheated, but I never caught him out.

I hold my hand out to Alice for the rest of the pack. She glances at her brother, then scowls and hands it over. I shuffle the deck and divide it into three, conscious of Danny watching me. My skin feels hot under his gaze, exposed and prickly.

"You go first, sis," Danny smiles across at Alice.

She doesn't look at him as she lays a card on the table. I place one on top, trying to focus on the game. Only my head is buzzing with confusion and it's hard to pay attention.

Danny lays a card, and we go through several rounds without a match. Alice keeps her eyes fixed firmly on the growing pile, her little face fierce with concentration.

"Snap!" she shouts, as she smacks down a three of

spades. She pulls the cards towards her with a proud expression, trying to gather them up into a neat stack. It takes ages, Alice's natural clumsiness making her struggle to hold them all in place.

I glance at Danny. He's watching her, that smile fixed on his face, but underneath I see him fighting to hide his impatience.

"Ready!" Alice throws down a card with a grin of challenge. Round and round we go. Danny lays a six of hearts. I cover it with a four of diamonds, and Alice puts a four of clubs on top.

"Snap!" Danny slaps his hand on the pile before Alice gets a chance to even register the pair.

Alice bites her lip and stares at the table.

I raise my eyebrows at Danny as he claims the cards, hoping he'll pick up on my meaning. Give Alice a bit of leeway, I'm trying to say. Make allowances for the fact she's slower than the rest of us.

Danny kicks off the next round and we play till half the pack is on the table.

"Snap!"

Danny grabs the cards again and places them underneath the pile in his hand. I can see Alice only has a few left. I nudge his foot under the table, but he ignores me.

We carry on till Alice is down to her last card. The five of diamonds. I peek at mine and sneak out a five of hearts, laying it down slowly so she gets a good look.

"*Snap!*"

There's triumph in Danny's expression as he grabs the remaining pile. Alice glares at him and bursts into tears.

"Hate you!" she screams, spittle forming at the corners of her mouth. "Go away, go away, GO AWAY!"

"What?" Danny says, looking first at his sister then at me.

I chew my lip and shrug. What can I say?

He glares at both of us for a few more seconds, then flings down the pack. Cards scatter and skid across the table, several falling to the floor.

"Sod this!" He rises from his chair so fast it nearly topples over. He glowers at Alice before turning and slamming upstairs.

I look back at his sister. She folds her arms on the table and buries her head, shoulders heaving with sobs.

Is this why Martha asked me to babysit? I wonder, seizing on the source of my unease. Doesn't Martha trust her own son any more?

The moment the thought unfolds into words, I know it's true. And more. On its heels a question I really don't want to face.

Do I trust Danny any more?

Just asking myself this leaves my breath catchy and raw. After all, Danny is…was…my best friend. Next to Mum… and Dad…the person I was once closest to in the whole world.

I cuddle Alice until she calms down, then help her stack the cards, one by one, into a new pile. My mind flashes back to all the other games Danny and I used to play. Ludo and Monopoly and Mousetrap, and that one where you have to guess who the murderer was. Back then, Alice was way too little to join in, but she loved to sit and watch, cheering and waving her arms in the air whenever either of us won.

Yet here we are. Alice and I alone in the living room, Danny lurking up in his room. How on earth did this happen? Has Danny really changed so much?

Have we?

As Alice hands me the pack to shuffle, it hits me. No matter how difficult this is for us – for Alice, for Martha, for me, for everyone – it has to be worse for Danny. What if something terrible happened, something so bad it changed everything? Something so awful you couldn't bear even to remember it. And then, when you finally made it home, everyone expected you to be the same. To act like nothing was ever wrong.

Wouldn't anyone find it hard to fit in? To be normal? To be just like they were?

All this churns around my mind as we start another game. But this time I make sure Alice wins almost every round.

"Snap!" She slams her card on top of mine right at the moment the phone rings. "Me," Alice says, getting up and lifting the receiver with a determined look. Recently she's insisted on answering every call.

"Alice," she says brightly into the mouthpiece. Her grown-up voice.

"Who is it?" I whisper when she doesn't say anything more. I'm hoping it's no one important.

She ignores me, moving the receiver closer to her ear.

"Who is it?" I hiss more insistently.

But Alice just stands there, listening as if mesmerized. I get up and prise the phone from her hands and lift it to my ear. "Hello?"

The line goes dead.

I look at Alice. "Who was it, Ally? Do you know?"

"Nobody," she shrugs, sitting down and picking up her cards.

"Was it Mummy?"

"No."

"Daddy?"

"I says nobody." She thrusts out her bottom lip in a way that tells me to drop it.

I check for the dial tone, then punch in 1471, but an electronic voice says the number is unavailable. Maybe someone misdialled, but I can't help thinking about those prank calls. Paul tried again to have them traced, back when Martha insisted they were from Danny. But he got nowhere. And they dwindled to almost nothing soon after.

When was the last one? I think back. When Martha went away to get Danny. At least that's the last time I know of.

Could they somehow be connected?

But that didn't make sense. If they were from Danny, he would hardly have rung after being picked up in Paris. Or now. It had to be someone mucking about after all.

"Hannah, come on." Alice looks impatient.

I sit back down and lay a card on top of hers, studying Alice's face as she loses herself in the rhythm of the game. It's easy to underestimate her, I think, to assume she isn't as aware of stuff as other kids her age.

But lately, I have the feeling Alice knows far more than she's letting on.

"Snap!" she yells with a grin. "Beat you!"

I look down, and see she's taken all my cards. I smile.

This time I didn't even have to let her win.

14

At lunchtime I spot Joe, sitting alone on the bank up by the sports hall. He's not reading, nor watching the impromptu football match on the tennis courts, but hunched over, staring into the distance.

"I'll catch you later," I tell Lianna and Maisy.

"Where are you off to?" Lianna asks as I stuff my lunch box back into my bag.

"I need to talk to Joe." I nod in his direction, see Maisy start to smirk. "It's *nothing* like that." I sigh. "I just want to ask him something."

Even so, I know they're both watching me as I walk over. It makes me feel ridiculously self-conscious, and for a moment I consider giving up on the whole idea. But Joe sees me approaching and swings round, shielding the sun from his eyes with his hand.

"Hannah Radcliffe," he says with mock gallantry. "To what do I owe the pleasure?"

I smile. "Mind if I join you?"

"By all means." He shifts his rucksack aside so I can drop down onto the grass beside him. I make sure I don't even glance towards my friends.

"So, what's up?" asks Joe, obviously curious as to why I'm here. It's not like he and I have ever been friends – we only know each other through Danny.

"Nothing really," I say, trying to think how to begin. But Joe beats me to it, nodding towards a small group over by the sports hall. I squint into the sun. See Danny and Dean Simpson chatting to Alison Heppall and a couple of Year Twelve girls.

"Danny looks on good form," Joe says. "He's a regular charmer these days, isn't he?"

I nod, watching Danny slouch casually against the wall, the girls leaning in, vying for his attention.

"That was quite a performance in French, wasn't it?" Joe continues. "Old Richards certainly met his match."

I smile at the memory. I can't believe Danny had the nerve. People are still talking about it a week later.

"Danny one, Mr Richards nil," Joe says. "No need for extra time."

I keep wondering how Danny pulled it off. How he seems to take every subject in his stride since he came back – even things he was rubbish at before. Did he go to school somewhere else? Study by himself?

"I guess he's the closest thing this school has to famous," Joe sighs, his eyes locked on the little group. "At this rate he's going to end up a bloody legend."

It's true Danny's return has caused quite a stir. Though only the older kids can actually remember him, even the younger ones know what happened. And despite only being back a couple of weeks, Danny's already in with the likes of Dean and Alison – people everyone agrees are somehow cooler than the rest of us.

Looking at the three of them now, laughing and nudging each other, you'd think they'd been friends for ever.

"I wanted to ask," I say, "if he's talked to you at all?"

"You're joking, aren't you?" Joe snorts, snapping off a length of grass. "I've been sat here trying to work out what on earth I might have done."

I look at him. "How do you mean?"

"I don't know," he shrugs. "I'm just wondering why he's avoiding me. He's barely spoken to me since the party." He whistles, shaking his head slowly. "I said hello the other day and he walked right past. It's doing my head in. All that stuff we did together, and he acts like he doesn't even know me."

"I'm sure he—"

"I mean, I know it's been a long time," Joe cuts in before I can conjure up anything reassuring. "I get that. But you'd think he'd make some kind of an effort."

He bites down on the grass stalk then tosses it away, trying to control the emotion in his face. I want to say something nice, something to make Joe feel better. But I can't think of anything convincing.

"So, you don't know either?" He turns back to me.

"Know what?"

"What happened to Danny?"

I shake my head. Glance back towards Lianna and Maisy, relieved to see they've gone.

Joe frowns. "Really? I mean, the two of you were friends, like, for ever. He must have told you something. Or is he avoiding you too?"

I get a sad, sick sort of feeling. Because hearing Joe say it makes me realize it's true. Danny has been avoiding me. Every time I call round at Dial House he's either up in his room or out somewhere, and he barely even acknowledges me at school.

Maybe this would have happened anyway, I tell myself quickly. Maybe growing up always means growing apart.

"I have asked him about it," I say, thinking back to my failed attempts to talk to Danny. "But he just says he can't remember. The doctor reckons he has amnesia."

"Yeah, I heard that." Joe pauses for a moment, scratching the end of his nose with his thumb. "But that's weird, isn't it? That you can forget everything that's happened for several years. I mean, can't they hypnotize you or something? Help you remember?"

"I doubt it's that simple." Though in truth I've no idea.

"Hasn't his mum taken him to see a doctor or anything?" Joe asks.

"I think so," I say. I don't mention the psychiatrist.

"I asked my uncle about it. He's a doctor. Not a head doctor, okay, but they all have to learn that kind of stuff when they're training. He says most people get their memory back sooner or later."

A clump of giggling, whispering girls from Year Eight walk past Danny, openly staring as they pass. He acts like he hasn't noticed, but I can tell by the way he stands up a little straighter that he's basking in the attention.

"And the swimming. That's weird, don't you think?"

I look at Joe blankly.

"You didn't hear?" He frowns in surprise. "Danny refused to rejoin the swimming club. Told Mr Cozens he wasn't allowed."

"Wasn't allowed? What do you mean?"

"Medical reasons, apparently. But I reckon he just didn't fancy it." Joe stares into the distance. "I mean, how mad is that? Danny was a bloody fish – always in the water. You could never get him out."

I picture those silver trophies. All that lunchtime and after-school training, practising turns and putting in the laps. Is Joe serious?

Judging by his angry, slightly bewildered expression, he is. And I can see too how badly Joe needs to make sense of it all.

But I have no more in the way of answers than he does. Just more questions as the days roll past.

"Do you think something bad could have happened to him?" I ask Joe. "While he was away."

"What do you mean?"

"I dunno." I shrug. "Maybe he got involved in something. Something dodgy."

Joe chews another stalk of grass as he considers this. "Yeah, I've been wondering about that too. I mean, how the hell did he live? He was, what, thirteen when he disappeared? We all thought he was dead, but he was out there, having to survive."

"It would change you, don't you reckon? I mean, you wouldn't be the same."

We both watch as Danny pulls his cap down over his eyes. God knows how he gets away with it at school. I guess it's another thing the teachers have decided to ignore.

"I don't know," says Joe, getting to his feet and heaving his rucksack over his shoulder. "And I'm starting to think I don't care either. Might as well leave him to it."

He looks at me. Studies my face for a moment.

"And that's my advice to you, Ms Radcliffe," he says, with the briefest glance back in Danny's direction. "Just let the whole damn thing go."

15

Ten days later I'm standing in the lunch queue with Lianna and Vicky when Ed Billington rushes in, cheeks flushed with excitement.

"Fight!" he yells to a group of boys sitting around the neighbouring table. "Danny Geller and Ross Jacobs. Main playground."

Those with packed lunches gather them up and hurry out. Others bolt their food in huge mouthfuls before diving out the door. By the time I make it outside, a small circle has formed around the fighting boys. I push my way to the front. Danny is sitting astride Ross, his hands pinned around his throat.

"Gerroff," Ross gurgles. "You're strangling me."

Before I can even think what to do, Danny releases his neck, then picks him up by the scruff of his shirt and bangs his head against the ground. At that moment Zach Brandon launches himself at Danny, knocking him flying. Ross jumps up and delivers a sharp kick to his side. Danny makes a sort of *urgfff* noise and curls up in a ball, his face a contortion of pain.

"What the hell is going on?"

Mr Brading pushes through the crowd and pulls Danny to his feet. He's pale, bent over, gasping.

Ross looks shamefaced. "He started it, sir." He nods at Danny. "He...he called my sister a..."

He doesn't finish.

"Spare me the details for the moment," Mr Brading barks. "Both of you, inside."

He yanks Danny towards the entrance to the dining hall, but Danny pulls away, kneels down, and throws up all over the grass.

Ross Jacobs gets away with bruises and a small lump on the back of his head. Danny is taken to the sickroom, and then on to hospital when the vomiting doesn't stop. I pick Alice up from school and when Martha brings him back it's hard to say which of them looks worse. Martha's face is crumpled with exhaustion and worry, Danny's pallor a vivid contrast to the large darkening bruise on his cheekbone.

If he notices me, he doesn't show it – just pushes through the kitchen and heads upstairs. There's a distinct clunk as his bedroom door slams shut.

Martha sinks onto a chair and stares into space.

"Is he okay?" I ask.

"I think so," she nods. "I didn't actually get to speak to the doctor – Danny insisted on going in on his own.

But they did a scan and apparently there are no major injuries."

"You don't exactly look relieved," I hazard.

Martha shakes her head. "No. Yes. I mean, I'm sure he's fine. It's just..." She stops.

"Just what?"

She sighs deeply, choosing her words carefully. "I don't know how to describe it, Hannah. He's so... He won't let me anywhere near him. Won't let me help. I wanted to talk to the doctor, but he..." Tears spring to her eyes and she tries to blink them away. "He swore at me. Told me to mind my own bloody business. But I'm his mother, for god's sake. I just don't understand."

I stand there, not knowing what to say. Martha wipes her eyes and turns to me. "Hannah, do you think... I was wondering if you've noticed anything different..."

"About Danny, you mean?"

Martha nods. "I simply wanted to ask if... Oh, I don't know." She rakes her hand through her hair. "It's just that he's so..."

I think about what to say. I think about Danny banging Ross's head against the ground. I think about the look on his face when he did it, the way his lips curled back from his teeth, the terrible energy in his expression.

How can I tell Martha I'm sure her son's been mixed up in something bad? That the Danny we knew is not the Danny we're getting to know now?

"Mummy!"

Alice bounds into the room and throws herself around her mother's neck. Martha nuzzles her face into hers, hiding her tears. "Hello, darling."

Alice wriggles. "Tickles," she laughs.

Martha smiles, but Alice places her hands on her cheeks and peers right into her eyes. "You sad?"

Her mother takes a deep breath. "Of course not, silly. Come on, let's get some supper on, shall we? How about a treat? What would you like…pizza?"

Martha goes in to see the head the next afternoon; Ross Jacobs's parents have already been. There's talk of exclusion, but as no one can establish exactly who or what started it, and with exams about to begin in a week or so, Mr Givens just suspends both of them for three days.

There are plenty of rumours, of course, but Ross refuses to give any more details.

Which is odd. Ross isn't the kind of boy to get himself into a fight – not like Luke Devenish or Alex Howarth or any of that gang. Ross is one of the quiet ones.

Even more odd is that Ross used to be one of Danny's best friends.

16

"I thought you might want these."

Danny doesn't even raise his eyes from the TV as I hand him the science revision sheets.

"Thanks." He tosses them onto the coffee table without a glance. I look for any sign that he's been studying, but there are no notes, no textbooks, nothing.

"When are you coming back?" I ask.

"Where?"

"School. Your suspension's over, isn't it?"

His shoulders shrug. "Exams start next week. Mum said I may as well study at home. Make sure I'm okay."

He goes back to ignoring me. I grit my teeth. Remind myself again how hard this is for him.

I'm about to give up and leave when my eye is caught by something on the TV screen. Two little kids running round a garden in swimming costumes, someone trying to spray them with a hose.

It's not a TV programme, I realize with a jolt. The kids are Danny and me, short and lanky, cheeks covered in freckles. Now Danny's chasing me with what looks like a worm suspended between his fingers, a gleeful expression on his face. I'm running away, squealing, but laughing too.

The image shudders as someone adjusts the camera. Martha, I'm guessing. She videoed nearly everything Danny and Alice ever did. I feel my spirits lift a little. Glad, I suppose, that he's even bothering to watch them.

Maybe I've been too harsh on him, I think. Maybe Danny cares more than he likes to show.

"You going to go through all of those?" I nod at the box of old VHS tapes by the sofa.

"Mum wants to get them digitized," Danny says. "I'm checking them for her, seeing what's on each one. She never remembers to label them properly."

I stare, fascinated, as the hosepipe scene cuts to a pool with half a dozen boys racing down the lanes. The swimming gala. The one where Danny won his first cup.

"Are you going to take it up again?" I ask.

"What?"

"The swimming."

Danny swings round and actually looks at me. "Why do you want to know?"

I shrug. "Just curious."

"The answer is no, I don't think so."

On the screen, a younger version of Danny hauls himself out the pool, his smile wide and his face glowing with pride. Martha's head bobs into view as she hugs him.

"Don't you miss it? The competitions and stuff?"

"Give it a rest, won't you?" Danny growls. "You're beginning to sound just like Martha."

I frown. *Martha?* Did I hear that right?

"Anyway, I can't," he says. "It hurts my back."

"Your back? Since when?"

Danny turns to face me, his features taut with irritation. "Hannah, for god's sake, stop interrogating me, okay?"

I pull my gaze away from the screen and stare at him. See the hostility in his eyes and remember Joe's advice.

Just let the whole damn thing go.

But something inside won't let me. "You're not worried about Ross then?"

Danny's jaw stiffens as he struggles to keep his cool. "Ross was fine – there's nothing to worry about."

I let him stew for a minute or two. Voices on the TV, one of them Danny's. His old voice – or rather his younger one – higher-pitched and brighter somehow.

I keep my eyes on the Danny right in front of me, refusing to be distracted. "What was it about then, the fight with Ross?"

His eyes flash towards me and away again. He sucks his teeth before he answers. "Nothing."

"But I saw you bang his head against the ground. It can't have been *nothing*…"

"Listen," Danny says, his voice rising. "I told you, Hannah, just butt out, okay? It was simply a misunderstanding."

"A misunderstanding? But he was your *friend*, Danny,"

I persist, determined to break through to him, to force him to open up to me. "How could you…?"

"Fuck off, Hannah."

I stare at him, stunned. Did he really just say that?

Danny turns back to the TV. I inhale slowly, my breath shaky, and turn to leave. Stop when I hear a voice. A woman's voice. Oh god…

I look back at the screen and there she is. Fair hair tied back in a ponytail, a twist of green glass beads around her neck.

The beads I have in the box under my bed.

Paul standing to one side of her, Martha and Dad the other. They've all got glasses in their hands, tall drinks with coloured straws, and they're laughing at something off camera.

She looks into the lens and smiles, says something about getting a sandwich. Then a much smaller version of me runs into the picture and throws myself at her knees. Mum staggers back, laughing.

A pain flares through me, sharp and hot, and tears prick my eyes. Oh god. Mum. I haven't seen her for so long. All I have are the few pictures I rescued before Dad hid them away in the loft.

"Turn it off," I hiss, swallowing hard.

Danny doesn't move.

"TURN IT OFF!"

"Why?" Danny's hand hovers over the remote as he studies my face. For a moment I think I see the faintest hint of a smile on his.

I don't bother to answer. Just walk straight out the house and into the garden, heat and humiliation coming off me in waves.

How could he? I want to scream as I gasp in fresh air and fight back the tears? *How could he do that?*

Because Danny knows what happened to Mum. And how much it hurt. And how there isn't a day when I don't feel like my life somehow ended with hers.

There's no way he could have forgotten that. No way at all.

I ride a tidal swell of emotion, anger and grief and pain, all cresting together. And with it a sudden awareness. Danny doesn't care any more. Not about me. Not about Alice or Rudman or Ross or anyone.

That much is clear.

The question is why? I don't know, I think, wiping my eyes. Forcing myself to breathe, to calm myself down. I have absolutely no idea what happened to make Danny this way.

But I do know one thing: I am damn well going to find out.

17

"Are you really sure about this, Hannah? I can still cancel."

Dad rolls up his trousers and shirts, lining them side by side in his suitcase like enormous sausages. He swears it keeps out the creases. He's a very tidy packer considering the mess he's happy to live in.

"I said it's fine, Dad. Really."

Dad looks doubtful. I know he feels bad about leaving right before my exams, but it's not often he gets offered a lecture stint in America. And I'm glad he's got his career back on track – after Mum died, Dad barely worked for nearly six months. He was lucky the university held his job open.

"It's only four weeks," I add. "I'm just going to be revising anyway."

Dad looks at me as he lines up the sleeves on another shirt. "And you're okay staying with Martha and Paul?"

"Of course I am. Anyway, Lianna said I could go to hers if I need a break."

"I still wish you were coming with me," Dad says wistfully, pausing to stare out the window at the lilac tree blossoming in the neighbours' garden. Homesick even before he leaves.

"Me too. But I'll be fine here. Really."

The truth is, I'm quite relieved I can't go. I did once, just for a week, the year before Mum died. It was fun at first – the malls and freeways and the sheer size of everything – but once I was over the novelty, I got really bored. I didn't know anyone on campus, so all the time Dad was working I ended up watching TV – all five hundred channels of it.

Besides, I'm glad of an excuse to stay at Dial House. I can keep an eye on Danny. Try and figure out what's going on with him.

Dad sighs then nods, looking both guilty and slightly relieved. He may have doubts about going, but I know he loves meeting all those biology geeks and talking about stuff the rest of us would never understand.

He lowers the lid over the suitcase to see if it will close. It's touch and go. Dad chews his bottom lip, examining the pile of clothes still left on the bed.

I laugh. "They do have washing machines over there, you know."

Dad grimaces. "Hannah…" He hesitates, looks back out at the wilderness of our garden, the tangle of plants and grass gaining momentum in the early summer heat. I've given up worrying about it – it all dies back again in winter.

"I was thinking," he says, "when I get back, maybe you and I should have a talk."

"What about?"

Dad looks shifty, his eyes unable to settle on mine. He scrapes a hand through his tangle of hair. "You're sixteen, you're growing up. There are a few things I should explain. Things you have a right to know."

He's thought about what I asked him outside the supermarket, I conclude. He must be planning to tell me what went on with Martha and Paul.

"Why not now?" I ask, feeling the need to know right away.

Dad swings his gaze back to mine. Really looks at me for once. "Let's wait till after your exams, love. Then I thought maybe we could go away somewhere for a few days. You deserve a treat and I could do with a break."

I smile. We haven't had a holiday since we went to the Isle of Wight with Mum. That was, what…six years ago?

"Sounds great," I say, forcing down my impatience. "I can't wait."

By the time I see Dad into his taxi and make it round to Dial House, it's almost dark. Alice is frowning when I walk in.

"Jolly angry," she says solemnly. "Everyone jolly angry."

Martha is ironing. A bad sign. Martha hates ironing and only ever tackles it when she's in the worst of moods. She looks up at me and smiles as I slip off my shoes. The sort of smile you know doesn't come easily.

"I was beginning to wonder where you were. Did your dad get away all right?"

I nod. "Is everything okay?" I ask, trying to sound as casual as possible.

Martha sweeps the iron across one of Paul's shirts, catching the cuff. Straightens it up with a scowl.

"Nah," says a voice behind me. Danny. "Mum's in a funk because I missed a dental appointment. Like it matters."

Martha swings round, almost brandishing the iron in his face. "You didn't just miss one though, did you, Danny? You missed two. And I wouldn't have known about either if the receptionist hadn't rung to complain."

Danny shrugs, leaning against the door frame. "I've said I'm sorry. Anyway, what's the big deal? There's nothing wrong with my teeth."

He curls back his lips to show them. It makes him look like he's snarling.

"The point, Danny, is that you lied to me." Martha's voice is slow and deliberate. "I asked you how the check-up went and you said fine."

"I told you. I had other things to do."

"What things? What's so important that you can't keep a ten-minute dental appointment?"

Danny doesn't answer, just glares back at his mother. Neither looks like they're about to back down, and I catch Alice eyeing them warily. Then Danny swings round and walks out the room.

I glance at Martha. Her face is red. I can't tell if it's because she's angry or she's about to cry.

"Christ," she hisses under her breath so Alice can't hear. "I just don't know what's wrong with him. He's getting moodier and more difficult by the day." She swipes the iron angrily over Paul's shirt, setting in more creases than she's removing.

"Here, I'll do that," I offer.

Martha shakes her head. "Don't worry, Hannah. You should be studying." She presses her eyes closed then looks up at the ceiling. "Perhaps you could encourage Danny to do the same."

She tips the iron the wrong way and a squirt of steam shoots all over the shirtsleeve.

"Give it to me." I hold my hand out for the iron. "I don't mind. I want to help out while I'm here."

Martha hands it to me with a grateful sigh. Pours herself a glass of wine and sinks into a chair. I wonder if it's a good moment to talk to her about Danny. Ask her what she thinks happened while he was away. Tell her my suspicions that Danny landed himself in some kind of trouble.

But no. Now isn't the right time. Alice is sitting at the kitchen table, chewing on a piece of toast and Martha looks tired and agitated, her face pale and lined.

I readjust the shirt and slide the iron across the creases, watching them dissolve beneath the steam. Wishing that everything in life could be smoothed over so easily.

18

"Hannnnnnnaaaaaaah!" Alice yells when I get in from my maths exam, running into me so hard I'm nearly winded.

She seems to have grown in the week I've been here, and her face looks happier, less pinched. Rudman bounds up behind her, tail wagging furiously. He's put on weight, and the scratches are almost healed – just a few strips of shorter fur where the vet shaved his coat before putting in the stitches.

Alice is wearing her party dress and a plastic tiara. She grabs my hand and drags me upstairs into her parents' bedroom.

"Hannah!" Martha turns from trying on a pair of black sparkly shoes and gives me a warm hug. "How did it go?"

"I think I did okay," I say, letting Alice push me onto the end of the bed. "I answered most of the questions."

"Did you see Danny? Is he back?"

"He was in the exam. I'm not sure where he is now." I don't tell her that he sat a few desks away from me, barely writing after the first half an hour. Just staring out the window, looking bored.

"You should ring your dad," she says. "Tell him how you got on."

"I'll give him a call him tonight. When he's finished his lectures."

"Well?" Martha does a little twirl to show me her outfit for the Rotary dinner. She's wearing a fitted green dress that does a sort of V across her shoulders and pinches in at the waist. With her cherry-red lipstick, she looks great.

Better than great. The best I've seen her in ages.

She spins around again, ending with a curtsy and a flourish of her hand and Alice bursts into giggles. Martha pulls a face, which makes her laugh even more.

"Fantastic," I say. "Really."

"These earrings –" she holds a dangly diamanté one up to her ear – "or these?" She puts a black stud up to the other.

"I don't know… You know me…I'm not really much good at these things."

"Black," Alice says firmly.

"Black it is then." Martha drops the other pair back in her jewellery box and locks it back into her cupboard.

"Why is Alice dressed up?" I ask. She can't be going out with Martha and Paul.

Martha laughs. "You know Alice, she always has to get in on the act. If I glam up, she does too. That's why it takes me so long to get ready."

Alice scowls, then flops back onto the bed and kicks her feet into the air.

"All dressed up and nowhere to go," I say, grabbing her ankles. "Come on, Bugsy. Let's leave Mum to it. We'll go and see if we can get Rudman to chase the squirrels."

"Gotcha!"

Alice squeals when she lands on my counter, sending it home for the umpteenth time. We're playing Ludo in her bedroom, a made-up version where you pile counters to block your opponent. It means it goes on for what feels like for ever, but Alice loves every moment.

"Maybe we should just declare you the winner," I suggest hopefully.

"No way!"

"Well, I need a drink. You do my go for me."

Down in the kitchen, I pour myself a glass of water and pick up the crisp packet Alice abandoned on the floor, shoving it in the bin. As I close the lid I spot the side of a box, shoved underneath yesterday's newspaper. It's the picture that catches my eye, a woman with long glossy blonde hair.

I pull it out. Sure enough it's hair dye, a shade called Golden Summer. Inside, an empty tube, a smear of grey-green gunk still clinging to the lid.

I stare at it, bewildered. Who on earth colours their hair? I know Martha dyes hers, but dark brown – she goes off to the hairdresser every couple of months to have the roots done. So who then? Alice is way too young, and Paul doesn't have much to bother with.

It must be Danny, I conclude. But why would he dye his hair? It's already blond.

Then I think of mine, how it's darkened over the last few years, from fair to mousy-brown. Lianna's always telling me I should get highlights.

Even so, I'm surprised Danny would go to that kind of effort. He never used to care about his appearance. Martha had to nag to even get him in the shower.

Somewhere in the house, a door slams. Instinctively I stuff the box back deep into the bin and hurry back up to Alice's room.

"My go?"

Alice is picking at strands of wool on the rug, her face sullen. "No. Tired now."

"All right then," I say, trying not to sound relieved. "Bedtime."

I tuck her in and kiss her on the forehead. Down in the lounge the blare of the TV starts up. Danny.

"Stay here," Alice whispers as she turns onto her side. "Please?"

I watch the rhythmic rise and fall of Alice's breathing, the way her eyelids move as she dreams, and think about going for a walk. It's still light and I'm itching to get outside and clear my head.

But somehow I feel uneasy about going. What am I

afraid of? I ask myself. That Danny will go out again and leave Alice alone?

Surely not if he knows no one else is here.

Or am I afraid of leaving Alice *with* Danny? The thought catches somewhere in my chest. Could that really be true?

I rest my head on the edge of her bed, studying the slight frown on her forehead, like she's concentrating, even in her sleep. Downstairs the TV goes silent. I hear a voice. Danny's.

I creep out onto the landing. He's talking on the phone, fast and urgent. A few moments of quiet, then he speaks again, lower this time, almost a growl, like he's angry and trying not to shout.

The silence returns. Followed by the clunk of the back door closing behind him.

Danny's gone. God knows where. He seems to be out later and later these days, returning long after I've gone to bed, and sleeping in every opportunity he gets. But still I go downstairs to double-check he's left before I grab his school bag from the kitchen chair and go through it quickly, looking in every pocket and compartment.

Nothing. Just a few pens and a couple of textbooks. Several loose coins, though no sign of his wallet. An exam timetable, crumpled at the bottom of the bag, like a piece of scrap paper.

I go back up to his room. The door is shut tight. I hesitate before turning the handle. Should I do this? What if Danny finds out? Or Martha and Paul?

A deep breath, then I open the door.

Right at that moment there's a flash of headlights through the landing window. The sound of the car in the drive. They're back.

I shut the door quickly, feeling strangely relieved.

"How was it?" I ask, as Martha walks in, smiling a slightly tipsy smile – a sure sign she's had a good time. Paul follows right behind, loosening his tie, nodding hello before going up to check on Alice.

"Oh, the usual." Martha flops down beside me on the sofa. "Ate too much, drank too much. Talked too much. You know."

I grin. "Not really."

Martha squints at me and smiles. "You're right, Hannah. You really should get out more."

I laugh.

"I'm not kidding." She pulls off one of her high heels and rubs her foot. "What about prom night? Anyone asked you?"

I feel myself flush. "No."

"How about Danny? Why don't you go with him?"

I look at her. Shake my head.

"You always swore you'd go together."

It's true. We had always promised we'd be each other's prom partner. Not in a girlfriend-boyfriend sort of way, but because we both agreed it'd be better than being stuck with someone else.

But that was then. Now I suspect Danny would rather skip the whole thing than spend the evening with me.

Martha is studying my expression. "What's wrong, Hannah?"

"Wrong?" I echo, feigning ignorance.

"Come on, it's not like I haven't noticed. What's going on with you and Danny?"

I look away. "I don't know what you mean."

"The pair of you barely seem to speak to each other."

I try to think what to say. But my head is bleary with tiredness and I can't find the right words. "I…I don't know. He's changed…things have changed, I mean."

There's a pause as my words sink in. Martha's shoulders stiffen as she sits upright and considers how to respond.

"Yes, he has, Hannah. And yes, before you say anything else, perhaps not for the better. Not in some ways." She sighs and closes her eyes, squeezing the lids tight. Then opens them and fixes them on me.

"But who knows what happened to him while he was gone – that's what I keep thinking. I mean, whatever it was, it must have been awful. Why else can't he bear to remember any of it? And that's bound to affect you, isn't it?"

So Martha has come to much the same conclusion as me. I wonder briefly whether to voice my suspicions about what Danny's been up to, but something holds me back. I'm still not sure Martha's ready to hear anything bad about her son.

"Hannah, look, I know it's hard – for everyone. But we

have to wait. Wait until he remembers or recovers… I'm sure Danny doesn't mean any of it. I'm certain he doesn't. It's just that…that he can't help it, that's all."

I nod, but can't quite hold her gaze or respond to the appeal it contains. Martha, I sense, is trying to persuade herself as much as me. The difference is she doesn't really want to know what happened to Danny – she just wants everything to be all right.

She leans over and cups my chin with her hand. "You have to give him more time, Hanny, okay?"

I chew the inside of my cheek and think of Danny and the videos. The cool way he watched my face as he played the one with my mother, gauging my reaction. Like a scientist scrutinizing a bug under a microscope.

I look back at Martha, her almost pleading expression, and smile. A brief, false, forced smile. And decide to say nothing.

19

Something flies over my shoulder and hits the back of Adam Jamison's head. He spins round, bewildered, his gaze fixing on something beneath my desk. I peer down and see a crumpled ball of paper.

I go to pick it up but Adam widens his eyes at me. I see Mr Watson heading towards us with that slow, deliberate walk teachers use when they're invigilating. Shit, I think, my heart thumping. What if he sees it? What if he thinks it's something to do with me? I have visions of being hauled out the exam, unable to explain the piece of paper by my foot. How could I prove it wasn't mine?

I inhale silently as Mr Watson strolls past. Bend down and grab the paper, unfolding the sheet under the desk.

Instead of physics formulae, just one scribbled sentence: *HAND IT OVER OR ELSE. D.*

As Mr Watson turns back to the front of the hall, I stuff it in my pocket. Adam bends his head to his exam paper, and I do the same, trying to focus on the question about mass and acceleration. But my mind keeps playing over the note in my pocket. The look on Adam's face when he saw it. What could it mean?

When Mr Watson finally tells us to put down our pens and collects our papers, I catch Adam up in the corridor. I hand him the note and watch his face grow pale and anxious as he reads it. And something more. A wounded look he gives me before he walks off – like I've just kicked him or scribbled all over his coursework.

"Are you okay?" I ask, going after him. Adam's quiet and clever, and his parents are well off, so that's enough to make some people give him a hard time. But surely he wouldn't think that about me?

He nods mutely, not slowing down. I'm practically jogging to keep up.

"What was the note about?"

"You mean, you don't know?" His expression almost a sneer.

"Why on earth would I?"

He stops and stares at me, then his face slumps. "I don't know. I just assumed…"

"Assumed what?"

He grips the strap of his rucksack. Checks briefly around us. "Look, sorry, Hannah," he says in a low voice, "I know it's nothing to do with you. Don't worry about it. Forget you ever saw it, okay?"

And with that he walks away.

* * *

Adam's words linger all afternoon. Why would he think I had anything to do with that note? I hardly know him. We've probably only ever spoken half a dozen times, but when we have it's been perfectly friendly.

I think about that line. What was Adam supposed to hand over? And who on earth was D?

Then it hits me, so obvious that I can't believe it's taken me this long to catch on. D for Danny. Danny must have thrown it – he was only a couple of desks behind us after all. And that would explain why Adam assumed I knew – he must have thought Danny and I were in it together.

In what together? I'm desperate to find out. I consider asking Adam again, but I'm pretty sure he won't tell me anything. I could threaten to say something to the head of year maybe, but what good would that do? Adam had taken the note and somehow I knew he'd deny ever receiving it. By the look on his face when he read it, Adam was far more scared of Danny than of Mr Rotherford.

Leaving just one option: confront Danny. Make him tell me what's going on.

But as soon as the idea occurs to me, I dismiss it. Danny, I'm beginning to realize, has plenty of secrets. And is hell-bent on keeping them.

20

A scream from the living room. Followed by a loud wail of protest.

I get there before Martha, in time to see Danny shove Alice backwards, hard enough that she nearly falls.

"He hurt me," she howls, holding her wrist up to her mother, her mouth a gaping "O" of shock and indignation.

"What the hell? I barely touched you." He swings round to face Martha. "I was just looking for my phone and she attacked me. Tried to bite me!"

Sobbing, Alice slumps face down onto the sofa.

"What's going on?" Martha looks dazed, like she's just woken up.

"I asked her where my phone is and she went mental."

"Why would Alice know where your phone is?"

"She's always messing around with it," Danny says, flashing a contemptuous sneer at his sister. "Changing stuff."

"Don't!" yells Alice, her face red with fury. "DO NOT!"

"Oh, shut up," snarls Danny, "you stupid—"

"*Danny!*"

We all spin round to see Paul standing in the doorway, his voice low and furious, his face revealing a turbulence I've never seen before. "Leave your sister alone."

"I just want to know what she's done with my phone."

"I don't care about your bloody phone," Paul thunders. "I care about you talking to your sister that way."

Danny tries to push past his father as he makes for the door, but Paul grabs his arm. "I think you should apologize."

"Who to? Alice?" Danny fixes Paul with a look I can't make sense of. "Oh right. We're all about happy families now, eh, Dad? Shall we talk about that? Shall we talk about my *sister*." He spits out the last word like something that tastes bad.

Paul holds his gaze, but I see him flinch. His hand trembles as it tightens round Danny's arm. "What exactly do you mean by that?"

Danny just glares at him defiantly.

"Well?"

"You sure, Dad?" Danny's face morphs into a smirk. "In front of everyone?"

Paul stares at his son a moment longer, then releases his arm. He doesn't look angry now. More defeated and… well…*unnerved.*

Martha snaps out of her trance and sinks onto the sofa, and in that moment I understand just how bad things have become. Her expression isn't the shock and surprise I'd expect, but something like panic. I realize

Martha's been putting a far braver face on it all than I ever suspected.

No one speaks. There's silence except for the sound of Alice's sobs. Danny hovers for an instant, then pushes past his father and out the room. Seconds later, the back door slams, a full stop to the explanation Danny never gave.

I can hear Martha and Paul arguing in the kitchen as I help Alice clean her teeth. Danny has been gone nearly five hours now, missing supper. Martha is insisting they go and look for him.

"He'll come back when he's ready," I hear Paul say.

Half an hour later Martha appears upstairs, looking pale and upset. "Hannah, we're going out to find Danny," she says, trying to keep the emotion out of her voice. "We need to sort this out. Do you have any idea where he might be?"

I shake my head. "I don't really know who his friends are any more."

Martha frowns, pinching her brow between her fingers. "Well, we'll try the usual suspects. Hopefully we won't be too long." She comes over and gives Alice a kiss on the forehead, then does the same for me. I feel an ache of concern for her. I wish I could be more help.

"Good riddance," Alice says, as the sound of the car fades down the drive.

"What, Mummy?" I ask, confused.

"No, silly. Not Mummy. *Him*."

I tuck Alice into bed, and my hand touches something hard under the pillow. I pull it out without her noticing.

It's Danny's phone.

I've no idea how long I've got, but I'm guessing they won't find Danny any time soon – wherever he goes these days, it's not round to Ross's or Joe's. And Danny, I suspect, will stay away until he thinks we've all gone to bed.

I wait till Alice has drifted off, then take the phone into my room and prop myself up on the bed. I wake it out of sleep mode, praying it won't be locked with any kind of code or PIN. One swipe of my finger across the screen takes me straight into the main menu.

So far, so good.

I go into Danny's contacts. I recognize a few: Martha and Paul, Dean. Alison Heppall and a couple of other girls from school. Mr Dickson, the social worker from London.

Mine, I notice, isn't on the list.

But there are several I have no clue about. They're not full names, just nicknames or abbreviations: FranB, Jul, Mat, Del, PTB. I click on FranB and feel a twinge in my stomach when I see the number. It's long, starting with 00 33. Doesn't that mean it's abroad somewhere? I look through some of the other names, find more foreign-looking dialling codes.

Who are these people?

I swap to the call log. Lots of incoming calls from Martha.

A few from Paul. Dean and Alison have rung a number of times. Then I spot one of the unfamiliar names: Mat.

Who on earth is this Mat guy? I scroll through the log. See he's called repeatedly, sometimes several times a day. I check the number. Another 00 33 code. Where is that? I could look it up on the net.

I put the phone down on the bedside table and get up to switch on my laptop. A few seconds later a loud buzz behind me makes me jump. I spin round and see the phone vibrating against the wood, shifting slightly with each ring. I grab it and look at the screen.

"Mat" is calling right now. Shit.

The phone vibrates in my hands for another moment or two, then goes dead. A second or two later the voicemail icon blinks up. How do I access it? I try the three-digit number I use with my phone, but it doesn't work. Perhaps it's different for Danny's network, or maybe he's changed it to something else. I think you can.

There's only one thing to do. I stare at the phone, hesitating. Then press *Return Call*.

A long silence, followed by a series of short clicks. Then a strange *brrr-brrr* tone I've never heard before, slower than the usual one. I feel my heart beat faster. Am about to hang up when there's a pause.

Then a voice. A female voice.

"*Allo…*"

I can't speak. My hand is shaking so much I nearly drop the phone.

250

"*Allo…*"

Christ, what am I doing? I should cut off the call…

"*Je sais que c'est toi, chéri. Je vois ton numéro. Pourquoi tu ne me parles pas…?*"

I press the *End Call* button, my palms sweating. Then check the number I just dialled.

It's her. It's definitely "Mat". And not a boy at all.

My mind runs through the possibilities. Maybe the phone is faulty or this girl has got the wrong number. What, dozens of times? And my French is good enough to know what she just said.

Mat could see who was ringing. Danny's number. She recognized it.

I put the mobile back on the table and sit on the bed, my legs wobbly, mind racing. How does Danny know a French girl? And well enough for her to call him "*chéri*" – "darling".

I press my hands between my knees to stop them trembling. Danny has secrets all right, I think, and this is obviously one of them.

But that's not what's making my heart race and my head spin.

The thing is, I'm certain Danny didn't know anyone in France before he disappeared. He'd never been there. He couldn't go on the Year Seven trip to Paris because he had a swimming contest.

And I can't imagine he's met this girl since he came home – after all, this isn't exactly the kind of place foreign tourists bother with.

251

No, there's only one conceivable way Danny could know her – from the time he was away. He turned up in France, after all.

It only adds up to one thing: Danny is lying. He hasn't forgotten everything from the years when he was missing.

Nor has he left it all behind.

21

"Croissant?"

Martha holds the tray out to Paul, who shakes his head then disappears back behind the Saturday supplement. Danny takes one without even looking at his mother. A glimmer of something flits across her face before she erases it with a smile.

I watch Danny out the corner of my eye. He seems perfectly at ease, tipping back in his chair with a casual air, a mug of coffee balanced on his knee. With his other hand he's punching text into his phone, which I left last night on the kitchen table, along with a note saying I'd found it down the back of the sofa. Enough to get Alice off the hook.

I take another croissant and peel the crisp flaky skin from the top and place it on my tongue, savouring the buttery sweetness while I try and work out what this is all about. Did I just imagine yesterday's argument? Danny storming off and staying out half the night?

Because Martha is acting as if nothing ever happened, and Paul confines himself to the occasional wary glance at his son. Though from Alice's quiet, furious expression, and the way she won't even look in her brother's direction, I can tell it's far from dead and buried for her.

Is Danny really going to get away with it so easily? I wonder, remembering how he grabbed his sister's arm. As if in answer he looks straight at me, treating me to a wide grin.

But I'm not fooled, not any more. This kind of smile has more to do with challenge than friendship.

I stuff the last of my croissant into my mouth and wash it down with a gulp of orange juice. It lies heavy in my stomach, like silt. Nothing feels normal any more, I can't help feeling. All the rules have clearly changed.

Martha suggests a trip to the shops, but I cut out, pleading revision. Yet as I help strap Alice into her booster seat and say goodbye to Martha and Paul, I get a flutter of unease and almost change my mind.

I push it away. Take myself upstairs, grab my biology notes and flop back onto my bed. Danny's still here, I know, but I reckon there's a good chance he'll go out soon. He spends most weekend days out the house. I may as well try and study till he leaves.

But it's hopeless. I can't take anything in. My stomach feels greasy and queasy, my mind buzzing with questions. Who is Mat? And those other people listed in his phone?

I lie back and stare up at the ceiling, running through

the possibilities. What is Danny hiding? Was he involved with some kind of gang? Maybe they kidnapped and brainwashed him. That might explain how much his behaviour has changed.

Or maybe Danny just fell into it, that other kind of life. But it must be bad, mustn't it, because why else would he hide it from us? Why else would he pretend to have forgotten everything?

The more I think about it, the more anxious I feel. I can't banish the conviction that I'm missing something. Maybe everything.

I sit up, feeling an emptiness inside, like homesickness. I'll phone Dad, I decide. Tell him what I've found, my suspicions, the lot. He'll help me make sense of everything, help me unravel the truth.

Then I remember it's still early in Chicago and Dad will be asleep. I feel a surge of disappointment – somehow these days we're always out of sync.

And anyway, what could I tell him? That Danny's changed? That Danny's been keeping secrets? That Danny doesn't seem to want to know us any more? But I know exactly what Dad would say. I don't even need to hear it.

Give it time, Hannah. Just give it time.

A noise from across the landing makes my stomach flip. And I realize. This dragging feeling isn't all about missing Dad…

I'm afraid.

But what of? The answer crystallizes in my mind.

I'm afraid of being left alone with Danny.

I grab the duvet and hug it around me. Oh god. When exactly did I become frightened of my best friend?

My ex-best friend, a voice in my head reminds me, and my queasiness grows. Because it's true. Danny isn't my friend, not in any sense of the word. Not any more. Danny is someone I no longer know, no longer understand.

Worse even. Danny is someone I no longer even like.

Seconds later, I hear his footsteps on the landing. Then silence. For a moment I have the unnerving feeling he's standing right outside my door. A pressure in my chest as my heart picks up speed, the sound of my blood booming in my ears.

Has Danny found out about my phone call? With a clench of panic I remember the call log – if he checks he'll see that someone dialled Mat last night. Or she might mention it to him, ask him what was going on.

Jesus. I could kick myself for being such an idiot. Why didn't I ring from my own mobile?

Calm down, I tell myself as the footsteps retreat downstairs. If he asks, I'll just act ignorant. Pretend I hit the call button by accident or something like that. He's no reason to suspect otherwise.

I force myself to breathe evenly again, then creep to the window as I hear the back door close. See Danny sauntering down the drive, hands thrust in his pockets, cap pulled low so his face is in shadow.

Without warning he spins on his heels and tips his head

back, looking right up at my bedroom window. I duck, heart fluttering. Did he spot me?

I don't think so. I was too quick. But it's several minutes before I dare lift my head again and peer back over the window sill.

The drive is empty. Danny has disappeared.

Even so I leave it ten minutes to make sure. Then check all the rooms downstairs to reassure myself he's really gone. When I'm certain I'm alone, I head back up and turn the handle to Danny's bedroom door. It opens easily, with the usual creak of the hinge. I half expected it to be locked somehow, though there's no way to do it. None of the internal doors have locks.

I peer round, and just when I think nothing can surprise me any more, I find myself ambushed. It's immaculate. The bed is made, the duvet smoothed and pulled up neatly over the pillow. The surfaces are clean and almost completely clear, only a clock on the bedside table, his laptop and a neat stack of textbooks on his desk.

No revision notes, I notice, nor any other sign of Danny having actually done some work. Not that I'm surprised; it's obvious he couldn't care less about his exams.

I survey the room, trying to take it all in. The walls are freshly painted in the steely blue-grey, and there's a new pair of cream curtains hanging at the window. I knew Martha was giving it a revamp, but the tidiness is freaky. The whole place looks empty and hollow somehow – more like a waiting room than a bedroom.

I open the wardrobe door. Inside are orderly rows of shirts and pressed dark jeans, arranged on wooden hangers. A few jumpers, precisely folded. A couple of pairs of trainers and black school shoes lined up at the bottom, several looking like they've never been worn. In the chest of drawers, underwear in neat piles. Socks tucked together in pairs. Some sports gear that looks brand-new.

And underneath, the thing that makes me gasp – Danny's swimming trophies, stowed away in a clear plastic bag at the back of the bottom drawer.

I pick out the little cup he won in the County Under-12s, running my finger over the engraving on the front.

Daniel Geller – Gold Medal Winner, 200m Freestyle

I remember him waiting for the start signal, poised to dive, looking more nervous than I'd ever seen him. The blur of bodies slashing through the water, the cheers and shouts of encouragement from the crowd. A couple of minutes later, Danny pulling himself onto the poolside, his skin wet and gleaming, his chest heaving as the tannoy announces his win. I can still see that look on his face, the pride and relief as he turned and waved at Martha and Alice and me.

I miss him. That Danny. The Danny that actually cared. Something like grief sweeps over me, and with it a desperate need to know where he went. And whether there's any hope of ever getting him back.

Placing the trophy with the others, I shut the drawer and go over to the laptop. Lift the screen and press the start button, wait a tense minute or two for it to boot.

A password box appears. Damn.

I glance out the window, checking for any sign of Danny. The drive is empty, but I know I can't afford to hang about. I type in *Rudman*. Nope. Think for a moment, then replace it with Alice's name and birth year.

No luck.

I rack my brains. What would Danny use as a password? I realize I have no idea. I haven't got a clue how his mind works any more. And I haven't the time to carry on guessing, so I power down the computer and scan the room, making sure I've covered my tracks. I'm just about to let myself out when I see a glint of something shiny, behind the radiator.

I walk over and peer down. Wedged between the radiator and the wall, the edge exposed, is a thin metal tin. I bend down and prise it out with my fingers. It's an ordinary tin, decorated with fir trees and a snow scene – the kind you get at Christmas full of biscuits or chocolates. But I've never seen this one before.

I lift up the lid. Inside is a small bottle of clear liquid – contact lens solution, half used. At least that's what the label says. I pull off the cap and give it a sniff. It doesn't smell of alcohol at least. I stare at it, puzzled. Does Danny wear contacts? I don't remember Martha saying anything about his eyesight. It's always been good, though I suppose that's another thing that can change.

Next to it is a little black notebook. I pick it up and flick through. Page after page of tiny writing, almost impossible to read. It seems to be in some kind of code, with no space between the letters. *dditsam.estdisp.ilya6a...metpsemar. ilya25a.* Occasionally a string of figures that could be phone numbers.

I give up. I can't make sense of any of it. I check the rest of the box. Just an envelope and a couple of photographs. The first shows a young girl with brown-blonde hair. *Souviens-toi de moi toujours, Mathilde*, on the back in that loopy handwriting French people have. *Remember me always.*

Mathilde, I take in with a start. *Mat.*

In the other picture, a couple with a little boy stand in front of a house. You can tell it was taken a while ago – their clothes, the car parked on the street behind them, all look dated. The 1980s, I reckon. Maybe a bit later. The photo is creased, a white line running like a scar across the face of the little boy, though you can still see he's staring at the camera with a sullen expression.

I lift out the envelope. It's not sealed so I peek inside. My heart almost stops. It's full of twenty-pound notes. I flick through them quickly. Over five hundred pounds, I reckon. I feel my chest tighten. Where on earth did Danny get so much money?

A noise downstairs. A sound like something dropping. I pause, heart beating wildly. It was probably Rudman, but I'm not taking any chances. I stuff everything back, then hesitate. Remove the notebook and shove it into the pocket of my jeans before replacing the tin behind the radiator and tiptoeing out the door. I close it behind me, as quietly as I can.

I'll put it back soon, I tell myself. Before he notices it's missing.

My hands are sweating and my heart beating so hard now I feel dizzy, though I can't say why I'm so scared. What, after all, would Danny actually do if he caught me snooping in his room?

All I know, as I slip back into mine, is that I really don't want to find out.

22

"Don't you think you should be in bed, Hanny?" Martha asks as I flop onto a kitchen chair.

"I'm okay," I say. "It's just a cold."

She lifts a hand to my forehead, testing my temperature. "Maybe you should take the day off. Have you got much on today?"

I shake my head. "Just an English revision class. It's my last exam tomorrow."

"I'll call the school in a minute. Tell them you're staying home."

I smile, grateful. I could do with some time off. I feel exhausted, limp as a damp towel. I've spent the last few days mulling over what I discovered on Danny's phone, and what it means. Coming to the only conclusion I can think of – I have to talk to Martha about what is going on with Danny. I've been putting it off for too long.

I watch her lift the cutlery tray out the dishwasher and carry it to the drawer, sorting the knives and forks and spoons into the right compartments. There's something soothing about it. So ordinary. It makes me feel I must be imagining things, that there can't really be anything so terribly wrong.

But there is. And I have to tell her about it. Now, while everyone is out.

"Um…" I begin.

Martha looks at me, a stack of plates in her arms. "What is it, sweetheart?"

I clear my throat. Force myself to speak. "Actually… I wanted to talk about Danny."

A shadow crosses Martha's face, extinguishing her smile. She stiffens slightly and sets down the plates.

"What about him?"

"I think maybe he's in some kind of trouble."

"Trouble? What sort of trouble?"

"I don't know," I shrug. "I just think he is, that's all."

"Well, Hannah, you're going to have to be a bit more specific."

I pause for a moment. How can I tell her that Danny has been lying to us all? I think of his notebook, which I managed to sneak back the day before yesterday. I couldn't make any sense of that code, but it's clear Danny's hiding something. I remember too the fight at school, the note he threw at Adam. And the money, still in the tin when I returned the notebook.

I take a deep breath. "I think maybe he got mixed up in something while he was missing. Maybe still is."

Martha stares at me.

"And I think he *can* remember what happened to him."

There's a long silence. Finally Martha pulls out a chair and sits down. "Okay, Hannah. And what makes you say all this?"

I can't tell her about snooping around on his phone. Or what I saw in that tin. I meant to, but in an instant I see how it'll look, that I did that, poking through his things. How furious Martha will be.

Oh god. I press my nails into the palms of my hands. I've dug myself into a hole.

"When I found his phone, it rang. I answered it." Not quite the truth, but close. Close enough to make Martha fix me with a look that drills right through me.

"Who was it?"

"I don't know, but she was French. At least she spoke French."

"It must have been a wrong number."

"I don't think so. Her name came up on his phone."

Martha doesn't say anything for a moment. "Couldn't it be someone from school?"

I shake my head. "I don't know anyone who's fluent in French."

She shrugs. "Well, anyway, it's Danny's business. What does it matter if he's got friends?"

"It doesn't," I say. "But the point is, she must be someone he met while he was missing. You know, while he was in France. And if they're still in touch, surely that means he can remember at least some of what happened?"

This time Martha has no answer at all.

"And if you think about it, if he *can* remember her, how come he hasn't told us who she is and how he knows her?"

More silence.

"Don't you see? It means he's lying about losing his memory."

Martha stands up so abruptly the chair nearly tips backwards. "That's enough, Hannah. I've heard quite enough!"

I stare at her. She returns my look with a hard expression.

"But don't you see?" I exclaim, my voice fast now and urgent. "Danny must be in some kind of trouble. Why else would he hide it from us? He must have done something bad and he can't tell us…"

"Stop it, Hannah!"

I shut up. I've never heard Martha so angry. I feel tears prick my eyes, a lump form in my throat.

She leans across the table, bringing her face closer to mine. Her voice trembles as she speaks.

"You know I'm happy to have you here, Hannah. As far as I'm concerned this house is your home, for as long as you need it—"

"I know," I stammer. "But—"

Martha holds up her hand. It's shaking slightly. "I've always made an effort to treat you…like our own daughter…" She pauses, inhales, like she's trying to calm herself down.

Made an effort? What the hell does she mean by that?

"I've done my best for you despite—" Martha stops

herself. Closes her eyes for a few seconds. "But I want you to remember that Danny is my son, and I really don't appreciate you calling him a liar…"

"I'm not…" I gasp. "I didn't mean… I was only trying to help."

I should tell her, I think, tell her about the stuff in his room. Take her upstairs and show her what Danny is hiding. Make her see that he has some kind of secret he doesn't want anyone to discover.

"Help?" The ice in Martha's tone makes me shudder. "How is this helping, Hannah? Danny is having a difficult time adjusting, and maybe his coming back has put your nose out of joint—"

"That's crazy!" I jump to my feet. "How could you say that? You know I wanted Danny back more than anything. I did everything I possibly could—"

"Really, Hannah?" Martha cuts in. "I'm not so sure. Frankly, you've been positively stand-offish towards Danny since he got back. You've barely said a word to him."

"That's not true… It isn't like that…"

I close my mouth. I don't know what to say…how to explain. I just want to get to the bottom of things. To get all this stuff straight so we can move on. A tear wells over my eyelid and wets my cheek. I wipe it away on the sleeve of my dressing gown, choking back the sob that threatens to follow.

This is all going wrong. Horribly wrong.

"All I'm saying is that you could make more of an effort,

Hannah. I know it's not easy. It's not easy for any of us. But you could at least make an effort."

"I *have*," I protest, something beginning to slip inside me. "I've tried. Lots of times. But Danny doesn't want to talk to me. He hates me!"

The moment I say it, I know it's true. The one thing I haven't wanted to admit to myself. Danny hates me. I see it in his eyes every time he looks at me. I feel it like a chill in the air whenever he walks into the room.

He hates me. He really does.

Martha glares at me, her expression a cross between disbelief and fury. And all at once the words spill out before I can stop them.

"It's not just me either. He hates all of us, even Alice. You can't pretend you haven't noticed."

The slap leaves both of us reeling. In the moment of shock that follows, I wonder if I imagined it. But then the sting rises like heat in my cheek and I know it really happened.

Martha just hit me.

For a moment I see something close to panic in her eyes and realize she is as astonished as I am. I stumble from the kitchen and run straight out the front door, too stunned even to cry.

23

I wake at seven the next morning, feeling shaky and weak. For a moment I'm lost, confused.

Where am I?

I look down and see I'm still dressed in the jeans and sweatshirt I was wearing when I ran out of Dial House. Memory rushes in to fill the vacuum in my head.

I'm back home.

I peer outside the window. The new day is dark and heavy, more like winter than summer. Clouds fill the sky, dark and ominous, obscuring all trace of the sun.

In the bathroom mirror I see my nose is red from my cold, the skin already peeling at the edges, and my eyelids swollen and puffy from crying. I swallow, wincing – my throat still rough and raw. The thought of school, of anything, makes me want to crawl back into bed and pull up the duvet to block out the light and everything that goes with it.

But I've got my last exam this morning.

So I dig out the uniform I'd thrown into the back of the wardrobe before Dad went to Chicago; the only one I've not left back at Dial House. It needs washing, but it'll have to do. I find a couple of aspirin in the bathroom cabinet and head into the kitchen. The bread rolls I unearthed in the freezer last night have gone stale, but there's nothing else, so I toast them and drench them in butter and force myself to eat, ignoring the pain when I swallow.

The walk to school seems twice as long as usual. I'm dreading seeing Danny, wondering what Martha will have told him. Not that he'll be interested – just pleased I'm gone.

But there's no sign of him in the English exam. My relief eventually gives way to curiosity. I catch up with Sophie Fox as we file out the hall, ask if she's seen him.

She seems astonished. "Haven't you heard?"

"Heard what?"

"Danny. He's been excluded."

I stare at her, dumbfounded. "Excluded? When?"

"Yesterday. Right before lunch. The head called his mother and she came to collect him." She looks at me quizzically. "But you know all this, don't you? Aren't you staying there at the moment?"

I don't reply. Just muster up a poor excuse for a smile. "Does anyone know why?"

"Well, it's only a rumour, but Aaron Boyd says he's been caught bullying some of the Year Sevens. One of them told his parents. Said Danny had been taking money off them, that sort of thing."

I swallow, thinking of the twenty-pound notes in the envelope. "Is he sure? Aaron, I mean."

Sophie nods. "It's unbelievable, isn't it? I don't think Givens believed it either – not until he pulled in some of the others and they backed up the story."

She leans in confidentially. "Apparently his mum went crazy. Accused the boys of making it up. Ryan Billinger said he could hear her shouting at old Givens right from the other end of the corridor."

My stomach contracts. Martha. The head must have contacted her after I fled yesterday morning. That explains why I haven't been bombarded with frantic calls from Dad – Martha hasn't got round to telling him I've gone. She clearly has other things on her mind.

I almost laugh. I'd spent the whole day at home dreading the ring of the phone. It wasn't that I didn't want to talk to Dad; more that I knew he'd insist on me telling him what had happened. He'd get the first plane home and it would all come out, all the things that could no longer be left unsaid. About him and Paul and Martha. Whatever it was Dad didn't want to tell me till after my exams.

And right now that's more than I can deal with.

I stand in front of Dial House, hesitating. Should I ring the front doorbell or let myself in as usual? I opt for the latter. It'd be just too freaky turning up on the doorstep, like a visitor or the postman or something.

I walk round the back, stomach in my shoes, part of me hoping I'll find Martha out in spite of her car parked in the drive. But the other part, the better part, wants to make sure she's okay – to make sure *we're* okay. I want a chance to explain, to sort this out.

And I want to give her a chance to apologize.

But as I raise my hand to knock on the back door, I catch sight of someone lying in the hammock beneath the apple trees. Blond hair, bare legs.

Danny.

My hand drops back to my side. I watch him for a moment or two, wary of movement, but he doesn't seem to be aware I'm here. After a few minutes, I realize Danny's asleep.

Suddenly I have the creepiest feeling that something is wrong.

At first I can't put my finger on it. I glance through the kitchen window, looking for Martha, but there's no one there. I move a little closer to the hammock, treading carefully to avoid waking him. He doesn't stir, even when my foot crunches a twig.

It's turned into a warm afternoon, the whole garden shimmering in the early summer heat. Danny is wearing a pair of shorts and a T-shirt. As I edge closer, I see the sleeve of his left arm has worked its way up, revealing the smooth skin of his shoulder, pale and unmarked, except for a light trace of freckles.

Shock stops the breath in my lungs. I freeze, staring,

hardly able to believe what I'm looking at.

Then turn and run from the garden.

Back home, I dump my bag on the kitchen table and head straight upstairs. I pull the loft ladder out of the airing cupboard, grab the torch from under Dad's bed and climb up into the roof space, swinging the beam around until I spot it – the box with all the old photo albums.

It's heavier than I expect, and nearly falls on top of me as I reverse back down the ladder. I wipe the dust off the first album and lay it on my bedroom floor, turning and scanning each page.

Where is it? Where? I'm sure it's here somewhere, though I haven't seen any of these photos since Mum died.

I flip right through, checking each picture carefully. Nothing.

I pull out the next album, trying not to get distracted. But I'm not fast enough. Images of Mum scorch my retina like flares. Standing in a lilac dress, one hand shielding the sun from her eyes; posing on the seafront, linked arm in arm with Martha and Paul, her skirt billowing in the breeze; pushing a pram with a skinny toddler in shorts…me.

So many photos, most taken by Dad. As if he was forever sneaking up on her, trying to capture her with the snap of a lens. You can tell how much he loved her just looking at these pictures.

A wave of grief hits me so hard it's like being winded.

Suddenly I miss her so much I want to lie down on the floor and cry. Scream and howl until I'm washed out and all this pain has flowed out of me.

More than anything in the whole world, I wish that Mum were here to help me now.

I wipe my cheeks. Gritting my teeth, I force myself on, reaching into the box and pulling out the last album. My desperation builds. Where the hell is it? I'm sure I haven't just imagined it.

It has to be here somewhere.

And then I find what I'm looking for. Right towards the back, near the last page. The four of us – Martha, Mum, Danny and I – sitting on the beach, eating ice cream. Martha and Mum are facing forwards, laughing at the person taking the photograph – Dad, probably, maybe Paul. In the lower right-hand corner, Danny and I sit at their feet. Me in a red swimming costume, looking cold; Danny in a pair of blue trunks. We're gazing out over the sea, distracted by something we've seen, and the camera has caught us sideways on.

I lift the album up to look closer, trying to keep my hands from trembling. There it is. No mistaking it. Exactly as I remember.

A birthmark.

Small and distinct. Dark, almost black, like a tiny tattoo on Danny's left shoulder. The birthmark Danny was born with – the type that never fades.

The birthmark that's no longer there.

24

I check my watch again. Half past six. I've been here just over half an hour, but it feels like for ever. My legs ache from crouching behind the bushes, and my throat still burns whenever I swallow. Even my brain hurts from an afternoon of thinking everything through.

Could there be some other explanation for Danny's missing birthmark? Would the photo in my pocket be enough to convince Martha?

My cheek feels hot as I remember the slap. No. This time I have to be sure.

I glance through the thick shrubs that border the driveway. I have a clear view of the front of Dial House, including the upstairs windows. We often used to hide here when we were kids, Danny and I, so I know I'm safe – no one can see me from inside.

But I can see him. Danny's blond head passing in front of his bedroom window. Just ten minwutes ago.

Right on cue, Martha emerges from the house and gets into her car. I retreat deeper into the bushes as she drives past, Alice strapped in the back, clutching her giant blow-up duck. Martha always takes her swimming on Wednesday evenings, when the pool is quiet and they have the shallow area pretty much to themselves – with any luck, they'll be gone for a couple of hours. And with Paul at a conference in London, I know he won't be home till late.

Even so, I give it another ten minutes, just in case Martha comes back for something. I shift my weight from side to side, trying to relieve the cramp in my legs. The ground smells damp and peaty, and my skin feels clammy and moist. I look up at the sky. The weather is changing again, grey clouds massing overhead. I pray the rain will hold off till I can get inside.

I recheck the time. Now should be okay. Pulling out my phone, I punch in a text. Short and sweet.

We need to talk. Urgent. Meet you at the bandstand at 7? Hannah.

Nothing to do now but wait for Danny to get the message, and hope that curiosity will drive him out to meet me.

Somewhere down in the town I hear the screech of a siren, fading into the distance. Before I have a chance to wonder whose day just got worse than mine, a sudden movement near my feet makes me yelp in fear and surprise. I look down. A grass snake slithers away, its long dark body vanishing into the shrubs further up the drive. It takes a couple of minutes for my heart rate to subside enough to pull my focus back on the house, and it's then I see Danny appear, the hood of his jacket pulled over his head and baseball cap, his mobile phone clasped in his hand.

He walks towards me, purposeful but not hurrying. I hold my breath as he approaches, half expecting him to sense I'm here, to swing his head and fix his gaze on the bushes where I'm hiding.

A rush of relief as he passes without a glance in my direction.

My eyes follow him down the road until he drops out of sight. How much time have I got? Ten minutes for him to get to the bandstand, maybe ten more hanging around waiting before he realizes I'm a no-show. Ten minutes to get back. About half an hour in total.

Long enough. Just.

I run round to the back of the house, legs stiff and numb, trying not to think about how tired I am. Bend down and slip my hand under the bird bath. Nothing. I feel around again, then heave it onto one side and peer underneath, eyes alert for the silver glint of the spare key.

It isn't there.

I look around me, mind blank with alarm. What on earth do I do now? I feel a surge of frustration. Why didn't I think to take my own key when I bolted from the house yesterday? I try the back door handle, but it doesn't budge. My heart rate ups a notch. I have to get inside – and fast.

I check the bottom windows round the back of the house, but they're all shut. Skirt round to the front, but it's the same, everything closed tight. My heart thumps harder;

I'm beginning to panic, sure I'm never going to get a second chance.

It's only when I circle the house another time, neck craning upwards, that I see it – Martha and Paul's bathroom window, slightly ajar.

I size up the wooden fence dissecting the back garden from the front – if I can climb onto it, I might be able to reach the window sill. I grab the empty plastic bucket Martha uses for weeding and turn it upside down. It seems sturdy enough, but buckles the moment I put my full weight on it; I just manage to lever my leg over the fence before it cracks and tips over.

Pulling myself into a sitting position, I slowly get to my feet, one hand on the wall to steady myself. Stupidly, I look down. I'm only about six feet up, but it's enough to make me dizzy and I nearly lose my balance. I grab the wall in panic. Narrowly avoid falling.

C'mon, Hannah, you can do this.

I close my eyes and take a deep breath, willing myself steady as I edge towards the bathroom window. I reach up and slip my fingers between the window and the frame, can just feel the metal bar holding the window open. I nudge it upwards with my fingertips, but it doesn't budge.

I try again. Nearly topple over and have to grab the sill to steady myself. Above me the clouds finally burst, sending down a sudden violent shower of rain.

Hell. I swallow, blink the water from my eyes, refusing to think about what will happen if I slip and fall. Gripping the sill with one hand, I raise myself onto the tips of my toes and, fingers aching with the effort, give a last desperate push.

The window flies open, nearly knocking me to the ground. I cling on to the edge of the wall, steadying myself, gulping air to stop myself crying out in fright.

You can do this.

Carefully, placing both hands on the wet window sill, I heave my body upwards, feet scrabbling against the wall. My arm muscles scream with the effort, and for a moment I think I'm going to collapse and fall, but I manage to get myself halfway through the window. Resting on my stomach for a few seconds, I dig my toes hard into the brickwork and pitch myself inside.

There's a crash as one of the bottles on the window ledge hits the floor, smashing on the tiles. Damn. I pick up the shards of glass and throw them in the bin, mopping up the liquid with a flannel and shoving it into the laundry basket. Then rearrange the jars and tubs of cream – with any luck Martha won't notice.

The door to Danny's room is ajar. The tin is still there, behind the radiator. I pull it out and lift the lid.

The notebook has gone. Along with the envelope of money.

Oh god. I have to get that notebook back. I'm sure if I can crack the code everything I need to know is inside. Certainly enough to convince Martha. Perhaps Danny's hidden it somewhere else. I run my hand under his pillow and the duvet. Lift the mattress. Look in the wardrobe, in the folds of the clothes in the drawers. Peel back the rug on the floor.

No sign anywhere.

I check my watch. Quarter past seven. I have to think. And fast.

Backing towards the door, looking upwards, I scan the very top of the wardrobe and the bookshelf. It's then I spot what I missed before. A glimpse of white peeking over the rim of the bookshelf. Balancing on the edge of the bed, reaching up on tiptoes, I manage to grip the corner between the tips of my middle fingers and yank it towards me.

A thump as several sheets of paper and something harder hit the floor.

My heart almost stops when I see what's lying there. A notebook – but not Danny's. I stare at it, hardly believing what I'm seeing. My diary. I pick it up and flip through the pages. Yep, my handwriting on every page.

What on earth is it doing here?

A shiver ripples through me as the truth sinks in. Danny. He's been in my house, in my room. I can't remember the last time I wrote anything in that diary, so I've no idea when he might have taken it.

I feel sick, shocked, outraged. And yet…here I am, doing the same.

But there's a difference, I tell myself, trembling. I don't want to be here, but I don't have a choice.

But Danny? What does he need to find out about me?

I grab my diary and shove it into the waistband of my jeans, then pick up the pieces of paper. They're letters, the first dated six weeks ago, from a Dr John Stanner at the Department of Psychiatry at Somertree Hospital. The shrink Danny saw.

Dear Mrs Geller,

I am writing again regarding your son Daniel Geller, who has attended several outpatient appointments with me. He has now missed three sessions in a row, and I have no choice but to terminate treatment.

I know that this will not come as welcome news, given your anxiety regarding his "missing years" and the possible trauma that may have resulted. I have indeed tried very hard to encourage Danny to speak freely about this time, but frankly with no success. I can neither confirm nor refute the diagnosis of amnesia, though I have to say that retrograde amnesia lasting this length of time is rare without accompanying severe head trauma.

But in my opinion, given my brief acquaintance with Danny, this is not a case of amnesia. It is not possible for me to formally diagnose what he might be suffering from, since he has avoided cooperating with me at every juncture. Danny, as far as I can tell, has treated his time with me as some kind of game – one whose object is to outwit my every attempt to help him.

While I hesitate to offer advice to a family member outside the remit of therapy, I would urge you to

encourage Daniel to seek further help, as he strikes me as
quite a disturbed, if not dangerous, young man.

I scan the next letter, short and to the point. It's from
Mr Givens, the head, asking Martha to come in urgently to
discuss Danny's behaviour.

The last has another official letterhead, the local hospital
in town. I glance at the name at the bottom – Dr Julian
Gray, a consultant in the Accident and Emergency
department.

Dear Mrs Geller,
I am writing to you with reference to your appointment
on 12th May for your son Daniel. As you are aware, we
did an abdominal ultrasound after the incident at his
school, to check for any injuries related to his persistent
vomiting. While we were happy to report that there
seemed to be no problems, we have since checked his
patient records and found an anomaly.

According to our records, Daniel Geller attended this
hospital ten years ago, age six, after referral from his GP
for acute appendicitis. As a result we removed his
appendix via laparoscopy and he made a full recovery.
However, this more recent scan appears to reveal an
intact appendix. Moreover, the radiographer has made
no note of incision marks on the abdomen.

As a consequence we can only conclude that there has
been some kind of mix-up with Daniel's hospital records,

though we can find no trace of any other Daniel Geller ever having attended here. I would be very grateful if you would contact me forthwith, as we would like to clear up this matter as soon as possible.

Have I understood right?

I think so.

I read through the letters again, fighting to keep the words in focus, letting the meaning sink in. Then fold and stuff them into the back pocket of my jeans. I've found what I need.

Proof.

25

I wander, dazed, down towards the seafront. Sit on one of the benches overlooking the slipway. With the evening so grim, there's hardly anyone around. Just a few people walking dogs, wrapped up in raincoats and cagoules.

I take the letters out my back pocket and read them again. Make sure I haven't made a mistake.

Should I go to the police? I wonder. I could ask for Janet Reynolds, tell her everything. She'll have to take it seriously.

Yet how can I let the police turn up on Martha's doorstep without warning? I must talk to her first. But the thought of another confrontation makes me feel sick and dizzy.

It's different now, I remind myself, my hand clutching the letters. Now I have proof even Martha can't ignore.

I take a lungful of salt air. Release it slowly. I'll wait for Paul to get home from his conference, I decide. I'll tell him and Martha together, and Paul will know what to do. And if Martha freaks out, tries to blame me, I feel sure he'll intervene.

I glance at my watch. He probably won't be back till nine or ten. That's a couple of hours away.

I close my eyes for a moment. Listen to the sounds around me. The *ark-ark* of gulls, the distant bark of a dog. The faint lap of waves on a rising tide.

But what about Danny? I think, with a lurch of anxiety that has my pulse racing again. Danny will have guessed something was going on when I didn't turn up at the bandstand. Maybe he's already checked his room, discovered what's missing.

He'll be waiting for me at Dial House. *He'll be prepared.*

What can he do though? I have the letters, the letters he stole before Martha could read them. How can he explain those away?

He can't, I reassure myself. But the sudden creepy feeling that he might still be down here, waiting for me, propels me off the bench and up towards the pier. As I approach, I get a sudden, prickly sensation on the back of my neck. Tiny shivers running across my skin, like ripples on a lake.

As if someone's watching me.

I spin round, checking behind. No one, apart from an old man walking along the promenade, a paper sandwiched in the crook of his arm. He doesn't even look in my direction as he passes.

Stop being paranoid, I tell myself, ignoring the thump of my heart. I have to calm down. Walk. Breathe. *Think.*

Where can I go? I can't go to Dial House, and I daren't go home, in case Danny is waiting for me there. I could turn up at Lianna's or Maisy's, but they'd soon sense something was wrong, and I can't talk to them before I've even spoken to Martha and Paul.

Besides, I need to keep moving, fast, to distract myself from my nerves. So I take the footpath that weaves round the coast to Ladd's Point. It should be quiet out there. No chance of bumping into Danny.

It starts to drizzle again, the sky growing darker. By the time I reach the steep flight of steps leading down to the beach, there's a sharp stitch in my side and my lungs feel hot and raspy. I slow down as I cross the pebbles to the edge of the cove, then begin to clamber up over the boulders, trying not to crush the winkles and limpets clinging to every surface. I pick my way carefully – lose your footing around here, and there's nothing but seaweed to break your fall.

I don't stop until I reach the ledge, the vast expanse of flat rock that extends right round the headland. There's no one here at all, not even anyone fishing. That's why Danny and I loved this place – you're hidden from the coast path on the cliff, and people rarely bother with the arduous climb to get here. There's nothing to disturb you except the screech of gulls and the slap of the sea against the rocks below.

The end of nowhere, Danny used to call it.

A quick glance behind me. The only way back is the way I came, and I don't want to get cut off. The tide's coming in, but the water has only reached the first line of rocks surrounding the little beach below. I should be fine for an hour or so.

I make my way further along the headland, hopping from rock to rock, avoiding the pools stranded by the receding tide, eventually reaching the little gully that forms a natural shelter from the wind. It was here we once saw dolphins swimming in the channel. And here that Danny caught the biggest fish he ever landed.

I shiver at the memory. How Danny has once again slipped out of my present and into my past.

Climbing down into the gully, I sit on a flat piece of rock splashed with yellow lichen, bright as spilled paint. Just at that moment the sun breaks through the clouds, brightening the grey-brown water of the Bristol Channel to an almost-blue, illuminating the Welsh hills in the distance. I inhale deeply, trying to clear my head. My mind feels dull and cloggy, still heavy with my cold. My clothes are damp and I'm a little dizzy; I remember I haven't eaten anything since breakfast.

I close my eyes, hug my legs and rest my forehead on my knees, listening to the rhythmic suck and swish of the waves. I'm exhausted, drowsy almost, yet a buzz of anxiety courses through me like electricity. I want to go to sleep and wake up when all this is over.

"Hello, titch."

My head whips up. I blink at the figure standing in front of me, blocking the evening sun. With the light behind him, I can't quite make out his features, but the voice is unmistakable. I scramble to my feet.

Danny.

But not Danny, I remind myself, my legs feeling shaky. Not Danny at all.

I squint to get him in better focus. His mouth is curled in something like amusement, but his eyes have all the concentration of a hunter eyeing its quarry.

"How did you know I was here?" I ask, forcing down the stammer in my voice. How come I didn't hear him approach? He must have crept across the rocks like a panther.

The figure in front of me doesn't say anything. Simply looks at me, the expression on his lips morphing into something tighter, more considered. The hairs on the back of my neck prickle again. I feel exposed. Vulnerable. And it's later than I thought; I must have drifted off after all. I glance around, hoping there might be someone about.

But we're alone.

"How long have you been there?" I ask. "Watching me?"

"A while." He smiles. "But I think I should be asking *you* the questions, Hannah." His voice is slow and deliberate. "Like exactly what you think you're up to?"

He's been spying on me, I realize. He must have cut back up from the bandstand the moment he knew I'd set him up, and followed me here. My heart picks up speed, my mind keeping pace, alert, racing. Should I act innocent? Pretend I've no idea what he's talking about?

One look tells me I'd be wasting my time. Whoever this is, I know he's not stupid. So I don't say anything. Just stare back at him, trying to hide my growing unease.

"Nice spot," he says. "Quiet."

"We used to come here a lot, Danny and I." I pause, gathering strength for my next words. "But I guess you don't remember that, do you?"

No reply. Instead he takes a step forward, watching me intently. I stand my ground, willing myself not to blink or look away.

"So, tell me," I ask. "What's your real name?"

I can see his features clearly now, see him wondering whether to try and bluff his way out of this, to carry on the pretence. But then his face slackens and he exhales deeply. The long sigh of someone coming to a decision.

"Eric," he says slowly, "Eric Fougère."

My mouth drops open despite myself. "You're French? But your English is so…"

"Good? Thanks. I grew up speaking it with my mother. I'm only half French – she was English – though I was raised in the South of France."

I study him, not bothering to disguise it. Try to absorb the impact of this confession. I mean, I knew. As soon as I saw the missing birthmark, I knew. Maybe before that even, some part of me knew.

But at the same time I was still hoping I was wrong, that there was some explanation that would make everything okay.

Hearing him admit it hurts like a blow. It's so…so final.

"*Why?*" I stammer. I'm shaking now, fear getting the better of me.

Eric shrugs. "Why not? You all missed Danny. I missed having a family. It was right for everyone, I think."

Even as he speaks, his voice is beginning to change, sounding different somehow, lower in tone. And with a trace of an accent I've never heard before.

Letting his mask slip. Allowing me a glimpse of the stranger underneath.

My skin creeps beneath my clothes. I should leave now, I think. I should run across the rocks and take the short cut and get as far away from him as I possibly can.

But I stand there, rooted by a sudden surge of fury.

"*Right?* How could it be right? You've come here. Fooled everyone. Made them believe Danny was still…"

I can't bring myself to say it.

"How could you?" The words spill out my mouth in a torrent of rage. "How could you be so…so cruel? How could you do that to Martha? What the hell has she ever done to you?"

Danny…Eric smiles. An amused, indulgent smile, like I'm some kind of backward child. "Who says I did her any harm? Wasn't it everything she wanted, to have her son back?"

"That's ridiculous," I spit. "That's just—" I stop, my thoughts a muddle. Words elude me. So many questions whirl around my head. So many answers in their wake.

"The hair dye…" I say finally.

Eric eyes me for a moment before pulling off his cap, tipping his head forwards, using his hands to flatten the parting. Along the white line of his scalp a thin band of darker hair is just visible. Really dark, nearly black. Not mousy like mine.

Then he lifts his face, puts a finger to his eye. Holds it out, upturned. On its tip sits a perfect circle of thin blue plastic with a clear centre.

A contact lens.

"Clever, huh?"

I look up at his exposed eye. Dark brown, flecked with green.

"Oh my god…" I'm giddy now, my anger fizzling away as I try to take in what I'm seeing.

"You can buy them almost anywhere these days," he says. "You can have different colour eyes every day of the week."

I examine his features and the stranger emerges, like a face hidden in a picture. He looks nothing like Danny, I see now. His nose is too angular, his eyes too closely set. And without his cap, I notice his ears for the first time. Danny's never stuck out that way.

My mind reels. How could we ever have thought this *was* Danny?

"You see what you want to see," Eric says, reading my thoughts. But then they must be written all over my face.

"How did you know?" My voice comes out as a whisper. "How did you know all that stuff about Danny? About us?"

Eric regards me carefully, as if wondering how much to reveal. "I saw the story on the internet, on that site for missing persons – it had a link to Martha's website. Then it was only a question of checking out Facebook, chat rooms, places like that. It's not hard to get information. People post stuff everywhere."

He takes a deep breath, gazing out across the channel. "Anything you don't know, you can find out. You go round any home, discover all those things tucked away in boxes, diaries or in files, in photo albums, wherever. All the past is there."

I think of my diary, what he must have read in it, and feel a tremor of disgust.

"You don't even have to bother with research," Eric says. "The whole amnesia thing means you can ask people pretty much whatever you like. You just pretend you can't remember."

I flashback to the party. Everyone talking, reminiscing, telling stories. He's right – it's not difficult to get people to fill in the gaps. You just have to play on their trust.

"It's all about secrets, you see." Eric eyes me with something close to pride. "Every family has them. It's like taking the back off a watch and examining inside, finding what makes it tick. Once you know people's secrets, what they most fear, what they most long for, you can get them to believe almost anything."

The accent in his voice is unmistakable now. And it sounds deeper. Older.

I swallow. "You sound like you've done this before."

"A few times."

I suck in some air. "Here?"

"France, America. This is my first time in the UK." He looks strangely pleased.

"So you planned it all? Being picked up by the police? Getting taken back to England?"

Eric nods. "It went like a dream."

"Even beating yourself up?"

His face lapses into a momentary scowl. "No, not that. That was real."

I'm lost for words as I try to get my head around everything Eric just told me. Somehow I can't make sense of it. Something doesn't add up.

"But why?" I gasp finally. "I still don't understand. Why go to all that trouble? What could you possibly hope to gain?"

Eric bends down, picks up a pebble and lobs it into the water. "I never knew my father. And barely my mother since I was twelve. Love, affection, attention – you take these things for granted, but not if you spent half your life in foster homes."

"But Martha," I splutter, my anger resurging. "How could you do that to her? This'll kill her when she finds out."

Eric spins round and looks straight at me. "So why does she have to?"

I stare back. "You're kidding, aren't you? Are you actually suggesting I don't tell her?"

"Yes."

"Jesus," I gasp. "That's absurd. I mean, what the hell am I supposed to do? Just carry on pretending you're Danny?"

"Why not? It wouldn't be so hard. Martha doesn't want to know the truth. Martha has never wanted the truth; it's been right in front of her all this time and she chooses to ignore it. All Martha wants is her son back – it makes no difference to her whether it's me or Danny."

I open my mouth to protest, then close it again. My mind flounders, confused. The ground seems to shift beneath my feet, like sand eroded by the sea. Maybe he's right, I find myself wondering. After all, what's the alternative? I show Martha the photograph and the letters, force her to believe me – and she loses Danny all over again.

Or I go back. Keep my distance and my mouth shut. And she's never any the wiser.

Would that really be the best thing to do?

I study my shoes, trying to think, trying to find solid ground. But the world feels like it's pitching, tilting at a dangerous angle, and I no longer know which way is up, which is down.

Then I see Rudman, lying in his basket, bruised and cut and shivering with shock. And Alice's face, filled with fear and confusion as she kneels beside him, stroking his head.

"Did you take him?"

"Who?"

"Rudman."

Eric snorts. "I shut him away, that's all. That animal was getting on my nerves."

"Where?"

"In an old shed, down by the allotments." He laughs at the look on my face. "Don't worry, I left him water. And some food. I figured someone would hear him barking sooner or later."

"But he was really hurt!"

He shrugs. "Must have been when he escaped."

I stare at him, wondering if I believe him. Then shudder as I realize it wasn't only Rudman who sensed the truth. It was Alice too. And if Eric could do that to Rudman, what might he do to her?

I take a step backwards. "I have to tell them. You know that. You can't seriously expect me to do anything else."

Eric regards me for a moment, as if sizing me up. I see his mind calculating his options, his odds of success.

"I really suggest you don't."

He moves towards me and fear floods me like a dam burst. I'm suddenly aware of Eric's height, his strength. And speed – if I try to run, he'll catch me easily.

He picks up on my nervousness, and his hand darts out and grabs my wrist. "Listen, Hannah," he hisses, "I'm warning you…"

An unexpected sensation of wet and cold hits my feet. I glance down. A wave breaks over our shoes, soaking them in seawater. Eric stares, appalled, then swings round to look behind him.

And sees what neither of us noticed before. How late it is. The sun is sinking behind the hills across the channel, and the tide has already reached the crest of the little beach, cutting off the way back.

"Shit." His grip on me tightens. "The water…" He glances up at the cliffs behind us, too steep and high to climb to safety, and groans. I see the panic on his features, feel his fingers dig into my arm.

"What do we do?" he asks, looking at me.

I don't say anything for a moment, watching him. Sensing his power over me begin to dwindle.

"We'll have to swim for it," I say. "Round the headland. I think there's a way up to the path there."

"Swim?" Eric gasps, jaw slack with horror.

"It's not far. Only round to the next bay." I glance at the sea. "At least it's calm."

"But I can't," he splutters.

"Don't be silly, you…" Then I remember. Danny was the champion swimmer – not Eric. "You can't swim?"

Eric's look of terror is my answer. I stare at him and stare at him and then the laughter spills out of me like something overflowing, the sound of it echoing off the rocks around us.

"*You can't swim!*"

I picture all the trophies in Danny's bedroom. His easy crawl up and down the lanes in the school pool. The dance of his smile whenever he won a race.

You can steal someone's secrets, I think. You can dye your hair and copy the colour of their eyes.

But there are some things you just can't fake.

26

"Shut up!" Eric's voice is a cross between a growl and a whimper. "How do we get out of here?"

When I don't answer, he twists my wrist until I squeal in pain. I wrench my hand away and fish my mobile out my pocket. Check the signal.

Nothing. No way to call for help.

Hell.

"How deep is it?" Eric asks, his face rigid with fright.

I look, but it's hard to tell. The shoreline around here is deceptive – shallow in parts, deeper in others – and the water so murky you can't see through it, especially in this light.

"I don't know," I say. "We could try and wade."

"Oh god." Eric's voice is rising towards hysteria. "I can't… I just can't…"

"We haven't got a choice."

I study the fear on his face. It would be easy to dive in, to swim away and leave him. He couldn't stop me.

But how could I? We're well below the high tideline; the water will come right up over the rocks.

He'll drown.

"Walk behind me," I tell him. "I'll test out where the deep bits are."

Eric stares down at his feet, at the waves lapping over his trainers.

"Come on," I urge. "We haven't got much time."

We hurry to the point where the water swallowed the way back. I start to wade in, trying to remember the lie of the rocks, where the shallow parts are. But as soon as I edge forward, the water engulfs my knees, rising to my hips as I inadvertently step off the brink of the ledge.

It's freezing, and with the clouds congealing overhead, the sky is darkening by the minute. It's getting hard to see where I'm going in the growing gloom.

I look back. Eric is watching me, his face paralysed with horror. I hold out my hand.

"Come on, just follow me."

"I can't," he whimpers.

"You've got to," I hiss. "There's no other way."

He stares into the sea and back at the dwindling area of rock behind him. He looks like he's going to cry. For a moment I almost feel sorry for him.

Then he steps gingerly into the water.

"I can't swim."

"You told me."

He grabs my hand and I feel his fingers trembling. I use my foot to find the next rock, letting my weight drop down onto it. Eric follows, a cry of alarm as he sinks right up to his waist.

We make our way slowly around the headland, the tide rising fast around us. Jesus, I'd forgotten how quickly it comes in.

I slip on seaweed, nearly losing my balance, and have to let go of Eric's hand.

"How much further?" he asks, fright shrinking his voice to a whisper.

I peer through the failing light. It can't be far to the next cove, and I'm fairly sure there's a way through there onto the coast path.

What if you're wrong? asks a fearful voice in my head. What if there isn't a way up?

"*Hannah!*"

I turn round barely in time to see Eric lose his footing and tumble into the water. He flails his legs and arms in blind panic, trying to stand. But he must have hit a deep patch. His head keeps sinking under the waves and re-emerging, mouth gulping for air.

"Help…" Eric vanishes again.

Oh god, he really *can't* swim.

"Hang on!" I edge my way back towards him and hold out my hand. He grabs it wildly, and immediately I'm dragged under, a mouthful of saltwater scalding my throat as I kick out my legs, trying to keep afloat. I wrench my hand away but Eric clutches at me, his arm encircling my neck. I can hardly move. He's so big and heavy, and his grip is nearly strangling me.

"Let go!" I manage to yell. "Let go – or we'll both drown!"

For a second I get a foothold on a rock beneath me and yank his arm away. Eric flounders in the water, his limbs thrashing violently, something like a scream escaping from his throat. I grab his hand again and press it to my shoulder.

"Kick! Keep your head up and I'll keep you afloat."

I plunge back in and try to swim round the tip of the headland. It's almost impossible. Eric keeps dragging me back down under the surface.

"For god's sake, kick your legs!" I shout, before going under and swallowing another mouthful of water. I fight my way back up, coughing and gulping air, my throat burning.

For the first time I'm really scared. The currents round this coastline are notorious – we could easily be pulled further out to sea. Second by second I feel more dazed and exhausted, but I force myself forwards, dragging Eric with me.

With every scrap of energy I have left, I swim, thrusting my arms and legs through the waves, trying to stop both of us from sinking. I think of Danny, of the strength in his stroke, the effortless way it propelled him through the water. I think of Danny and try to swim, Eric's weight pulling me forever downwards like an anchor.

I struggle until the muscles in my arms and legs scream with agony and the salt blurs my vision. But the beach isn't getting any closer.

Danny, I think, as I realize we're not going to make it. Danny, I'm sorry.

I can see his face so clearly now, so vividly, that it's like he's here with me. Danny, I'm sorry, I repeat to him silently. I'm so sorry. I really tried.

I'm so tired now it's easier to let myself sink, to take a final breath then allow the waves to pull me under and the water to close over my head. It feels almost comforting to stop struggling, to let the tide suck me down into oblivion.

Then another face fills my mind. Mum, whose last moments were flooded with fear and desperation and the cold, cold river rushing in around her. I think of Mum and how she must have struggled to get free, and know her final thoughts were of me, and know that this, here, now, is the very last thing she'd ever have wanted.

I force myself to make one last effort, striking out against the current, fighting for air, ignoring Eric's weight on my shoulders and the exhaustion in my limbs and the voice in my head telling me that it's useless, it's hopeless, it's all over.

And then my foot scrapes something hard. A rock, I realize, legs floundering, hope resurfacing like a gasp. I smash my ankle against another, causing a flash of pain that's almost welcome.

Moments later we're on solid ground.

27

We scrabble to the shore and drag ourselves up onto pebbles at the top of the cove, beyond the reach of the sea.

We're safe.

I can hardly let myself believe it. Even if we can't find a way back up to the cliff path, we're safe. Cold, wet, exhausted, but we won't drown.

I flop onto the stones, unable to stand any longer. Eric lies panting beside me.

"You okay?" I ask, once my breathing has settled enough to speak.

A choking sound.

"I think so." He coughs violently for several seconds, then rakes more air into his lungs. "Thank you," he says hoarsely.

I shrug.

Eric clears his throat. "I nearly drowned once."

I gaze at him. All his self-assurance has gone. He looks so limp and bedraggled that my fear seems a distant memory – Eric is no threat to me now.

"In a swimming pool. My mother's boyfriend thought

it would be funny to throw me in. I was only two."

"Jesus. You can remember that?"

"I never forget anything," Eric sighs.

"Anything? That must be handy." I consider all the stuff he had to remember about Danny. About all of us.

"It's a curse," he says, shaking his head. "Believe me."

I think for a moment, trying not to focus on how cold I'm growing now we're no longer moving. I lift the leg of my jeans and examine the gash on my ankle, at the blood mingling with seawater, edging towards my foot.

"You okay?" Eric nods at the wound.

"Yeah." Even if it needs stitches, it's better than drowning. I cover it with my wet sock, ignoring the sting that follows. Then look back up at Eric.

"How old are you anyway?"

He coughs again. It's almost a laugh. "You wouldn't believe me if I told you."

"Try me."

His look weighs me up. "Twenty-two."

Five years older than Danny. He's right. I'm lost for words. I search his features again for clues as to how I could ever have thought he was my friend, but the darkness is deepening around us and it's hard to see much.

Eric inhales, lets out a long sigh. The relief of someone who almost died. "Like I said, it is easy to convince people of something they want to believe."

I laugh, though I'm not particularly amused. "No wonder you weren't bothered about your exams."

"I didn't need to bother," Eric says. "I've done much harder stuff than that. I got a distinction in my bac."

His baccalaureate. The exams they take in France. I've heard they're hard.

We sit for a minute or two, listening to the screech of the gulls coming in to roost for the night. All my anger has been dowsed by the ordeal of getting us both back to safety. I just feel wrung out and empty.

"So who's Mat?" I ask.

A long pause before Eric speaks. "My sister."

I give myself a moment to process this. "Does she know you're here? I mean, why would she let you do this?"

"She doesn't know anything," Eric says hastily.

"You're not close then?"

"I never saw much of her – we were both put in different homes – but we're closer now." He turns away, stares out across the water. I have a feeling I've touched a nerve.

"Eric," I say, breaking the silence. "You know I can't…"

"Yes." He sighs again, wrapping his arms around himself. "Never mind, the game's up anyway. It's no fun if it goes on too long. Especially with your awful English food."

He wrinkles his nose, and I'm reminded of the rice pudding, his grimace of distaste. I feel another rush of indignation for Martha.

"Eric, for Christ's sake, this isn't a bloody game." I jump to my feet and stare at him aghast. "Nobody's winning here."

"No?" He looks up at me and laughs. "Never wonder why I didn't better hide that box? Or burn those letters?"

So someone would catch him, I realize. Eric would never be that careless. Eric didn't really want to play happy families – he was more interested in playing cat and mouse.

"You wanted to be found out," I say. "So we'd all know how clever you are. Was that what all this was really about?"

A silence. When Eric speaks his voice sounds softer, more serious. "Not so much. It's hard to explain. All my life I wanted a family. A proper family, not all those different people I was sent to live with. So I go to parents who need a child, their missing child, and for a while it's everything I dreamed of."

He gazes at me, his eyes glinting in the dusk. "But it's not real, Hannah, don't you see? It's only a dream. In the end you can't escape that – it always catches up with you and then the spell is broken."

I shiver, and not just from the chill of sitting in wet clothes. For a moment I get a glimpse into Eric's world, and it's a cold, hard, desperate sort of place. Not somewhere I want to be.

He gets to his feet and scans the darkening beach. "Anyway, I'll be glad to go. All this mud and seaweed. Your freezing, dirty water."

I glance out over the channel and for a moment see it through his eyes. I guess it's not much to look at if you're used to the sandy beaches and bright blue waters of the Med.

"So, you win, Hannah," Eric sighs. "It's time for me to leave. For me to move on – if you'll let me."

I consider the appeal behind these words. He's asking me to give him a chance to get away. He knows I could go straight to the police and it's likely they'd catch him, even if Eric Fougère isn't his real name.

Though somehow I suspect it is.

"I can't, Eric. I have to tell…"

Eric moves towards me and I resist the urge to step back. "Just remember, Hannah," he whispers, "you and me – we're not so different."

"What do you mean?"

Eric leans forwards and peers right into my eyes. I force myself not to blink or look away. "Let's face it, it's not like you're above a bit of snooping, is it? Or breaking and entering, for that matter."

"How did you know…?"

"That call on my phone, my missing notebook." He eyes me, amused. "Not to mention the house was locked today – you left your key and I took the spare from under the bird bath. So how else did you get in?"

Despite the chill in my body, I feel my face flush with heat. "That was different – I was only…"

"Face it, Hannah, we're more alike than you want to admit. Only you're the lucky one – you have people who are there for you." He gives me a look that almost pierces. "Though not perhaps in the way you assume."

"What do you mean by that?" I snap.

Eric eyes me for a few seconds. "Never mind. All I'm asking for, Hannah, is a few hours, okay? Nothing more."

I press my lips together and force myself to think. My phone must be wrecked, but if I ran back now, I could go to the police and they'd pick Eric up before he had a chance to get away. After all, how far could he get in half an hour?

And then what would happen? Getting Eric arrested wouldn't bring Danny back. And very soon Martha will be forced to face the truth anyway. Her son is gone, and he's never coming home.

"Hannah?" Eric is still staring at me, his wet clothes clinging to his skin. He looks ghostly pale in the near darkness, and up close I can see his face betrays a shock and exhaustion he's not quite managing to hide.

Where's he going to go now? I wonder. What on earth will he do?

"Let me go, Hannah, and I can offer you something in return."

"What?" My mind is spinning. What could Eric have that I could possibly want?

"The truth."

I look up at him in panic. What does he mean?

He holds my gaze and suddenly I understand. What would I rather – to live like Martha, happy to believe a stranger is her son? Or to know what's really going on?

Just for a second I'm tempted. Just for a second, I choose an easy life.

But only for a second.

"Tell me." Suddenly I'm shaking rather than shivering. Have to clamp my jaw shut to stop myself from stuttering. Eric remains silent.

"It's about Danny, isn't it?" I say, my heart sinking.

But Eric shakes his head, then smiles. The way a teacher smiles when you're struggling to find the answer to a difficult question. When you're close, but not quite there.

"Martha's bedroom," he says. "The cabinet in her wardrobe. The key is in the drawer beside her bed."

"What cabinet? What am I looking for?"

But Eric is on his feet now and already backing away. "You'll know when you find it."

Before I can react, he's heading off towards the cliff, scrabbling over the rocks until he's nearly reached the path. I stare after him for a moment, and then it hits me.

There's something else I have to ask him. Something I should have asked him much earlier. The only thing that matters at all.

"Stop!" I yell, running after him, stumbling and nearly falling in the dark. "Eric, please…wait!"

The shadowy figure in front pauses long enough for me to catch up.

"You called me 'titch'," I gasp, grabbing his arm and pulling him round to face me. "From the first time you saw me you called me 'titch'."

Eric just stares at me, saying nothing.

"Only Danny ever called me that. You couldn't have got that from a website or anything."

Eric still doesn't respond.

"And you knew what he said, the last time we spoke."

I see Danny now, as he pushes off on his bike. See the little wave he gives me as he glides off down the road, out of my sight and out of my life.

"See ya, wouldn't wanna be ya." The last thing he ever said to me.

"You've met him, haven't you? You know Danny, don't you?" I grip his arm tighter. "Where is he, Eric? *Tell me!*"

Eric's eyes are fixed on me. For the first time in all these months, he appears flustered, indecisive.

"And those phone calls. The prank calls we've been getting. It's him, isn't it?"

Eric looks like he's going to say something, then hesitates.

"For Christ's sake, Eric. At least just let me know if he's still alive."

"I can't talk about this, Hannah." He looks past me into the gloom surrounding us.

I tug on his arm. "You have to!" I'm shouting now, my voice harsh and desperate. "Please, Eric. You have to tell me. I *have* to know!"

He grips my fingers and gently prises them off his arm. "I can't tell you anything, Hannah. I'm sorry." He starts to back away.

"Why, Eric?" I scream after him. "WHY NOT?"

"Because I gave my word," he says, picking up speed. "I made a promise, and some promises you just can't break."

I watch as he moves into a run along the cliff path, heading towards the distant lights of town.

This time I let him go.

28

"Hannah!"

Martha's face registers surprise when she sees me, a flush colouring her cheeks as she watches Alice bound towards me and hug me tight around the waist.

"I called round at your house yesterday evening," Martha says, facing me. "Just to check you're okay. And to, you know...apologize for the other day." She masks her discomfort with a thin smile.

"Sorry. I was round at a friend's," I fib, feeling relieved I missed her. I doubt I could have explained away the state I was in when I got home – clothes soaked, freezing cold, a gash on my ankle that I had to cover with some gauze and an old bandage I found in the bathroom cabinet.

But none of that as painful as having to wait till morning to be here. I spent half the night plotting how to get into Paul and Martha's bedroom, anxious to see if there's anything in what Eric said. And the other half dreading what's going to happen when Martha discovers that "Danny" has gone.

Clearly she doesn't know yet. We wouldn't be standing

here, having this awkward conversation, if Martha had a clue. With Eric often out late and sleeping well into the morning, she must be assuming her son is still in bed.

"Have you phoned your dad?" Martha asks, studying my face. Probably wondering why I'm here.

I nod. Easier than lying outright.

She pulls Alice away from me and scoops her hair into a neat ponytail, securing it with a band. Alice winces and scowls, then sticks her tongue out at me for good measure.

For a moment I hesitate. It's stuff like this that makes a family, I recognize – normal families doing normal things. It makes me think of Eric. Where he is now and what he'll do next. Where he'll go.

"I need to talk to you." I keep my voice calm and steady and look Martha straight in the eyes.

She returns my gaze, her expression devoid of emotion, then glances up at the clock. My timing is perfect – Alice has to be in school in ten minutes and Paul has already left.

"All right." She ushers a sullen Alice towards the door. "Wait here till I get back."

The moment the sound of the car engine fades, I go straight up to Martha and Paul's bedroom. The key is in the drawer in Martha's bedside table, exactly as Eric said. A plain gold key, smaller than my little finger.

Kneeling on the carpet, I part the dresses and skirts in the wardrobe to reveal a small metal cabinet with a lock.

It's well hidden, though I'm surprised I never stumbled across it in one of those games of hide-and-seek. I pull it towards me, then slide in the key and feel a slight click as it turns. Lift the lid carefully and peer inside.

A dozen or so files hang from a ridge on each side of the cabinet. I flick through them, glancing at the documents they contain. Birth certificates, exam certificates. Danny's and Alice's medical notes. Nothing here that anyone might want to keep secret. I check them all again, making sure there's nothing I've missed.

So Eric was just winding me up. Playing me one last time.

But as I shove the box back into the wardrobe, I glimpse something below the files, crammed into the thin cavity beneath. I reach in and my hand closes around a small brown envelope. I lift it out carefully. The flap isn't sealed. I remove a thin pile of papers.

The first is a cutting from a newspaper, folded in half. My heart misses a beat as I open it up. I'm staring at a grainy, black-and-white picture of my mother. She's smiling, and scrunching up her eyes slightly, like she's looking into the sun.

Underneath, a headline: *Mother, 42, Dies in Freak River Accident*. It's dated 11th October five years ago – a week after my mother's death.

I scan the paragraphs below, skin tingling. I know what happened already, can still hear Dad explaining it to me, his voice shaky with shock, after the police had left. How

Mum had been driving in the rain and had lost control at a bend, skidding off the road and into the flooded river. How the seat belt had jammed and she hadn't been able to get free before the car filled with water.

But the last paragraph chokes back the breath in my throat. "The coroner gave a verdict of accidental death on Wednesday, despite several witness reports that Ellen Radcliffe was experiencing marital difficulties, and had been distressed in the days running up to her death. The coroner, however, was adamant that there was no evidence of suicide."

Marital difficulties? What did they mean? Mum and Dad had always been happy, hadn't they?

Then I remember. The argument, the one I'd overheard down in the kitchen right before the accident. Dad's raised voice. The sound of Mum sobbing. Everything that happened later was so awful that I'd almost forgotten all about it. Hadn't understood it was so serious.

Hands shaking, I unfold the other piece of paper. Blink hard as my vision goes blurry when I recognize my mother's handwriting.

Dear Martha,

I know you don't want to speak to me, let alone give me the opportunity to apologize, but I want you to know how very much I regret the pain I have caused you. Please believe me when I say I never meant to hurt you in any way. It was all a terrible mistake, one we both regretted as soon as it happened.

I am sure too the news about Hannah is as much a shock for you as any of us, but I beg you, please, Martha, not to say anything to her. None of this is her fault, you know that, and I know you care for her deeply and would not want to cause her any pain.

I am going away for a few days to give David some space to think things through. I hope more than anything that we can move beyond this, for Hannah's and Danny's sakes as much as anyone else's. I hope too, in time, that you will be able to forgive me.

Ellen

The only thing left in the envelope is a photo. I pull it out. It's a picture of me and Danny, just our faces, leaning in so the side of our heads are resting one against the other.

I gaze at it, the lump in my throat growing so big I can hardly swallow. It must have been taken in summer, when we were eleven or twelve. We look tanned and healthy and there's a sprinkle of freckles on both our noses. We're grinning at the camera, looking insanely happy, like nothing was ever going to touch us in the whole of our lives.

"Hannah, what the hell are you…?"

I raise my head, the photo in my hand, to see Martha staring down at me. The anger in her face fades as she sees just what the hell I am doing. She hovers for a moment in the doorway, then sits across from me on the bed, smoothing out her skirt with her hands.

I see they are trembling.

"You shouldn't be in here. You've no right…" she begins, then thinks better of it when I fix my eyes on hers without flinching.

"Hannah…I…" Her voice tails off.

"What's this all about, Martha?" I lift my hand from the envelope so she can see clearly what I'm holding.

Her face twitches, and she squeezes her lips tight together. "I'm not sure now is the time…"

"Just tell me."

Martha looks away and back again. I sense her searching for some version of the truth that might let us both off the hook. I hold her gaze, not even letting myself blink, until her expression slumps and a long sigh escapes her.

"This is really something you should talk to your dad about."

I flashback to our conversation before he left. Him saying he had things to tell me.

"Dad's not here," I say plainly.

Martha pulls her hand through her hair, her eyes darting away again. "It's hard to explain, Hannah."

"Try."

She takes a deep breath, releasing it slowly. Buying herself time.

"Okay…your mother…your mum and dad had a big argument before she died. Your mum was very upset. They weren't sure it was an accident…"

"I know that, Martha. I just read this." I wave the newspaper article towards her. "But what's this letter from

Mum, the stuff about me? What is it I'm not supposed to know?"

Martha swallows. "Oh god, Hannah…" She looks down at me with a kind of pleading in her eyes. "I really think your father should be the one to…"

"Just tell me."

"Okay…" Something surrenders in Martha's face, like she's come to the end of a road and found there's nowhere else to go. "Your mum and Paul… You know that they were friends before he and I got together, back at university?"

I nod. Remember Dad joking once about being Mum's back-up plan.

"Well, something happened…"

Martha pauses and looks down at her hands, spreading her fingers and placing them on her knees. "Later on. Briefly."

I stare at her, my brain trying to unscramble her meaning.

"You mean…Paul and *Mum*?"

The movement of Martha's head is so small you could easily miss it. But I don't. It was a nod.

Blood thumps loudly in my temples. "You're saying… what? That they had an affair?"

Martha swallows and sighs. "It was a long time ago, Hannah, before you were even born."

"And you knew?"

She shakes her head vigorously. "No…no, I didn't…not till later, just before your mum died."

I pause to let her words sink in. To give my mind a chance to make sense of them.

"Why then?" I ask. "I mean…how did you find out?"

Martha's head droops. "Look, Hannah, I really don't think…"

"*Just tell me!*" The vehemence in my voice surprises us both. Martha stares at me for a moment, as if seeing me for the very first time.

When she speaks her voice is shaky.

"Your mum and dad had been trying for another baby, after you. In the end your dad went in for some tests. And they found that…well…he couldn't."

"Couldn't what?" My mind feels foggy and confused.

Martha closes her eyes briefly. When she opens them again I see something softer there. Something worse than sympathy.

Pity.

"Have children," she says slowly.

I stare at her dumbfounded, my thoughts a blank of incomprehension. Her face is pale and drawn and she looks almost afraid.

"But that's ridiculous." I swallow. "That can't be right… I mean, how could they have had me?"

Martha flushes and looks back down at the floor. For a moment I think I've misunderstood something. Like one of those maths equations where you make some small mistake and none of your answers add up.

Then it all falls into place, and my heart slowly collapses in on itself.

Mum and Dad didn't have me.

Dad isn't my father at all.

I try to breathe but I can't get in enough air at once and I have to keep taking small, short gasps. Dad... Oh god...

Martha's hand on my shoulder. "Hannah, I'm sorry. I shouldn't have said anything..."

"B-before," I stammer. "Why didn't anyone tell me this before?"

"We meant to, sweetheart. Despite your mum asking us not to." She nods towards the letter in my hand. "Your dad was going to talk to you, explain everything, but..." Her voice falters, stumbles on again. "Well...then Danny... then Danny disappeared and everything was such a mess. It was all so hard on you...on everyone...that we felt it would be better..."

"How?" I find my voice and it crackles with rage and disbelief. Tears prick at my eyes, and I blink them back. "How could that possibly be better? All this time I thought Dad... Jesus, I had no idea..."

"Hannah, I know it's hard. Please believe me, no one planned it this way. Your dad was in such a terrible state when your mum died. I'm sure you remember."

The awful question finally surfaces in my mind. But even the moment I ask it, I know.

"So who is...?"

I look down at the photo. Danny and I. All those times people mistook us for brother and sister. We thought it was because we were always together.

I raise my eyes back to Martha. She's staring at me helplessly.

"So Paul is my real father."

Martha doesn't say anything. She doesn't need to.

All the pieces start to fall into place.

The way Paul seems to hover around me. Hesitant. Attentive. Trying to find a way to get close.

Paul and Dad and Martha, circling one another, keeping their distance. Keeping up appearances, the fiction that nothing had changed.

And Dad. God, Dad. A pain in my chest, sharp as knives, as I think how awful this must have been for him. Having to pretend all this time. Knowing I'm not really his daughter. Knowing his genes and mine have nothing in common except the building blocks of DNA that all of us share.

No wonder things have been so weird between the two of us. I thought it was just losing Mum. But Dad lost everything, all at once: Mum, his closest friends – and me.

My eyes smart with the urge to cry, but I force back the tears. If I start now, I won't be able to stop. I need to keep a grip. I need to *think*.

Because that's not all of it, I realize, as the truth carries on unravelling in my head. Oh god… A cramp grips my chest so tight I'm almost gasping for air. Eric's bargain – my truth for his freedom – I had no idea it would blow my life apart so completely.

Martha reaches a hand towards me. "Hannah…"

"He knew," I say, looking back at the picture of the pair of us, smiling into the camera. "Danny *knew*."

Suddenly I understand. Everything. What drove him away. Why Danny abandoned me even before he disappeared. He must have found out, stumbled across this letter. Or heard something, his parents arguing.

"What do you mean?" The concern in Martha's voice sours into accusation. "What did Danny know?"

"Don't you see? That's why he was being so weird towards me…towards us…before he ran away. He knew. About me. About Paul and Mum and everything."

It made sense now. Total sense. How the only way he could cope was to keep his distance, so he didn't have to lie to me, to pretend he didn't know.

And in the end even that became too difficult.

It's not you. His words echo in my head, that one time I asked him what was going on. *It's not you.*

Martha is staring at me in disbelief. "That's absurd, Hannah. No one said anything to Danny."

But there's fear in her eyes. I can see her mind winding back to the past. Assembling all the clues.

She knows I'm right, I think, and something snaps inside me.

He knew. Danny knew. *They all knew.*

And they all hid it from me.

A cold thrill of resentment seethes through me, drowning my misgivings. "Actually, I have some letters for you, Martha." I pull the sheets from my pocket and toss them onto the bed beside her. They're crumpled and stiff from a night drying out on the towel rail, but they're still legible.

Martha eyes them for a moment, then picks them up and unfolds them. I watch the colour seep from her cheeks as she reads.

"Where did you get these?" She looks up, her expression confused, bewildered.

"Danny's room."

She flips through the sheets again, scanning every word. "I don't understand. They're addressed to me. How come I never saw them before?"

"Because Eric got to them before you did."

"Eric?" She stares at me, perplexed. "Who's Eric?"

I look at her and, even now, despite everything, I hesitate. My next words will tear Martha's world to pieces. The thrill that possessed me a few moments ago has vanished, leaving the awful weight of someone's life in my hands.

And then I understand. This is how Dad felt. Martha and Paul. *Danny.* This is why no one was able to tell me the truth about my father.

This is why it was easier for Danny to disappear.

Martha's still gazing at me with that dazed expression, like someone looking up from their steering wheel to see a juggernaut heading straight towards them. I could lie to her, I think, explain away those letters. I could do what Eric suggested. Let her carry on believing he was Danny.

But no. Not any more. Eric has gone – I don't even need to check in his room to be sure of that.

And I'm equally certain he's never coming back.

"Eric is Danny." I say it quickly before I can change my mind. "Or rather, he isn't Danny. He's just been pretending to be him."

I watch Martha's look of bewilderment morph to scorn. "Don't be ridiculous, Hannah. You're making this up. I understand that you're very upset about—"

"Look in his room."

Martha blinks. "I don't need to. I don't know exactly why you're doing this, Hannah, but—"

"Just *look*, Martha!"

My voice comes out louder than I intended, almost a shout. Martha flinches in surprise, then gets up and walks out. I hear the door open to Danny's room, its telltale little creak. Then silence. A long, long silence.

I sit, unmoving, thoughts and feelings swirling like a cyclone in my head, gathering momentum. A maelstrom of emotions. Anger at Mum, at Paul, at Martha. Even Dad. How could they do that? How could they lie to me like that?

And Danny…how could he see me almost every day, knowing what he did…and say nothing.

Then I think of that last day, his hesitation on the beach. The words I sensed playing at the corner of his mouth.

Was that it? Was he fighting the urge to tell me the truth?

In an instant I see how hard it was for Danny. How *impossible*. His dad had cheated and his mum had lied, and then his best friend was suddenly his half-sister. And he couldn't talk about any of it – least of all to me.

How could he face taking away my father when I had only just lost my mother?

My head is reeling so much I lean it back against Martha's bed. Just at that moment I hear a muffled thump from Danny's bedroom. I scramble to my feet and run in. Martha is crumpled on the floor, looking like her legs simply collapsed beneath her.

"Oh god…" I grab her under the arms and pull her over to the bed. I can feel her body trembling, the terrible weight of her despair.

"Martha…"

"He's gone. Taken half his things…he must have left in the night."

I nod.

"How did you know…? When did Danny…?"

"He's not Danny, Martha. He never was. His name is Eric Fougère. He's half French. He's twenty-two years old."

Martha recoils as if slapped. "That's impossible," she stammers. "Ludicrous. I'd have known…"

"But we *didn't* know, did we?" I say, letting the words sink in. "And it's not the first time he's done it, pretended to be someone who's missing. He's had plenty of practice."

"I can't believe…" She shakes her head. "I just can't believe…"

But I can see she does. All those things that didn't add up. All those clues. All those doubts. I'm watching the penny drop, slowly, like a stone sinking down towards the seabed.

She slumps on the bed, head in hands, a terrible wailing noise coming from deep inside her. A howl, like an animal in pain. I stand, transfixed, watching her, unsure what to do. Wait until the moaning subsides and Martha lifts her head and finally looks at me. Her face has drained to the colour of pale sand.

"But how could he know…? I mean, everything about Danny? About us?"

"The internet," I shrug. "The TV programme, photographs, videos. He pieced it all together. He's very clever."

Martha sinks her head into her hands. Sits there for a minute or two, then raises it again. She looks ghastly, like someone in shock.

"Where is he?" she asks abruptly.

"Who? Eric?"

Martha nods.

"I don't know. I haven't seen him since yesterday evening."

"Did he say he was leaving?"

"No. But he knew he couldn't stay."

Martha lapses back into silence. Something has broken inside her. She looks utterly defeated. And I feel sorry then. Desperately sorry to be the bearer of the worst kind of news.

Because Martha has done her best for me, I know that.

Despite everything. When even the sight of me must remind her daily of Paul's betrayal, of Mum's, she still tries to be there for me.

"I still don't see how he could know so..." she stammers, then falls quiet. Seconds later she looks back at me, her expression suddenly hopeful. "Hannah, do you think it's possible...this Eric, might he have met Danny? Could he know where he is?"

I stare at her, my thoughts crashing around my head like waves trapped in a gully.

Some promises you just can't break. Wasn't that what Eric said? And what is a promise, except a pact between two people?

Between Eric and Danny.

Martha is looking at me, a terrible pleading in her eyes. And I think of all those weeks, months, years she spent looking. All that time. All that grief.

And I know that if I tell her what I suspect, all that will start over again. The searching, the waiting. The endless, restless hoping.

The disappointment.

I swallow. "No," I say evenly, "I don't think so."

The lie leaves a taste in my mouth, bitter and sour. But what Eric said about the promise – that told me everything. That if Danny ever wanted to be found, he would be. It was his choice.

And one I knew he'd already made.

EPILOGUE

"*Qu'est-ce vous prenez, mademoiselle?*"

I look up from my book to see the waiter standing over me. The one that served me yesterday – and the day before. Indeed, there's recognition in his smile, and I wonder what he thinks of this strange English girl who's spent most of the week sitting alone in his little beach cafe.

"*Encore un coca, s'il vous plaît.*"

He pauses as he removes my old glass, cloudy with melted ice. He wants to talk, I can see that. To ask me what I'm doing here.

I wish I knew. What seemed like a good idea a few weeks ago, in the euphoria of finishing my A-levels, now feels completely mad. Not to mention boring.

I dig in my purse for another five euros, trying not to flinch at the cost. Nothing comes cheap in the South of France.

"*Non.*" The waiter waves away my money. "*Gratuit.* On the house," he adds in his heavily accented English. "To thank you for your loyal custom."

He looks at me, obviously hoping I'll say more, but I

stick to a grateful smile. When he's gone, I take a sip from the fresh glass of Coke, enjoying the cool fizz against my tongue. It's late afternoon, but the air is still sizzling with heat, and all of me feels hot and sticky.

And restless. I try to focus on my book, but can't get back into the story. I let my eyes wander across the beach, taking in the view of the sea, the little yachts out in the bay, the sunlight glinting on the tops of the waves. The crowds that clustered along the sands are beginning to thin now, I notice, as people head back for aperitifs and a leisurely dinner.

Café sur la Plage, Almanarre, Hyères.

That's all the email said. One line, from an address I didn't recognize. No name, only the date it was sent, three weeks ago. And the date I should arrive.

An invitation. One I couldn't refuse.

Dad, as I still insist on calling him, thinks I'm on holiday with Lianna and a bunch of other friends from school, to celebrate the end of our exams. It's true enough, I tell myself, though it doesn't stop the ache of guilt. I hate pulling the wool over his eyes – especially after everything that's happened.

But if I told him the whole truth, he'd worry. Ditto Paul, who no longer has to hide his concern when I go round. He lives alone now, in the flat he rented after his split with Martha. I see her too, and not just because of Alice; I want to stay in touch, make sure she's okay. Martha's never been the same since Eric left. I guess it finally broke her.

Which is one reason I'm here, though I know it's insane coming all this way with no idea what awaits me at the other end. But I want to tell Eric about Martha, about the damage he's done. About the damage he might now be doing to some other family. I want him to understand something I learned in science years ago – that every action, no matter how small, has a reaction.

Though in life, as opposed to physics, I'm learning it's rarely the one you expect.

I rescan the beach, searching the crowds for a familiar face. I know he's here somewhere, watching, waiting for the right moment.

Just as he knew I'd come. Out of curiosity, if nothing else. I've spent the last two years thinking about Eric. I've cycled through every possible emotion – anger, disbelief, sympathy and back again – always ending up right where I started. Nowhere near understanding what really went on in his head.

Or Danny's. I've spent countless hours thinking about why he left. How it all became too much. How he couldn't bear to lie to me. And yet…the fact that my best friend could keep such a huge secret proves you don't know anyone. Not really. Not deep down. There could have been anything going on in his life.

I'll never know the real truth. I've accepted that.

I pull my eyes back to my book, but something in the distance snags my attention. A man, walking towards the cafe, baseball cap pulled close over his eyes, jeans slouching on his hips. I study his progress, my heart rate beginning to quicken as he approaches. I can see the hint of blond hair round his neck, a slight strut in the way he walks.

Is it him?

I crane my head as the figure disappears behind a couple still lounging under their parasol. Just when I think I've lost him, he reappears a few metres away. I'm about to get to my feet, to run over, when he looks right at me.

I bite my lip in disappointment. Too short, the wrong build. Not even Eric could disguise that.

I slump back into my seat, feeling almost tearful with frustration. Is this another of Eric's elaborate games? Why drag me here if he's got nothing to say?

After all, he owes me. For letting him vanish as quickly and neatly as he appeared, like a genie returning to its bottle.

I snap my book shut and toss it onto the table. It skids on the polished glass, nearly tipping into the sand as I grab my handbag and walk fast down towards the sea. A young girl strolls past with a dog nearly as big as herself, practically dragging her across the beach. With her long ponytail, she looks a bit like Alice, though the dog is black and much too large to be Rudman.

The sight of her makes my heart contract. I know how much Alice will be missing me. She hugged me so hard when I left I nearly fell over.

"Come back very soon," she said, before she finally let me go.

"Promise," I replied, meaning it. After all, Alice is the one person in my life who doesn't make it feel more complicated, the one person I can be sure will never let me down.

"*Maman!*"

The little girl spots her mother over by the edge of the water, and runs to meet her, the dog bounding alongside, panting in the heat. The woman gives her daughter a quick hug and takes her hand. I can see they're busy talking, but I'm too far away to catch what they say.

An image of Mum flashes into my mind. Us paddling back at home, on that thin band of sand that lies between the pebbles at the top of the beach and the mud below. It was nothing like here, of course, the water brown and murky compared with this dazzling blue, but I loved it all the same. We'd take off our sandals and roll up our jeans and jump, feet together, over the tops of the little waves as they rolled in towards us, one after another after another.

I can smile now at the memory. I'm over hating Mum for what she did, and back to missing her all the time. Dad's right, there's no point in blame. We all screw up, all do stuff we're not proud of.

What counts is getting past that. Making the best of what you have. Another thing Eric taught me – however hard my life is, however messy and imperfect, it's a great deal better than his.

I walk along the edge of the sea for a while, then turn round and make my way back to the cafe. The waiter eyes me discreetly as I skirt round to the loos. When I return he's busy talking to a man sitting at the bar with his back to me. I sit down in my seat and drain the last of the Coke, checking my watch. Ten to six.

Time to go back to the hotel. I want to shower and change and get down to the restaurant before it's too crowded. Maybe tomorrow I'll go and see the islands, I tell myself as I grope in my purse for a tip. Make the most of the few days I have left. Stop playing along with whatever game Eric's cooked up this time – and clearly lost interest in.

I pick my book up from the table and stuff it into my bag. Take a couple of steps towards the bar and call "*Au revoir*" to the waiter, raising my hand in a wave. He looks up, a white tea towel in one hand, glass in the other, and nods goodbye. The other man glances at me briefly as I pull the strap of my handbag up onto my shoulder and turn away.

And freeze.

I stand there, scarcely breathing. *Why can't I move?*

Something isn't right. I feel my jaw clench and my skin tingle as my mind tries to make sense of what I just saw.

Slowly, heart thumping wildly, I turn back round. The man at the bar is facing away again, but even from behind I can see his blond hair is darker now, his body strong and lean.

The waiter is watching me, noticing my confusion.

"*Mademoiselle?*"

The man looks up at the waiter, then twists round to follow his gaze. I take in the hint of stubble across his cheeks and chin, the puzzled expression as he sees me staring back at him. I feel faint with shock. I want to look away, but can't tear my eyes from his, from their perfect fathomless blue, the colour of the sea in the bay.

"*Vous avez oublié quelque chose, mademoiselle?*" the waiter asks. "You have forgotten something?"

A surge of disappointment knocks the air right out of me, and it's all I can do to shake my head.

No, I want to say, I haven't forgotten anything. Nothing at all.

But Danny has.

He drops his gaze from mine and turns away. For a moment I think I'm going to pass out from the pain, just fall to the floor with its force.

He doesn't recognize me. *He doesn't know who I am.*

I'm about to turn and disappear, to run across the beach as fast as I can when I think of Eric.

He set this up, I understand. To repay his debt. To make amends.

I hesitate, knowing I have a choice. To leave Danny to his own life, to the one he has chosen. Or to force him back into mine.

My mind reels with indecision. I'm standing on a ledge, peering into dark water. I'm dizzy and confused and I want to be anywhere but here.

This shouldn't be something I get to decide.

Then I think of Mum – how we never got a second chance, how I'll have to spend the rest of my life wondering what might have been. I think of her, holding my hand as we jumped over the surf, and I take one last, long deep breath…and dive in.

"Danny."

His back tenses. The hand raising his glass pauses in mid-air, drops back down. He lifts his head and slowly turns towards me. I see his stunned expression as this time he looks right into my eyes.

"*Tu la connais?*" The waiter asks him. Does he know me?

I feel like I'm sinking as I wait, tears beginning to blur my vision, for his answer. But he doesn't move, doesn't speak. Just stares at me blankly, watching me drown.

Get out of here, insists a voice in my head. Get as far away from this place as you can and never, ever look back.

I drag the air back into my lungs. Will my body to turn and my legs to walk away. Suppress the sob rising in my throat as I stumble and almost drop my bag.

"*Hannah?*"

His voice. Deep and strange and utterly familiar. Like a day hasn't passed since he rode off on that bike, leaving a rip in my life I thought would never mend.

My feet stop. I swing round. See the dazed expression on his face, the uncertain way he's standing there, like someone staggering from a blow.

"*Hannah? Is that really you?*"

The tears break free, running down my cheeks as I turn back towards my brother. I see the shake in his hand as he grips the top of the bar, as if he might fall. See him wavering, just for a moment, before taking the plunge.

And that smile, that glorious smile, breaking across his face like a wave as he sweeps towards me, and folds me into his arms.

ACKNOWLEDGEMENTS

I'd like to thank my agent, Jo Williamson, everyone at Usborne, especially Sarah, Rebecca, Amy, Anna, Elisabetta, Becky and Peter, and everyone else who worked on the book.

Book consultant Shelley Instone, for her generosity and excellent critiquing, and for giving me a decisive kick up the backside when I needed it.

My beta readers, particularly the lovely Wendy Storer, and everyone at Arvon, Writewords, Book Frisbees and YA Think for their invaluable advice and support.

Chris Murray, for helping me keep domestic chaos at bay during the writing of this, and Marie Adams, for doing much the same with my head.

And of course, the ever-patient James and my four quite patient offspring: Josh, Flan, Chip and Hetty. Oh, and Stanley and Mrs Perkins. Woof.

Don't miss the next stunning thriller
from **Emma Haughton**,
coming soon…

BETTER LEFT BURIED

Brother dead.
Best friend missing.
House ransacked.
Stalked by a stranger.
Attacked in the street...

…And Sarah has no idea why. She never knew her brother
was hiding a dark secret when he died. But now his deadly
actions have led the wolves to her door.
And the only way out is to run.

ISBN 9781409566700

www.usborne.com/fiction